The Mind
Hack

Stewart McDowall

SRL PUBLISHING

The Mind Hack

Stewart McDowall

SRL Publishing Ltd
London
www.srlpublishing.co.uk

First published worldwide by SRL Publishing in 2024

ISBN: 978-1915-073-31-0

1 3 5 7 9 10 8 6 4 2

A CIP catalogue record for this book is available from the
British Library

SRL Publishing is a Climate Positive publisher offsetting more
carbon emissions than it emits.

To everyone who asked when the next book was coming out, thank you, this is for you

One

McQueen pulled on the headphones and moved the microphone a little closer. He was sitting in an impressive, sound-dampened professional recording studio and was slightly awed by the expensive feel of the place. This was clearly the big league, and he momentarily wondered if he was up to it. It was only a fleeting hint of self-doubt that he easily managed to quash. Of course, he was up to it. It was only an interview.

While he'd been waiting in the reception area, buried deep in the hug of a sofa, a young assistant had handed him a mug of coffee. Amazingly, given his usual clumsiness around hot drinks, when ushered into the studio moments later, he had somehow managed to struggle from the furniture's embrace without spilling a drop. Inside the quiet cocoon of the studio, he laid out his notebook on the big round table in front of him but was concentrating harder on not knocking over the mug than on drinking the coffee.

Emma Cullen was a well-respected journalist,

commentator, and television presenter, and her true-crime podcast, *The Cullen Report*, had a huge following in the UK and many more fans across the world. Guesting on it was a great opportunity for McQueen to increase his media profile and, if nothing else, it was free advertising for his private detective business. Emma also fronted a television show on which she talked about infamous serial killers from the past. It featured some re-enactments of their gruesome crimes along with insightful comments and opinions from professionals. McQueen was hoping to be included on one of those shows as a criminology expert but first he needed this podcast to go well. It felt like a test, and perhaps that accounted for his uncharacteristic nervousness.

The topic under discussion today was predatory grooming, and Emma started the show with a strong introduction delivered with her usual bluntness. From his seat facing her across the table, McQueen watched with interest as the true media professional did her thing.

Watch and learn, he thought.

'Just a few short years ago,' she began, 'if I had mentioned the word "grooming" to you, it would have conjured images of nothing more sinister than beautifully manicured dogs.' Here, she paused, as if waiting for the chuckle from her digital audience and subtly encouraging her listeners to indulge in a little comforting nostalgia. 'Not anymore,' she continued, as her voice hardened. 'Now, it's a word steeped in evil. In case you aren't quite sure what I'm talking about, here's a definition.' She glanced down at her notes and her voice took on a different timbre to indicate to the listeners that she was reading something important. 'Grooming is the predatory act of manoeuvring another individual into a position that makes them more isolated, more dependent, more likely to trust and more vulnerable to abusive behaviour'. Then in a softer voice, she added, 'Wow.' She smiled across the desk at McQueen so he knew he was about to be called into action.

'My guest today is a celebrated Doctor of Criminology. He also has a master's degree in forensic psychology, but many of you will know him from his more newsworthy work as a successful private investigator. Recently, he has been on the front page of many of our papers due to his success on some high-profile criminal cases, but it's in his capacity as an academic that he joins us today as we delve into the twisted psychology that lies behind predatory grooming.'

She lifted her eyes from the words printed on her script and looked right at him. It struck McQueen that Emma had the classic good-for-television face, meaning it was attractive and smooth and virtually expressionless. It was a beautiful blank canvas viewers could invest with their own emotions.

Probably some Botox involved there, thought McQueen, looking at her lineless forehead, above which her layered blonde fringe never moved, even when she shook her head. Television close-ups tend to exaggerate any small facial movements. They're amplified so even slight gestures can make your features seem as if they're jumping around, especially on a fifty-inch HD screen. Although McQueen sported a nice covering of thick, grey hair, as he had done since his twenties, his own brow was far from smooth. "Deeply furrowed" would have been a better description.

He had a good-for-podcast face, as a friend had joked.

'Dr McQueen, first of all, could you just explain for our listeners very briefly the difference between criminology and forensic psychology?'

'Sure, Emma.' He was trying to keep it light and he certainly didn't want his credentials to intimidate or alienate any of the listeners.

'Put simply, criminology is about trying to answer the questions around why people commit crimes, whereas forensic psychology is the use of psychology in the criminal justice system. Forensic psychology can involve everyone from victims to prisoners.'

'Okay, thanks. So I suppose what we are more concerned with here today is criminology. At its heart, grooming starts slowly with everyday language and friendly words, often in the form of innocent-sounding texts or emails. Is that why it's so easy for people to become embroiled before they realise what's actually going on?'

This was it. Finally, it was McQueen's moment to shine. Years before, he'd had the opportunity to start a lucrative career as a TV psychology expert but had ruined it due to his excessive drinking and resultant unreliability. Thankfully, those drunken days were behind him now, and his newfound tabloid fame seemed to be reopening some slammed doors.

Fortunately, even with all the attention now focused on his reply, his voice didn't desert him or creakily give away his nerves. The show wasn't going out live, and he knew there would be a chance to make edits if anything sounded odd, but still his pride wanted it to be right the first time.

And although he didn't like to admit it to himself, he also wanted to impress Emma.

'You're absolutely right, Emma,' he answered, in a clear, authoritative tone, the tone of an expert who has all the answers. 'It is easy to miss the red flags, but we are often talking about very clever psychopaths here.' He paused to let the statement land. 'They're not just playing a harmless game. They learn the words and phrases that work best, then they use them like verbal keys to unlock a person's deepest fears and desires. First they find vulnerable victims and then they manipulate them to get exactly what they want.'

Emma said nothing. She was letting him run.

'And what they want,' continued McQueen, adding another pause for effect, 'often turns out to be devastating or even fatal for their unfortunate victims.' He felt himself growing into this podcast game. 'And remember, Emma, we're not only talking about sexual groomers. Yes, they're the ones who make the tabloid headlines, but the term covers a wide range of criminal activity.'

'Yes, could you expand on that, Dr McQueen?'

One of the advantages of the long-form podcast format was that it allowed a real conversation to develop rather than the series of trimmed sound bites required in other media interviews where brevity triumphs over clarity.

'Well,' said McQueen, relaxing as his nervousness abated and he began to relish his place in the spotlight. 'Predatory groomers operate on so many levels in our society. Obviously, as we've said, there are the sexual predators. But think about the financial scammers who gain trust in order to fleece investors of their savings. Or the romance scammers who use grooming to cultivate a relationship before asking for money. Another example would be street gangs who use grooming techniques to recruit new members before introducing them to an inescapable life of crime. And think how powerful the force of grooming is for terrorists. They can convince victims they've never even met to commit appalling crimes.'

Emma nodded vigorously and then said, 'It sounds like modern communications technology, such as the internet, plays a key role in all this.' She was offering the easy-option technology scapegoat, but McQueen wasn't ready to take the bait.

'Yes, but remember, this isn't a new phenomenon, Emma. The internet is just the latest very efficient mass-reach delivery method, but religious cults have been involved in the process of grooming for centuries. And all these grooming strategies, whether it's Charles Manson indoctrinating young hippies into a killing spree or the American pastor Jim Jones convincing his followers to drink poisoned Kool-Aid, they all have certain key very basic human factors in common.'

'Okay. Well, both those terrible cases you've mentioned have been covered before on this show, and so the listeners will be very well acquainted with them. So, Dr McQueen, can you outline some of those common grooming traits for us?'

'Of course. As I said, it starts with vulnerable victims, often damaged people searching for something, people who are missing something in their lives, people who need something. The groomers are exploiters who are experts at spotting the giveaway signs and targeting their weak spots. Then they ingratiate themselves, using nothing more than words to persuade their targets to do unspeakable things.'

'And when you talk about vulnerable victims here, you're not necessarily talking about gullible fools, are you?'

'No, far from it, Emma. Often, they are highly intelligent people who are plagued by their own desires. If you want to use a technology analogy, then you can say their minds are hacked and turned against them by clever programmers. We all know how much damage a computer hacker can do, how much they can steal. Well, these people are mind hackers. All they have to do is get a victim to believe, and once a person truly wants to believe something, then they start to do the groomer's work for them.'

'How do you mean?' The seasoned host already knew the answers to these questions, but her role was to anticipate what an average listener might want to hear, bury her own ego and ask the things they would ask as if she didn't have a clue.

'Okay, let's take a typical scenario. A lonely man gets an unexpected email from a woman which includes a stunningly attractive picture. She's his dream woman. He may look at that picture and his mind builds his perfect fantasy woman. She's being friendly to him, and maybe he doesn't get that anywhere else in his life. He wants to believe in that woman so much he doesn't even see the holes in her story. He ignores her unrealistic reasons for contacting him. He doesn't want to believe the message has actually been sent by a man, a criminal who is after his money. He fills in any gaps in the logic himself with his desperate need for it to be true.'

'Okay, and you mentioned groomers are very good at looking for telltale signs. What might those be?'

'Well, as a particularly disturbing example, men who groom young teenagers for the sex trade will often start by noticing the young person who's apart from the crowd, doesn't have the latest trainers or the latest mobile phone. All signs that this might be a person who is starved of attention. Online, they'll hang out in chat rooms and start conversations with kids who are having a hard time at home. And let's face it, how many teenagers *aren't* having some kind of parent issues?'

'Right, well, that sets the scene, but what we'd all like to know is, What is really going on in the twisted minds of these groomers?'

McQueen smiled. He was on home turf now and he could feel that it was all going to be fine.

Two

It was three in the morning, but a wide-awake Ian Bridger was sitting up in bed. The room was mostly dark, except for his illuminated face and the halo thrown onto the wall behind him by his painfully bright laptop. The harsh screen light washed out the nondescript features of an unremarkable thirty-six-year-old man. It was a face that was easily overlooked in a crowd, easily ignored, and easily forgotten. Such personal invisibility would have been a cause of ego-bruising distress to most people but, for Ian, it was a trait he used to his advantage. Eyewitnesses were notoriously unreliable at the best of times, and without glaring visual clues, they were almost useless.

He was listening very carefully to *The Cullen Report* while staring at the smiling publicity shot of its host on screen. Underneath Emma's image, the red and black time bar steadily ate its way through the remaining seconds of the podcast. Outwardly, Ian showed no emotion and, to an observer, it would have been hard to tell whether he liked what he was hearing or not. But there were no observers. Ian lived alone. He listened to the episode to the very end, even paying close attention to the closing credits and various thank-yous that the producers had tacked on. Eventually, he shut the lid of his computer and nodded into the gloom. He listened to true-crime podcasts for one reason only: research. He wanted to hear about methods and mistakes, about new law-enforcement techniques, about traps that had caught perpetrators, and clever behaviours which had kept criminals from being traced. It wasn't often he actually got anything useful from the broadcasts, but tonight had been different. *The Cullen Report* had shown him something very important. It had introduced him to two very dangerous people. It had introduced him to a threat to his existence and shown him two people who would be better off dead. It wasn't a difficult calculation for him; it made perfect sense. The logic was indisputable, and any dispassionate computer algorithm would come to the same conclusion. If there is a threat to you, you must remove it before it can hurt you, like finding the wasp that's buzzing in your kitchen and killing it before it stings you.

The logical progression that led Ian to believe this know-it-all criminologist and his smug podcaster colleague were particular threats to him would have been harder to follow. All Ian could have said was it was a strong feeling, an impulse, and he always acted on his impulses. McQueen and Cullen had talked about certain specific detailed situations Ian recognised as his own. They'd almost been talking directly to him, taunting him with their knowledge. Maybe they were after him? Cullen had said McQueen was also a private investigator, hadn't she? Even if they weren't tracking him now, they might be soon, and that was enough.

He abandoned his attempt to sleep. With his computer closed, the room was dark, so he flicked on the bedside lamp and got out of bed. He had far too much to do now for his mind to allow him to rest.

Badly insulated and barely carpeted, the house was cold, but he hardly noticed. It was a large, old three-bedroom semi-detached that had once comfortably housed a growing, happy family, but time had reduced the number of family residents to one. It had not been Ian's family, or his house, but now the property was legally his.

He had befriended an elderly woman after noticing the state of her front garden. He'd spotted the unloved, overgrown tangle as he walked past one day and took it as a sign. It spoke to him and told him something about the person who lived there. Preparation is everything, so for the next week he had sat outside in his car, observing everything in the quiet street. He had been there long enough to see the stooping home-owner shuffle past her window a few times and to see she had no visitors. At one point she had come outside in her heavy winter coat, even though it wasn't yet winter, to visit the nearby shop. He'd climbed out of the car, closed the door carefully without slamming it and followed her. He watched as she bought bread, milk, and some other uninspiring essentials before returning home.

A few days later, he had knocked on her door and told her he'd been sent by a local charity to see if she needed any help or someone to clean up her garden. Of course, lonely as she was, she offered this kind, young man a cup of tea. Over the next few weeks, with constant visits and a smiling face, he ingratiated himself and infiltrated her life. He didn't touch the garden, as he'd never intended to, and glad of his company, she didn't care.

During one of their friendly chats which were, in reality, carefully calculated fact-finding missions for him, he had learned that the old woman, Mary, had a grown-up son whom she rarely heard from. She knew he lived alone in Surrey but didn't visit her, not even at Christmas, and they hardly ever spoke. She seemed sad but stoic about the situation, and Ian gently sympathised. Her own flesh and blood certainly wasn't showing Mary the attention Ian was lavishing on her but her son was next of kin, so he was a problem for Ian. He thought it through, applied logic and reasoning to assess the least suspicious sequence of events and then took a week to deal with the son before he could become any kind of issue. While kindly "tidying" her paperwork for her, he'd found all the information he needed on the doomed young man.

People drink and then they drive and then they have accidents. That's what happens, and a roadside tree is an uncompromising stopping place. It was one of the trickiest accidents Ian had ever arranged, but he felt it was worth the effort.

For Ian, the convenient death of Mary's son was a double win. As well as clearing the way ahead, it also let him show her exactly how caring he was by supporting her through her grief. Now that she had no close family left and was more vulnerable than ever, it wasn't hard to subtly steer her towards revisiting her will to leave the house to him "just-in-case", "god-forbid", and "you never know". He even managed to convince her that her generous gesture of gratitude had been her idea all along. She trusted him and couldn't think of anyone else who deserved to live there more. In fact, she insisted. And with the instincts of a true manipulator, to seal the deal, Ian pretended to resist the idea.

Two weeks to the day after signing the updated will, before she'd had a chance to have second thoughts or change her mind, Mary sadly died.

Old people fall. That's what happens, and uncarpeted stairs are a tough landing place for an old neck. Ian made sure he wasn't the one to find her by getting her to book a nurse's home visit for that day. That had made him giggle, her thinking he was showing concern by insisting she ask for a visit, when all he was doing was distancing himself from the murder scene.

Three

McQueen was new to his purpose-built office on the outskirts of the city, having given up his old, converted town house in Leeds city centre when the developers had come knocking. The rotting building with its creaky stairs and unreliable electrics hadn't been ideal as offices, and now after some investment, it was going to become gentrified flats for the up and coming. It was a sign of new affluence in the resurgent city that many years before had been reliant on the wool trade. Some cities had ships, some had coal, some had steel, and Leeds had wool.

Even though it had been a crumbling relic, he'd been emotionally attached to the other office because it was where things had started to click professionally for him. When progress rolls your way, it's best to stand back or you'll get crushed by it. Ideally, he'd have liked to have moved to somewhere like Park Square, the pretty Georgian square in central Leeds, where a grassy area is bounded by rows of prestigious buildings housing mostly solicitors, barristers, private clinics, and financial companies. The address would have added some respectability to his business and counteracted the seedy image of private detection, but those places were still out of his price range. Instead, he'd gone for "modern and convenient" as the agent had described it. The new place was better decorated and digitally connected than the previous one and, due to being slightly out of the city, it had cheaper rents and the holy grail: free parking.

He hadn't owned his old office building and neither had any of the other four companies in there. Like them, he'd been a tenant, and the landlords had been offered a better deal. It was sad really. He'd liked the location and the way he could watch normal people fighting against the driving rain as they trudged into town passing his window. He romanticised the scene as keeping him in touch with the struggles of the stoic Yorkshire people. Their battles were his battles. Unlike the quaint, medieval tourist trap of York only twenty-five miles away, Leeds felt like a modern city to him. Gritty and real. It had thriving, diverse businesses and a multi-cultural energy featuring plenty of people working to make it, which is the lifeblood of every local economy. It also had proper crime, that was for sure.

When McQueen had started his career as a private detective, he'd spent a lot of time with his camera, trailing furtive husbands through the Holbeck Managed Zone. The zone was one of a kind, absolutely unique in Britain, but it didn't feature in any of the "Welcome to Leeds" promotional brochures. Some men even travelled a hundred miles or more to visit the area, but that still didn't make it something any council funded adverts featured.

In 2014, the streets in the north of an area called Holbeck had been designated as a progressive social experiment and bravely championed by the Leeds City Council. It was an area where the sex trade was made legal without fear of prosecution for the women. Maybe it was based on a dreamy vision of the canals of Amsterdam, McQueen didn't know, but he did know it had never reached that level of cool. Its commendable aim was to make it safer for the vulnerable women involved, but this was real life, and they were never safe. As the agreed street boundaries were ignored and the unofficial footprint of the area grew, things inevitably got rough. Local mothers on the school run with children were accosted by kerb-crawling men, and tensions grew. Horrified locals who were much more interested in buying a loaf of bread than getting a blow job were propositioned by desperate working women and girls, and the sparks of outrage flew in every direction. Terrified residents closed their ground-floor curtains in their terraced houses as clients banged sex workers right outside their windows. Crime breeds crime: where there's a sex trade, there are drugs, and where there are drugs, there are violent men. After almost seven years, the knock-on effects of constant protest saw the zone's eventual demise.

As bad as it had been for local people and businesses, the managed zone had made McQueen's job a lot easier. There were no hotels to stake out while waiting for a suspected husband to come out. Instead the ugly, hunched humping against barely hidden fences was easy to photograph for evidence. He hated those jobs, but ironically echoing the claims of the very sex workers he was photographing, it was how he was paying the rent at the time. Sometimes he had wondered if his activities technically made him a pornographer, but his paying audience was usually one weeping or raging wife. It was unfathomable really, men with big houses and double garages from expensive areas such as Linton, Shadwell, and Cookridge, men with Mercedes and BMWs and adoring children, all men who would risk it all for down and dirty sex. The Hugh Grant effect, perhaps? Something pulling at the thousands of years of genetic programming buried in their brains? Who knew? He didn't and he was a celebrated psychologist. The upshot was McQueen wanted to get as far away from that kind of work as he could. He'd got into the private detection arena to solve murders, not chase after men with their pants around their ankles. So, as soon as income would allow, he stopped taking on marriage disputes.

McQueen checked through the spreadsheet of his current work opportunities and allowed himself a satisfied smile. He had been sleeping very badly for months but it certainly wasn't due to the same money worries that had dogged his previous years in the detection business. His current nightmares didn't feature unpaid bills or pound signs, but the demons of his recent dreams wanted more from him than cash. Even though he was a little weary that the bulging columns made good reading, they would keep his accountant, Angus, happy, that was for sure; the man loved a healthy-looking spreadsheet. One of the advantages of becoming almost-famous was that as a previously struggling detective, he was now able to pick and choose his work and leave behind a lot of the run-of-the-mill divorce surveillance cases that used to fill his hours and ruin his nights. As the result of cracking a couple of high-profile mysteries, he had been able to increase his hourly rates, and that tended to put off most of the smaller, grubbier cases.

Another benefit of being in demand and the resulting increase in his income was McQueen had been able to employ an office manager. Originally, he'd advertised the post as "Office Administrator", and there had been a lot of eager applications for the position, but the response had been a bit overwhelming for McQueen. It had been exactly the kind of thing he hated. There were too many emails to sift through because he didn't have an administrator yet. His approach had been to solve the problem as quickly as possible by looking to hire the first person he thought would be able to do the job. After a couple of fairly short and unproductive interviews, he lucked out when he plucked an impressive CV from the list and invited Sekalyia Campbell to come in. Almost as soon as the interview had started, she had made it clear, in a confident and politely assertive way, for future CV purposes she wanted "Office Manager" as her title rather than "administrator". He was slightly taken aback. It was a bold move, cheeky even, and McQueen had immediately liked her style and poise so he'd been happy to oblige. It was something he'd heard that Billy Butlin, the famous holiday camp owner, had discovered many years before: people will do more for a grand title than a wage rise. This young woman was a recent graduate with a first in sociology from Leeds University and was way over-qualified for the role. It did beg the question as to how long she intended to stay at this job, but she gave off such an aura of confident authority and competence that McQueen decided to ignore the risk. She wanted to get her first real job, to start to climb the ladder, and McQueen was perfectly willing to let her miss out on a couple of the bottom rungs. McQueen had read a lot of studies about the psychology of interviews and the assessment techniques one should use to weed out bad candidates, but at the end of the day he relied on his instincts. Sometimes you just hit it off with a person, and that was an automatic reaction he couldn't ignore. He knew statistically rated personality tests had been proven to be much more reliable than gut instincts, but there it was. He liked her, she seemed very capable and he was the boss.

Although making sure the invoices were paid and all case evidence documentation was kept up to date, McQueen primarily saw Sekalyia's job as sifting the wheat from the chaff for him, because there had been enough chaff to choke him. She was his filter so he didn't have to deal with time wasters. He wanted serious cases that were challenges to his intellectual talents, and his new office manager was sharp enough to see which of the many enquiries those would be. In short, without too much explanation, she just got it. She picked out the cases she said would interest her, and that formula seemed to work. She kept the spreadsheet updated and he stopped worrying about any of it. Within a week of her starting, he didn't know what he would do without her.

There were a couple office ground rules McQueen and Sekalyia quickly came to an agreement over. One being she wasn't there to make coffee. She would make him one if she was having one but she would appreciate it if he would do the same. It was fair enough. She also told him her friends and family shortened her name to Lia, and it would be okay with her if he wanted to use that. He reciprocated by saying she needn't use Dr McQueen, and McQueen would be fine.

He was hopeful the hiring of Lia was going to be one more step towards making his agency the business he'd originally dreamed of. McQueen had left the successful and comfortable world of academia behind to use his criminology knowledge to do good. It was laughable really, a naïve and childish notion and one that had lost him a marriage while almost bankrupting him. It had plunged him into a life of chasing petty cheats when what he wanted to be doing was solving murders. It had also put him in extreme danger from time to time, but he'd survived in more ways than one. At last things seemed to be on an upswing, and the Cullen podcast was the latest of the bonuses.

The Cullen Report had gone very well, and afterwards Emma had seemed genuinely pleased with his expert contribution, or so she said as she wowed him with her bright, white smile and the thrilling squeeze of his arm. More importantly, the online feedback had been great. It seemed the topic of groomers had struck a chord with the public, and Emma was talking about a follow-up show to answer some of the listeners' questions. McQueen couldn't help allowing himself a smirk when he read that email from her. He felt the warm glow of peer approval none of us can resist.

Four

Sitting on the tattered couch opposite the living room window, Ian closed his eyes and thought about the details of the last person he'd killed. It was a man who had brushed past him in a quiet street. A stranger he had choked from behind with the stranger's own woollen scarf, perhaps knitted for him by his wife. That would have been a nice touch. Even though he had no capacity to imagine the pain of others he knew the physical effects of his actions. She would cry and berate herself for knitting the scarf. That was funny.

The victim was about five feet nine, medium build, probably around forty years old. He had looked right at Ian in a very knowing way as they had passed. What on earth could he know? It didn't matter. It was a threat, and Ian's instincts had been alive to it. Ian let him walk a few paces and then turned and silently rushed after him. Surprise was always a great weapon. The man didn't even turn, and Ian hit him hard on the back of the head with a cosh made from a slim leather pouch that was full of pound coins. If searched, he wasn't carrying an illegal weapon, only his man-purse. Then, as the stunned man sank to his knees, Ian had grabbed the trailing ends of the scarf and pulled it tight, then dragged him into the bushes at the side of the road. He kept the pressure up for a good minute after the flailing man had stopped struggling and then turned the choked man onto his back so he could see his face. Ian liked to see their eyes. He liked to try to see what the dead could see, what they knew, how they were different. He desperately wanted to take a picture so he could remember this, but the risk of having that evidence on him was too great. Besides, Ian stood alone in the world having no camera on his phone. He did own a disposable phone, an untraceable burner he kept because some of the criminal contacts he'd used in the past insisted on encrypted SMS messages, but he always left it at home. The police can track suspects through their phones. Suspects' positions can be accurately triangulated, and timings can be calculated. Anyway, most of the time he didn't need a phone; he had no one to call.

When Ian's eyes were closed, he saw nothing, no gory pictures or constantly running mental video. He saw nothing visual, only blackness. He only knew the facts and figures of what he had done. There were no pictures to go with his thoughts. That was why he liked to see the effects of what he could do to people in the flesh. It was sculpting with blood and bones. He could decide on the process of choking a man but then he wanted to be able to see what that actually looked like. He did remember a catalogue of details, though, a checklist so he would never carelessly repeat a pattern. He also kept a spreadsheet on his laptop, all in a personal code he had devised of dates, times, and methods, just in case he forgot anything. But he never forgot.

Having made an exhaustive study of the failings of other murderers, he'd noticed early on they were often caught because they had a recognisable pattern to their work. It gave the police something to focus on, and then they could set traps. For that reason, he tried to avoid any hint of similarity in his crimes. It would have been impossible for the authorities to link any of his victims because, quite simply, there was no link. Their only connections were that they had come to Ian's attention as a threat in some way and he had decided to kill them. Murders can easily appear to be bafflingly motiveless purely because the police can't comprehend the motive. Ian killed people who were a danger to him, but it would not have been possible for anyone to see that. Ian saw threats where others wouldn't have, because he had a sixth sense. He believed he was gifted and he knew more than other people. He could spot threats others didn't. That's why he would never be caught. Another big factor which played a part in the capture of the guilty was stupidity. Some very intelligent killers had done some extremely stupid things that had resulted in their downfall. Maybe it was complacency. When you've done something several times and got away with it you can begin to think you are somehow protected. Ian was never complacent or stupid.

He was also willing to learn lessons. For instance, when he had killed a woman who had been trailing him as he walked through town he'd almost made a mistake. She had taken the same turns as him for a good ten minutes, and it was clear she was following him. So when he reached the top of a set of concrete steps were near the carpark he turned and punched her hard in the face so she clattered down the sharp edges head first. There had been CCTV cameras nearby, and his fleeing image had been captured for a split second. Fortunately, the pictures were poor quality, and even though the video was shown on the local news, no one could recognise him and the story was soon dropped. Still, it was a warning. City centres and carparks are hot spots for snooping cameras. These days, even private houses are dotted with them. It was something to bear in mind, something to plan for.

And then there was Mary and her son. In lots of ways, they had been an exciting new direction for him. They were a very positive change, different from all the others. He was sick of living in rented accommodation, too many close neighbours. He wanted a house to himself, so he'd found a way to get one through them. To kill two people from the same family and then to take their house was the riskiest thing Ian had ever done. It went against everything he'd tried to teach himself about self-preservation, but in the end, he surrendered to this new recklessness that took hold and guided him. However, he hadn't lost all his senses and so had taken as many precautions as he could. It was why he'd spent so long researching the mother and son and taken such care to make sure their deaths looked like tragic accidents. For anyone to see a link they would have to be looking, and there was no one left to be interested in their deaths. There were no family members around to raise a stink, and who else would even notice? Ian had made sure Mary had used a faceless, soulless will-writing company to produce the documents so there was no busybody family solicitor involved.

Yes, it was true Mary had died falling down stairs like the woman at the carpark, but it wasn't the same, not at all. No one could make that link.

The other fresh element to the crime, one which had thrilled Ian, was Mary wasn't even a threat. She was something new, a blockage to his plans. Ian liked that idea, the idea she was not an actual threat, because it added another random element to the killing he knew kept the cosmos from aligning against him.

And now there were Cullen and McQueen. Their deaths wouldn't have to appear to be accidents, but unlike for Mary, everyone would be interested. Cullen was a TV personality after all, and that was exciting. There would be quite a stink. Many serial killers seemed to love notoriety and got a thrill from seeing coverage of their exploits. Ian liked to slip right under the radar. He wanted things to be as quiet as possible, so this would be different.

Researching the esteemed Dr McQueen and media queen Emma Cullen wasn't hard. They both loved the limelight, and a lot of their showboating was online for anyone to see. Ian studied McQueen's old cases, the ones that had made the papers anyway. He was impressive, definitely a threat. Ian looked at his website. A private investigator who wasn't an ex-cop, which was slightly unusual, but from news website reports of McQueen's past cases, it was clear he had ties to the police through a detective called Tracey Bingham. They had solved a case together and caught a serial killer. She had been promoted, and he had gone on to other triumphs. Ian read for a while, trying to get a sense of this man who may well be hunting him even now.

He looked at McQueen's picture, a prematurely grey-haired man, who was a little overweight and had a kindly, craggy face. He was mentioned as divorced by one journalist called Anne Kirkpatrick who seemed to have done a number of stories about him, not all flattering, but without any details of his ex-wife. By trawling the internet and searching around, Ian managed to track down some footage of McQueen on a TV show some years before. It wasn't great quality, and although he looked younger, he was perhaps a little drunk. He was giving his valuable insights into what makes people kill and he seemed way off the mark to Ian. He was observing the subject from the outside and basing his guesses on academic studies. A typical educated fool, he knew nothing. He did talk about his psychology background a lot, the fact he was a criminologist and how clever he was. Ian giggled. A psychology doctorate wasn't much use when there was a cord tightening around your neck or a knife slicing through your flesh.

Ian studied the McQueen Agency website; all the necessary contact details were there. The psychologist-detective had an office on the outskirts of Leeds. There was even a picture of the redbrick building with some poplar trees visible in the background. This was all good information because it meant McQueen was easily accessible.

There was a lot more information about Emma Cullen, too much in fact, and it was carefully managed by someone who had a main eye on publicity. Of her various shows, her podcast in particular attracted obsessive followers, and some of them took unsolved cases into their own hands. They used their combined information and internet connections to track down criminals. They had achieved at least one success by tracking down a man who had killed his wife and then gone into hiding. Emma was obviously a threat.

Five

Life being what it is and human bodies being what they are, if you are a GP, you have to get used to giving people bad news. It's an uncomfortable and often heartbreaking part of the job but it has to be done. It's the same for private detectives: there's often bad news to share, and McQueen always tried to mirror the same professional, no-nonsense, fact-based delivery doctors had used on him in the past. There had been a fair amount of bad medical news for him over the years, including he'd needed open-heart surgery, but he was still alive, and whether the news had been good or bad, he'd always appreciated medical honesty.

Telling a distraught wife her missing husband wasn't dead should have been a joyous moment. It should have been one of the perks of the job. Unfortunately, that isn't true if the missing husband has been found alive, living a happy new life with a new woman in a new town.

McQueen looked across his desk at the shell-shocked wife and her frozen face. He'd tried to let her down softly, but in the end, he'd still given her the details and shown her the pictures. They were the facts, and he couldn't change or hide them. She had paid a lot of money to find out what had happened to her husband once the police stopped showing any interest, and now she knew. From a professional perspective, he'd done his job, and it hadn't really been very hard to trace the husband. Fairly straightforward for a private detective with access to some specialist databases and a bit of experience. The police could certainly have found him if they'd had the time or the inclination. McQueen had only taken on the case because the wife had presented it as a possible murder scenario and there had initially been enough circumstantial evidence to suggest she could be right, but it turned out to have been a false trail laid by her fleeing husband. McQueen had been suckered into the kind of work he was trying to avoid, but the wife had been fooled, too, and her loss was greater.

The detective looked at her now as she took it all in, and although he'd seen it all before, he couldn't help feeling sorry for her. He would have liked to have given her a fraternally comforting hug, but it would have been awkwardly inappropriate and probably unwelcome, so he kept his seat.

She was a very slightly built, almost delicate woman in her mid-thirties, and although McQueen was no expert on fashion labels, as far as he could tell she was expensively dressed. He'd certainly noticed her hair, which was a lovely cascading flow of various shades of auburn that were now being picked out by the sunlight sliding through the half-closed blinds of his office. By any standards, Marina

Markham was a very pretty woman, but so too was the woman her husband had absconded with, who predictably was also a few years younger. That was one of the things he didn't like about these kinds of cases, the utter mind-numbing predictability of them.

McQueen hadn't been sure how she was going to react to the grim truth he'd uncovered, but as yet there had been no tears.

'So he's not dead?' she repeated, nodding more to herself than him.

McQueen shook his head. Seeing the pain cross her dark eyes for a second, he almost said, "I'm afraid not". It would have been an automatic response based on sympathy, but he managed to stop himself. It wouldn't have been very professional to wish someone's husband dead, no matter what a cruel shit he'd been to her. Instead, McQueen continued to present the cold facts.

'He's very much alive, Mrs Markham, but I'm sorry, he clearly didn't want to be found. He wanted to give the impression he may have been murdered so you would stop looking for him, I suppose.' He could have framed this positively as her husband trying to end her anguish quickly, once and for all, so she didn't have to deal with the thought of the other woman. But it wasn't for McQueen to second guess the man's motives, and a guess is all it would have been.

She snorted derisively, her first show of anger. 'Coward,' is all she said.

'I managed to retrieve a coffee cup he'd used, and it had a good set of prints on it, so I can confirm it's definitely him.

It's your husband, Toby Markham.'

'Did you speak to him?'

'No, I didn't. I didn't want to alert him to anything.'

She sighed and leaned over to take one of the A4 printouts from the desk. McQueen's printer wasn't great, but it showed a handsome man in his late thirties, laughing, hand in hand with an equally happy-looking, beautiful young woman as they walked in a park. There were a lot of shining teeth on show, and it looked like an advert for a holiday. It must have been sickening for Marina to see.

She studied it for a while and murmured, 'She looks nice.' And then she took a deep breath and straightened her back in the chair.

There were still no tears, and the pain that had momentarily haunted her eyes had been replaced by a look of resolve. It was as if all the information he'd given her had been processed and decisions had already been made. It was a quicker than usual turnaround, and McQueen wondered if perhaps she wasn't quite as delicate as he'd imagined. He silently admonished himself. Judging books by covers was a very bad habit for a detective and could even be dangerous, but not in this case.

'Okay,' she said. 'Give me that, please.' She was pointing at the large folder of evidence McQueen had collected, which he then pushed across the desk to her.

'It's got everything in there,' he said. 'His current name and where he works.'

'And his address?'

'Yes, and his phone number.'

She carefully added the picture she'd been staring at to

31

the file and then stood up. 'Please send me your invoice, Mr McQueen. You've done very well. Very thorough, so thank you.'

'Can I ask what you intend to do?' he asked gently. 'Will you contact him? The insurance company will, of course, need to be notified, and there could be fraud charges pending.'

She didn't answer. Her face was set and unflinching. Nothing showed, but she was still an injured human being. McQueen suddenly felt very moved by her plight, and all thoughts of being professionally distant left his head. Although it wasn't his place to do it, he wanted to extend some comfort.

'For what it's worth,' he continued. 'I think it was very cruel of him. Anger and revenge will probably be your first thoughts. You wouldn't be the first to go down that route, but I would advise against doing anything hasty. Give yourself some time to absorb this. You can always come back to talk to me if there's anything more you need.'

McQueen was also now standing, and she extended her arm to shake his hand. Her thin fingers were small in his, and he tried not to squeeze too hard for fear of crushing them.

'Goodbye, Mr McQueen,' she said without responding to any of his comments, and she was right; it was none of his business.

In the outer office, Lia spoke quietly to her and handed her some more paperwork. Then, with a buzz from the security door, she let Marina out into the fresh air and her newly defined and shaken-up life. After Marina had gone,

Lia came across the office and stood at McQueen's open door. She leaned against the frame, her arms folded across her pristine blue blouse, her short, straightened hair neat and perfect. She looked every inch the successful businesswoman. He felt for a second as if he was being scrutinised by his boss rather than his assistant. McQueen looked at her face for clues but saw none. She knew everything about the case, and she'd been very helpful in the tedious work of collating all the evidence, but so far she had passed no judgement.

'Poor woman,' said McQueen.

Lia pursed her lips and nodded slowly. 'I guess. And she still maintains she didn't know he was still alive? She had no clue?'

McQueen sat back down and cocked his head to one side as he regarded her closely. In the short time she had worked with him, he had already discovered her opinion was always worth listening to.

'You don't believe her?' he asked.

'I don't know, but there's something off about her.'

'Really? I didn't get that.'

'Right,' she said, turning away. 'But you're a man.'

Six

It was such a lovely restaurant. It was like stepping into a warm, pleasant dream, reassuring and comforting. Dark enough to provide a welcoming ambience but light enough to see your dinner partner's smile. Background jazz loud enough to lend atmosphere, but quiet enough to be able to hear what your companion is saying. Judging by the other diners' meals he'd spied as he'd weaved his way through the tables, McQueen was certain the food would be equally impressive. He'd checked online, and the menu described the tapas-style small plates as *Cajun-inspired dishes and tastes from all over the world*. He already had his mind set on the sticky glazed pork belly as one of his choices.

Emma had chosen the venue, and McQueen had to remind himself this was an important business meeting rather than a date. On the phone, she'd mentioned opportunities to work together, which was very exciting considering her standing in the industry. He was still finding it hard to shake that date frame of mind, though, because he'd been on a few app-arranged restaurant visits recently. It was, after all, the modern way to find love, or sex at least. A picture, a bio, a call, and then a meeting, boom, you had a date. At forty-six, McQueen was old enough to remember when it hadn't been this way. Lonely hearts columns had been a thing of ridicule when he was a teenager, an admission of relationship defeat. Now, proudly announcing to the digital world you couldn't find someone to go out with was accepted as the only way to meet.

How values change, he thought, and that was true across the full spectrum of intimate personal exposure. He recalled in the late eighties, the actor Rob Lowe, a very handsome young fledgling star, had lost his career because of a self-starring sex tape. But about fifteen years later, Kim Kardashian had initiated a billion-dollar empire with hers. Who could guess what the next ten years would bring? Maybe sex tapes would become the default resumé for every celebrity. Meanwhile, McQueen was trying to negotiate the various hurdles of down-to-earth internet dating without much success.

So far, all of McQueen's attempted courtships had proven to be disappointing, and he was sure the women on the other side of the table had felt the same. No follow-ups had ever been organised, which said it all really.

After his divorce, McQueen hadn't been particularly interested in meeting anyone new, and his work had made him very busy, especially late at night. It was the same detective work which had helped his marriage to disintegrate, that and the fact that he drank too much. Also, he had impulsively abandoned a comfortable, secure life as a lecturer to become a hero. His wife hadn't seen a hero. Instead she'd seen an empty bed, mounting bills, and a man having a self-destructive midlife crisis. But all that was before a case involving a couple called Baxter had made McQueen's name as a private detective and thrust him into the national spotlight for a week.

Recently, however, McQueen had thought it might be nice to have someone to talk to away from work and. after some initial reluctance. he had put himself "out there". His last two restaurant hook-ups were with very intelligent, great-looking women who had both seen his name and his picture in the papers but whose delightful faces gradually fell when they met the man behind the myth. Now he'd given up drinking he could no longer kid himself everyone around him found him hilarious at all times. He was sure he talked too much to compensate for his sobriety, and not everyone is interested in psychology case histories. The women had both wanted to know more details about his gory tabloid sensations, but it was exactly what he'd been hoping to get away from.

Tonight, however, the meal with Ms Cullen was meant to be work, so he was expecting to have to trot out some of the racy highlights of his exploits. Meanwhile, now he was more used to seeing her, Emma looked even more attractive than ever, which he felt was going to be something of a distraction. She was a serious player in the media world, and McQueen was keen not to come across as a creepy fanboy.

Emma glanced at the menu, but as a regular in the place, she already knew what she wanted. He squinted at the lists in the gloom. Overthinking on romantic liaisons meant even choosing the dishes felt like a test. *Don't let yourself down by ordering anything that's difficult to eat* was the general rule, and he was starting to think the sticky pork might be a bit messy before he remembered this was business so it didn't matter.

'Thanks for coming,' she beamed.

As McQueen saw her perfect features smiling so warmly at him across the tablecloth, he found himself wishing there could be just a touch of romance about this business.

'More than glad to, Emma. Such a pleasure to see you outside the studio.' He said this perhaps a bit too eagerly and then pointed at the wine list. 'Listen, I'm afraid I'm going to have sparkling water, but feel free to get wine for yourself. It's not a problem for me.'

'No, it's fine,' she said. 'I rarely drink these days.'

He wondered for a second if she was avoiding the wine as a favour to him, but again he was overthinking it. It was more likely she wanted to stay sharp for the discussion.

Out of the corner of his eye, McQueen couldn't help noticing several of the other diners were looking over at their table and one of them was trying to surreptitiously level their phone to take a sneaky picture. Emma was looking straight at McQueen and she must have noticed him frowning. He thought she hadn't seen the gawping neighbour, but she'd seen.

'Ignore it,' she said. 'People see a face they've seen on TV and they lose their minds a little bit sometimes. I may even get to do a selfie or two later.' She was grinning, and it obviously didn't bother her, but for McQueen this was a new experience.

Even when he'd been featured in newspapers, no one had ever recognised him in a restaurant. He hadn't realised quite how well-known Emma was, and it was a bit weird to witness the effect.

'And do you get this a lot?' he asked.

She shrugged. 'A little, but it's part of the job. If you want to be on TV, you have to expect it. Mind you, most people who know my face can't remember where they've seen me before. If they get rude, it's annoying, but I'm aware there are millions of people out there who would give their right arms to be recognised in public, so I don't complain.'

The pressures of fame were not something McQueen had ever needed to think about much, although the dehumanising downsides of living in the public eye were well documented in psychological literature. When he'd been studying for his doctorate, he had met a young patient who had suffered the mental health consequences of having lived the classic child-star nightmare. He had presented with severe depression and suicidal tendencies and he was a case study for McQueen. As far as he could remember, the patient was called Barry something-or-other, and McQueen had never heard of him before meeting him, which was part of the problem. How do you adapt to adult life when all your best moments are behind you at fourteen years old? Fourteen years of never having to face the fact that shit happens and feeling you are exempt from the boring and mundane. That case was less about the pressures of fame and more about the devastation of no longer being famous.

Barry had loved being recognised and being treated like a prince. Who wouldn't? But once it stopped, he struggled to adapt to the obscurity most of us take for granted. Once hopelessness for the future dawned on him, the bad behaviours started, which only hastened his descent. The so-called self-medication of drink and drugs hadn't soothed Barry at all, and he'd finally achieved his goal of ending his own life even though he'd been under supervision in a private hospital at the time. Late one night, he'd managed to swallow enough toilet paper to choke himself on wadded paper and vomit.

McQueen started to open his mouth to tell Emma the story but given their location and the gruesome choking part, thought better of it and instead left her to start the conversation.

'Soooo,' she said, stringing the word out playfully, 'as you know, the podcast went really well. It turns out you really know your stuff, Dr McQueen, and more importantly, you can communicate. Let me tell you, in the brains-for-hire game, that's rarer than you'd imagine.'

He feigned some humble embarrassment and said awkwardly, 'Oh, thank you, but it wasn't difficult. You've got a great show. It was the perfect platform for me to ramble on. I love my subject. It's my life, so it's something I could talk all day about.' He shrugged. 'It was good you were there to shut me up, Emma.'

She dutifully chuckled at his weak joke, which he felt was a good sign.

He pressed on. 'I've heard a lot of your work, and your

TV programme is very good, too.' He wondered if his unsubtle drift into the topic of her television show was a little clumsy, but she didn't recoil.

'And that's exactly what I want to talk to you about,' she said, leaning across the table a little and subjecting him to the full force of her gleaming smile. 'But first, how about we just enjoy our dinner and forget about the office for a while?'

'You mean we could mix business with pleasure? I thought that was one of those cardinal rules kick-arse executives weren't supposed to break. Not in the mafia anyway.'

'Well, I've never subscribed to that stupid rule and I've never been in the mafia,' she laughed.

McQueen sat back a little in his seat and tried not to look as surprised as he felt.

'I have a hectic work schedule,' she continued. 'Busy, busy, busy, and it doesn't leave much me-time. It's not often I get to relax with someone who interests me, so could we just get to know each other a little? Take the pressure off a bit?'

She was looking at him quizzically from under a perfectly shaped arched brow, as if she didn't know what his answer was going to be. For his part, McQueen couldn't believe it. He'd misread the signs, and in his eagerness to not trivialise the meeting, he had missed the fact that he'd actually been invited on a date.

Wow, he thought, *Emma Cullen, TV star, you've thrown me.* He knew according to Wikipedia she'd never been married but had been linked with a number of rich, high-achieving men. Not that he'd been stalking her, but he'd done some basic background research before the podcast. In one interview he'd read, she said she liked to be in control of her own life and that sometimes men found that intimidating. McQueen didn't feel intimidated but he had been wrong-footed.

'But of course,;' he said, regaining his composure. 'Nothing would give me more pleasure, Emma.' And he meant it.

'Great.' She raised her glass of bubbling water. 'So tell me about your hopes, fears and dreams, McQueen. Tell me what you want from life.'

Seven

The internet had been designed especially for Ian Bridger. It had emerged from deep within the infinite power of the universe, a gift for him. He was certain of that. The people who sent their money to him via the impenetrably anonymous online connections that had been put at his disposal were not really people at all, they were a digital creation. They came from a vast, bottomless, gently swirling cyber ocean of big, fat money-fish waiting to be hauled in. The electronic water stretched off into the horizon and it would never run dry. It had been put in place by cosmic forces as a resource for him, so that he didn't have to work in some stupid job somewhere to get money for food. It left him free to do the other things the universe needed for balance. He had worked in so-called normal jobs in the past, but they had always ended badly, and now he realised that was because they jarred with the natural order of things. He wasn't cut out for that type of ordinary work, so the invisible forces didn't allow him to stay there. It was so simple. The right mixture of words was all it took to attract the money-fish and then to pull them in, and Ian always knew the right words no matter who was reading them at the other end.

Some of Ian's financial contributors believed him to be a woman, some a man. Others thought he was a young girl or a young boy. It didn't really matter what they believed as long as they believed. It did mean there were a lot of different stories for him to remember and sometimes he got them slightly mixed up, but that was never a problem. There was always a way of explaining any slips. As the detective, McQueen, had said on the podcast, these people wanted to give their hearts and souls to the fantasy Ian provided so much there was little that would shake them off. He could usually get them to apologise for questioning him if they got too curious. Although they were a varied bunch, they all had one thing in common: they all thought they were helping a desperate person, a person who was relying on them, and them alone, for financial salvation. It was so funny.

There were a few basic guidelines that Ian followed to keep it all working smoothly. For a start, he made sure he chose a credible image to send to them, nothing too unbelievably beautiful or startlingly handsome, but attractive enough to be desirable. There were plenty to choose from on the web, and he always knew the ones that would work best. Then he let their imaginations do the rest.

He always said he was from a foreign country or that he had to work away from home a lot. He didn't want any surprise visits. He would have lied about his address anyway, but it might have got tricky. Once they had engaged with him and began to trust him they usually wanted to have a video call, but he always refused. It was easy to deflect those requests with phrases like, 'I can't. It's too dangerous'. That had the extra benefit of adding some underlying tension to the relationship, which set up the next steps. Once the person had been chatting for a few weeks, Ian would introduce some tragedy and ask for a financial helping hand. He started small. It depended on the situation he'd invented, but money for a winter coat or something desperate like that usually worked. There were so many ways to ask for money, they were limitless. Sympathy was a powerful motivator. To pay off loans to violent people was a good one, to pay rent or buy tickets for a visit were others.

Once they had sent a small amount, it was easy to ask for more, and their need to believe they hadn't wasted the money they had already sent kicked in. The bigger the sacrifice, the more they needed to believe in the fantasy. It had always been the same: sacrifice your favourite bull to the gods, and how can you not continue to believe in the god? Who wants to admit to themselves that they've been fooled?

Ultimately, however, all the time he put into grooming, the faceless mass was just for money, and money was meaningless. He didn't have expensive tastes but he did keep his technology up to date, which cost money. He wasn't interested in fancy foods, it was tasteless fuel to him, and most of the time he could survive perfectly well on cans of baked beans. He never got bored with his diet because there was nothing to compare it with. There was no joy to be found in eating.

Yes, money was how he paid for the few things he needed but it wasn't the essence of life, it wasn't what made the cosmos flex and spin around him. Death was the essence of life, and the making of death, the removal of all threats, was what had kept him alive. Money was just a by-product that spun out of keeping things aligned and in balance, and now Ian had some more balancing to do.

He had two murders to plan and he couldn't afford to be impulsive about them. These two people who thought they knew everything about everything, who thought they knew Ian and how he could be brought down, the TV woman and the psychology man, were about to find out the things they didn't know and could never know.

If Ian killed McQueen first, that would mean Emma Cullen would be compelled to talk about it on her show, never knowing she would be next. That would be funny. Or he could kill Cullen first. Then the detective would try to solve her murder, which would make him easier to find and kill. If he could kill them both together, that would be even better, that would be so powerful. He'd never killed two people at the same time before, and that thought was very exciting. There were a lot of options, but he didn't have to decide yet. His instincts would tell him the right order.

What he was sure of was this was the perfect time to use the gun. He had acquired a handgun a few years earlier through the dark web. It was an untraceable weapon that, as far as he could tell, had come from somewhere in Eastern Europe. At the time he'd bought it, he'd been seized by an overwhelming impulse to own a gun. It had become an obsession, and although he had no immediate plan to use it he just knew he had to have a pistol. Night after night, he trawled through the cesspit of the web's underworld and eventually found a source he felt he could trust. He'd paid a lot for the weapon, using cash, and he had travelled to Manchester to swap the packages at a drop-off point on a country lane. It was all very cloak-and-dagger, and he had been very nervous about the whole transaction. By definition, the seller was a dangerous criminal, and there were so many things that could have gone wrong. But it had all worked out, and Ian had got his gun and a few rounds of ammunition.

The heavy matte-black pistol looked quite old, but it fitted so nicely in his hand he didn't want to put it down. He'd had pretty convincing toy guns as a child and air pistols when he was a teenager, but this had a completely different feel. It carried with it a powerful psychological dimension, because right there beneath his index finger was life and death. A precision machine engineered for one purpose only: to take a life. Since buying it, he had been biding his time and waiting for the right time to use it. At last, it seemed, that time had come. It was an ideal way to kill Emma Cullen. The police would immediately think it was some kind of gangland killing, perhaps done by a criminal she had hounded on her show. It would send them spinning wildly in circles. In Leeds, a shooting wasn't unheard of by any means but it was still unusual enough to stand out. Stabbings were so common they sometimes didn't even make the news, but a shooting was still a story, especially of a celebrity.

Unlike for every other murder he'd ever done, Ian wanted these two victims to make a lasting impact. He was growing as a person, developing and evolving, and he wanted every person in the country to be aware of what he'd done, even though they would have no idea it was he who had done it. He wanted the world to be scared of what was possible.

That was the paradox at the heart of Ian's existence he struggled to contain. While he wanted the cover of anonymity and the ability to safely pass everywhere unseen, he also wanted people to recognise how clever he was. It was his history of achievements he didn't want to go unheralded, the things he had done that no one else could, the things that made him unique.

All his life, Ian had lived alone in a world of one. Like an astronaut in an abandoned capsule spinning in space, he had no way to tell up from down. He was his only judge. There was no one to watch or to listen to his thoughts other than him. There was no one to notice the changes and to tell him his thought processes were becoming more erratic and his thinking more muddled by the day. His logic didn't hold water, and his conclusions were measured against no calibration. His only monitor was himself, and to him everything was absolutely normal. It was exactly the way it had always been. He had always trusted his instincts, and the guiding powers of the cosmos had never steered him wrong.

It was while he was checking over the pathetic messages his financial victims had sent, making sure payments had been made, that he had the revelation. Of course, Dr

47

McQueen was just like everyone else. He had things he wanted, things he craved. Now that Ian had read some background about McQueen, he could see very clearly what they were. McQueen could be hooked in like any other fish, probably not for money, but for something better. McQueen was a do-gooder. He wanted to solve difficult murders, he wanted to be a hero, he wanted to show how much he could help the world. If he could be shown an opportunity to do that, he would not be able to resist. Vulnerability wasn't always about being poor or unloved; sometimes it was simply about having a weakness. Ian could see McQueen's weakness as if it were a huge neon sign hanging over his head. It would be fun to play with McQueen until Ian was ready to kill him.

Eight

'You okay?' Lia had bustled into McQueen's office and found him staring blankly into the distance, the coffee in front of him untouched.

'Yeah, fine,' he said, snapping out of it. 'Things on my mind.' He didn't admit that what had been dominating his thoughts hadn't been challenging criminal cases but the softness of some particular pillowcases. Emma Cullen had soft pillowcases, and the towel he'd used in her bathroom after he'd showered the next morning had been as luxurious as any brand new one, fresh off the shelf. How did people manage that? It was something he never seemed to achieve in his own laundry. No matter which powder, conditioner, or spin cycle he chose, he always ended up with slightly scratchy covers for his pillows, along with his limp abrasive towels.

The evening had developed very nicely in the restaurant, the conversation had flowed freely and everything had felt very easy and natural between them.

She was an impressive, knowledgeable woman and not the shallow, self-absorbed media entity he'd wrongly feared she might be. He scolded himself for being so judgmental. But as fascinating as she was, he somehow managed to keep up with her, and she seemed genuinely interested in him. She was funny too, something that had never come across on screen. As a lovely evening, it easily leaped to the top of his dating charts.

And then it got even better. At her suggestion, they'd gone back to her house to continue getting to know each other, and for once it couldn't be blamed on boozy abandon by either of them. It turned into one of the most memorable nights of his year so far, and when he'd awoken from a dream-free night to the sounds of Emma showering, the softness of the pillows had almost overwhelmed him.

It was while he was still enjoying the morning glow that she had come back into the room, a towel turbaned around her wet hair, and told him about her latest business proposition. She sat on the edge of the bed and explained she was about to start fronting a new ten-part documentary on one of the digital streaming platforms that had a massive worldwide reach. It was very exciting for her. The show was going to be the biggest she had ever done, and it was going to be an enormous commitment. And then she dropped the bombshell: she wanted him to be a part of it. Rather than simply including him as a guest, she was hoping he'd come on board as a technical advisor on the production team. She wanted expert guidance on the criminology that was going to underpin the programme and she felt he was the perfect candidate to provide it. She wanted authenticity and accuracy but she also wanted the credibility backup of having his name in the credits. It was a lot to take in, and he realised in some ways he was being steamrollered into something while his resistance was weakened, but it didn't feel like a bad thing at all. It felt like a lottery win.

He still had a faint smile playing across his face when Lia said, 'Well, you'd better get up to speed, McQueen, because you have some visitors.'

Flustered, he checked his laptop. 'There's nothing in the calendar until eleven,' he said, feeling he'd been caught out in some way.

'These are unexpected visitors,' she replied, raising her eyebrows, 'of the police variety. They insisted.'

McQueen's professional relationship with the police had never been smooth. He put it down to the fact that he was not one of their own. A lot of private detectives were ex-coppers, which was useful for them because they could usually rely on a helping hand and inside information from their ex-colleagues. In turn, the police felt they could trust their old buddies. But they didn't feel the same way about McQueen. At best, they viewed him as something of a hindrance to their work because he had no loyalty to them and, as far as they could see, he simply got in the way. At worst, in their eyes, he was simply obstructing the course of justice. His cause hadn't been helped when he'd pursued, solved, and taken national headlines for a case they'd completely given up on. He did have police help on that one, but it had come from one brave lone woman, Detective Tracey Bingham. She'd become a friend, but on the basis that he never asked her for her professional help. She said it was hard enough running the gauntlet of police politics as a gay woman without having the millstone of a needy private detective to lug around with her. She wanted to keep their friendship on the down-low, and he had to respect that.

The two plainclothes male detectives were shown into the office by Lia, who then went out and closed the door behind her. They introduced themselves as Detectives Reed and Chambers and then sat down on the client chairs opposite McQueen's desk. They were both in their early thirties by the look of them. Chambers was what McQueen would have called a "bulky unit", and they'd obviously been briefed about him because neither was smiling. After formally identifying themselves, they didn't waste any time with pleasantries before they got to their questions. McQueen noted they deliberately referred to him as Mr rather than Dr, perhaps to rile him, but it wasn't something that ever bothered him at all. He rarely used the title anyway and he certainly wasn't going to be unsettled by it now.

'Mr McQueen, do you know a Toby Markham?'

McQueen didn't have to think about that name. It's hard to forget a guy you've been hunting for weeks and following around with a camera. He was the disappearing husband McQueen had tracked down for Marina Markham. He was the man who had preferred to leave heartache and grief behind him to give the impression he was dead rather than tell his wife he was running away. McQueen could now guess what this meeting was all about. Presumably, the insurance company wanted to prosecute Toby Markham for insurance fraud, and the police probably wanted to see what evidence McQueen was holding.

'Yes, I know who he is,' said McQueen. 'I tracked him down for his wife after he proved to be too elusive for the vast resources of the police force.' He grinned and looked at the two humourless faces in front of him and thought he detected a sneer from Reed. He knew he shouldn't antagonise them, it didn't help anyone, but he just couldn't stop himself. 'The thing is, officers, you'll have to speak to his wife. I gave all the evidence to her, and it's for her to share it with you if she wants to. She has client privilege with me, so I can't really discuss the case.'

Detective Chambers was taking notes, but it was Reed who spoke. He had a deeper, more resonant voice than his partner and perhaps they had decided that was more compelling. 'We have spoken to Mrs Markham, but now we're talking to you. Can you tell us your whereabouts on the evening of Friday the seventeenth?'

The atmosphere had changed dramatically with that question, and McQueen knew enough about the legal process to know it wasn't the kind of question he should be answering without a lawyer present.

'I don't understand,' he said. 'What is this about? Why are you asking me that?'

There was no perceivable change in the expression on either policeman's face but then Detective Reed said, 'Because Mr Markham has been murdered, Mr McQueen.' It was said flatly in a monotone, as if it was almost a casual aside, but there was nothing casual about it, and both sets of police eyes were focused very intently on his reaction.

McQueen was shocked and he was sure it would have

registered on his face. 'Really?' was all he could manage to say.

'Yes, really,' continued Reed. 'Someone has killed him, Mr McQueen, someone who knew all about his movements, where he'd be and what he'd be doing.'

'Like you did,' said Chambers, speaking for the first time.

'Oh, right, I get it now. You're thinking that because I had been trailing him, legitimately for a client, that I'm a suspect?'

Neither of the policemen spoke, and McQueen knew they were hoping that their heavy silence would turn on a guilty verbal torrent from him, but he'd played this game himself in more than one consultation. They were just fishing. If they had anything concrete at all, they'd have arrested him. He shook his head.

'Well, gentlemen, as it happens, I do have an alibi for that evening but I choose not to share it at this time. Should it become necessary, we can talk again with my solicitor present.' He didn't want to drag Emma Cullen into this unless he absolutely had to. Hopefully, it would all blow over before he needed to do that. He was also hoping his abrupt tone would end the interview, but the detectives weren't moving from their chairs. Reed looked at his notebook as if it contained some damning evidence.

'Mrs Markham seems to think you might have something to do with the death of her husband,' he said. 'Now, why would she think that?'

'She said that?' For the second time in a minute, he found it difficult to contain his surprise. 'Marina Markham?

I have no idea why she'd say that.' He was slightly rocked but was already re-evaluating the fragile Mrs Markham and beginning to calculate all the options.

'Yes,' said Reed. 'She seems to think you took a particular interest in her husband. She said it was as if you took his behaviour personally. She felt you might have been encouraging her towards revenge.'

Chambers butted in now. 'Maybe you were feeling protective towards her? It happens; she's a good-looking woman. A chance to play the hero, maybe? Do you have a bit of a hero complex, Mr McQueen?'

McQueen let out a long sigh through his pursed lips. He couldn't believe it. Now they were trying to use amateur pseudo-psychology to make veiled accusations against a professional forensic psychologist. That was just plain insulting.

Someone was telling lies in all this, and he wasn't sure whether it was these two charming detectives or Marina Markham. He had a few smart answers he could have fired back but he kept them to himself. He wanted to say that the only way to track down a missing person is to show a particular in interest in them, and if the police had shown a similar interest they might have found Markham themselves, but instead he smiled.

'Okay,' he said. 'Thank you, gentlemen. This interview is over. It's time for me to get formal with legal representation.'

Detective Reed turned to his colleague as if McQueen wasn't there. 'Why would he need a solicitor if he didn't have something to hide?'

'Good question,' said Chambers.

McQueen laughed out loud at this clumsy attempt to make him start talking. 'Goodbye, gentlemen.' He pointed at the door.

The two detectives looked at each other again then slowly got up. They knew full well how shaky their reason for being there was.

'Well, if you don't want to be cooperative now, Mr McQueen, to clear this up nice and easy in the comfort of your own office, we'll be in touch soon to arrange an interview down at the station.'

But McQueen still wasn't biting. 'Sounds good. I'll look forward to it.'

Chambers dropped a business card onto McQueen's desk and pointed at it. 'Just in case you get a sudden rush of guilty conscience, any time, day or night, I'm at your service.'

As soon as the detectives left, McQueen called Lia in. He motioned for her to sit down and then went and made them both a cup of coffee. She looked at the cup that he put down in front of her.

'Are things that bad?' she asked when he'd sat back down.

'Nothing I can't handle,' he said. 'But I think you might have hidden psychic powers, Lia. If I remember rightly, you had a feeling about Marina Markham, didn't you?'

She nodded. 'Don't tell me she had her husband beaten up? Or his girlfriend? Some people blame the guy who strays, and some people blame the woman for being a wife-stealer.'

'I'm not sure if anyone was beaten up, Lia, but I do know Toby Markham's been murdered.'

Lia seemed remarkably unsurprised.

'And what's more,' he continued, 'Marina is vaguely pointing the finger of suspicion in my direction.'

Lia sighed and took a sip of her coffee. He studied her as her mind whirled through the same options that he had explored. As always, she was dressed impeccably and her makeup was perfect, but her features remained impassive. She was always ready to give her best impression to the clients, even on the days when there were none scheduled to come in. In her role, she was doing everything he'd asked of her, but he couldn't help feeling he wasn't tapping her full potential. Right now, he needed a sounding board, one who could also add intelligent insights, and this was as good a time as any to see if she was up to it.

'Okay, true,' she said at last. 'I did have a feeling about her, but nothing on that scale. I'm not sure she's up to murder. How did it happen?'

'I don't know any of the details yet, Lia, but we'll make some phone calls and find out what we need to know.'

'We?'

'Yes, and that's something else I wanted to talk to you about. I was wondering if you might want to take a more active role in some of the investigations, starting with this one. I think you might have a talent for it.'

'You think?'

He grinned. 'Well, truthfully speaking, I don't know, but I thought it might make things a bit more interesting for you, and it would help me a lot.'

Lia was hesitating, so McQueen added, 'What I mean is that as ridiculous as it sounds — and I don't know how serious the police are — I seem to be a suspect. It might not be a good idea for me to be poking around personally in this.'

'Okay, I get that,' she said, 'and I want to help. And yes, I'd like to extend my experience. But the thing is although I appreciate the offer, I have a social life. I have a boyfriend, and there are things I like to do when I'm out of the office. I've seen the hours you keep and I'm not sure I would want to commit to the after-hours time. I couldn't do any late-night surveillance or weekends, for instance.'

He held up his hand to indicate this wouldn't be a problem. 'Oh no, of course not. That's fine, I'd only ask you to do office hours. There'd be nothing dangerous, either. I'm not talking about crawling through the undergrowth or anything. I'm talking about making a few phone calls, chasing up information, online research, things like that. And yes, as it is more work, it would eventually be more money, but that would depend on how well it went.'

'Okay,' she said, smiling and lifting her coffee cup in a toast. 'Let's give it a shot. Where shall we start?'

'Well,' said McQueen, after gulping down the last of his coffee, 'my first job is to call Max Goodson.'

'Who is?' She got up from her chair.

'My solicitor. Those two cops might have been bluffing, but if they are going to haul me into the station over this bullshit, I'll need expert representation, and Max is the guy.'

After Lia had gone back to her desk, McQueen opened his top drawer and saw the red flashing light from his recorder. He always recorded client meetings. He wasn't a great note taker, and his memory could be unreliable, so it was helpful to have the actual words recorded when it came to writing his reports. It also gave him some security should there be any dispute, financial or otherwise. He thought it would be good to check the recordings from Marina Markham's visits before he rang Max. It took him a few minutes to find her last visit, but then he listened carefully until he found the relevant section.

He heard his own voice say, *Anger and revenge will probably be your first thoughts…* Was that what Marina had been referring to? Had she taken that the wrong way? He listened to more and heard, *…you can always come back to talk to me if there's anything more you need."* Could she have misinterpreted that as an offer to kill her husband? He thought it was a stretch, but you could never know how someone else was reading into your words. He sighed and shook his head. Either way, it was something he thought Max should know about. McQueen dialled his number.

Nine

Ian was standing at the front window, watching the street beyond his overgrown hedge. He checked his watch: 8:30 p.m. Like clockwork, the old, stooped man in the dark blue duffle coat passed by. Every day, he passed at this time walking a small dog, and in an hour's time he would return. But then there was the important part. Every day he looked in at Ian's window. Why? Ian knew why. Walking a dog was a perfect cover for a snooper. What was he seeing and what was he telling people? Had he known the old lady who had lived in the house before? Was he wondering what had happened to her? Was he going to be asking any questions? Was he the one who had gone to the police?

About a month after the old woman had died, a uniformed policeman had come to Ian's door. Even innocent people can sometimes get nervous at the visit of a policeman, but Ian had remained serene. There was nothing to panic about. Panic was an enemy which could give him away, so he didn't tolerate that emotion. The officer had asked if he was the owner of the property. Ian told him he was and that he could prove it. He didn't let the officer inside the house, but the young copper waited patiently on the doorstep while Ian fetched the paperwork. He barely even read it when Ian showed him. He seemed satisfied enough, bored even, with the fool's errand.

'Can I ask what this is about?' Ian asked politely.

'Nothing to worry about, sir,' said the young man. 'I think one of your neighbours thought you might be a squatter or something, so we received a complaint.'

'Complaint?' asked Ian, keeping his cool. 'But I'm as quiet as a mouse.'

'Oh, it was something about suspicious behaviour. Anyway, it all seems to be in order, so thank you.'

The policeman had gone away and never returned, but Ian had thought long and hard about what could have prompted the visit, and the dog walker was the conclusion he came to.

Ian waited the hour, then when the man crossed in front of his gate again, Ian left the house and followed him. He kept back far enough to go unnoticed. Not being spotted was a subtle skill, but practise had made him an expert. He watched as the man arrived with his little yapping dog at a slightly battered front door and unlocked it. No one came to greet him, and he shouted no hellos. No lights were on inside the house yet, even though it was quite dark now. With the door open, the man made his way into the hall and bent down to fuss over the dog. Even from across the street, Ian could hear him. He was talking to the dog like it was a person. Why did people do that? It was not a concept Ian could in any way comprehend. These owners always asked their stupid mutts questions in those high-pitched, sing-song voices, and of course the dogs couldn't answer. So what was the point?

Much later, when it was properly dark, Ian returned and watched from across the road until the upstairs light eventually went out. After half an hour, he circled the building and then, with a small crowbar and the minimum amount of noise, forced his way through the back door. The growling dog came scuttling across the slippery floor towards him, emitting little yaps and barks. Ian easily kicked it to one side. It yelped once and shuffled back to its basket, and he shut it in the kitchen. He waited for a second or two at the bottom of the stairs, but there was no sound of movement from upstairs. Too deaf to hear? Too tired to wake? People rarely got out of their beds at the first sound of a disturbance anyway. Their natural instinct was to wait and listen and hope it would stop.

Ian moved quickly up the stairs using his torch so he wouldn't clatter up any missed steps. Based on where he'd seen the last light go out from outside, he located the bedroom. He stood outside the door for a second listening and almost giggled when he heard a snore. He tried the door. It wasn't locked, so he opened it, then flowing without pausing and using the beam of his torch, he found the old man in his bed. The man woke in total confusion, watery eyes blinking against the harsh light, but before he could muster a shout, Ian pulled his pillow from under him and jammed it over his face. He pressed it down tightly. The vague outline of the man's face was visible and there were muffled sounds that gradually got weaker.

The man's arms were trapped under his covers, which were being pinned down by Ian's knees, but he wouldn't have put up much of a struggle anyway. Ian wondered how many times in his life the old man had said to a grieving friend, *When it's your time, it's your time*? Well, it was his time now.

After the nosy old codger was dead, Ian removed the pillow from his face and placed it back under his head. He stared hard at the lifeless features, but there was nothing in them, no clues about his final thoughts. He leaned closer and began to mimic the sing-song dog voice as he asked the man some questions.

'What did you see in my house then, eh? What did you see? What did you see? Did you talk about what you saw? Did you tell the police? Eh? Who's a bad boy, then? Bad boy.'

He pulled back the sheets and rolled the bag of bones onto his front so his face was buried in his pillow, then covered him again. Ian didn't need this to look like an accident or natural causes, but it wouldn't hurt if it did. The guy could easily have choked in his own pillow. If they did a post-mortem they might be able to tell the guy had been suffocated but maybe not how it happened. There might be some bruising somewhere. And if the police bothered to check the doors they'd find signs of forced entry. But maybe they'd force their own way in? And if they did decide it was murder they would question suspects, maybe distant family members, maybe neighbours. They would look for a motive but they would find none. He had taken all the usual precautions, and there was nothing they could trace back to him. He wouldn't look for money or valuables. He was stealing nothing other than the man's life, which had a value only in Ian's universe.

The dog didn't even growl as Ian passed back through the kitchen. It had already accepted him as a new family member. When he opened the back door, he checked the frame for damage. There were some telltale marks but no visible splintering. The lock was old and hadn't given much resistance but it wasn't broken and relocked behind him when he closed the door. The police might not even notice. That depended on how overworked they were and how carefully they looked at how an older man had died. It didn't really matter one way or the other to Ian. Natural causes or murder, he would never be caught, and the man wouldn't be passing his house anymore to spy.

As he stepped back into the night, he did it boldly. He was in no danger; the only person who could possibly be in danger would be anyone who confronted him.

Once he was back in his own front room, Ian washed his hands and checked his clothes for any incriminating evidence that he might have picked up. There had been no blood in this murder, which made cleaning up easier, and there was nothing visible, but he knew all about microscopic fibres and trace DNA. He carefully took off his outer garments and put them in the washing machine on a hot wash.

Dressed now in loose-fitting tracksuit bottoms and a baggy sweatshirt, he opened his computer on the kitchen table. He went through the lengthy process of logging on and accessing various international servers through his virtual private networks, where he dipped into the dark web. It slowed things down a lot but it was essential to hide his identity. He checked his messages and accounts, and as expected, the cosmos had seen what he had done with the old man and had liked his work. The ripples had spread quickly and now he had received the reward. A woman who lived in Spain had sent his "David" account £500 because she believed David was dying of cancer and needed to pay for his experimental drugs. A man in London who was madly in love with his "Katie" account had sent £1,000 so that Katie could buy tickets to visit him from the US, where he believed she lived. Ian's face showed no emotion as he made some notes on his computer. David's health would pick up a bit, but then he would need more drugs, maybe £1,500 worth this time, and Katie would need to pay for visas and buy clothes for the journey and also pay for some vet bills. She had a cute dog in her photos and her internet boyfriend had been very taken with that.

And then there was Cynthia. She was a little bit older than the others and she thought she was in love with a pilot called Sebastian. She lived somewhere on the outskirts of Leeds, so Ian had to be extra careful to keep Sebastian abroad or in London.

You reap what you sow, thought Ian. *If you do good work, the rewards will come, karma will see to that.*

Ten

The whole McQueen situation was placing Detective Tracey Bingham in a very difficult position. McQueen was a friend and she trusted him, but she couldn't let it cloud her judgement. She didn't believe for one second he had any involvement in the Toby Markham murder, but the officers handling that case had every right — in fact they had a duty — to follow him up as a person of interest. The problem was that everyone in the station knew she had a strong connection to McQueen, which was making them even more distrustful and careful around her than usual.

She had transferred into the West Yorkshire authority from the Devon and Cornwall constabulary after successfully helping to bust a high-profile drug smuggling ring that had been operating from the Cornish coast. She'd been a keen but inexperienced rookie constable at the time. Even though she had played a pivotal role in that bust, she hadn't got any of the credit, and following, she felt the colleagues around her couldn't see her in any other light than a female PC who'd got lucky. But Tracey knew better. She was good at her job and she had ambition, so she'd chosen to transfer away from the area, a long way, all the way up north. She had applied to West Yorkshire because it included the busy city of Leeds that she hoped would really give her a chance to establish herself.

Initially, things in Yorkshire hadn't been any easier for her than Cornwall and, in her new position, she also had to contend with being the newbie with the funny accent. The banter culture in the closed shop of the police force was strong. She had tried to focus on the work and began to devote her spare time to a murder case that was proving to be difficult, but after a short while she'd been told to leave it alone. She had been instructed to move on from the case and to let it go cold but she couldn't bring herself to do it. That's when she'd contacted McQueen as an outsider with no links to the force, because he wouldn't be leaking any information back to her colleagues. They worked well together, and between them they had caught a killer.

Meanwhile, Tracey had some new cases of her own to follow up. There was a male victim, forty-three years old, dragged into a bush and strangled with his own scarf for no apparent reason. A man with no enemies in his life. A man who had been walking home when he appeared to have been killed on a whim. There was no visible motive, no signs of a struggle, which suggested a surprise attack from behind. They had one small break on this one: the scarf had shown some trace DNA that didn't belong to the victim, an eyelash, but it unfortunately didn't correspond to anyone on their database.

Tracey had spent a lot of time chasing up his friends, relatives, and work colleagues and taking DNA samples but had drawn a blank on all of them. In that respect, it was similar to another case she had been investigating a few months before. This one was of a woman who'd been struck in the face, probably punched, at the top of some concrete steps and then had fallen backwards and cracked her head open. Again, no motive, but there was a clue. Some very grainy CCTV footage had captured a figure moving away from the area seconds after the victim had passed through the shot. Unfortunately, the images were very poor. You couldn't even tell if the person was male or female, just a dark shape who was probably the murderer. The local news had reluctantly featured the video on a late evening slot, but the coverage had given the police no leads other than the usual sprinkling of useless tip-offs that all had to be followed up, taking up precious time and resources.

She had mulled the two separate cases over for a long time until they had started to fuse together. They were becoming the same case in her head, and she knew she couldn't allow that to happen. But still, the questions kept coming back to her: Could no connection be a connection? Could the thing they had in common be that they had nothing in common?

Both of these dead-end cases had been handed over to Tracey, once all the juice had been sucked out of them. If the assignments were designed to break her spirit, the ploy wasn't going to work. If her bosses had known anything about her, they'd have known that the challenge would only strengthen her.

She slid back from her desk, stretched her aching shoulders, then went to the coffee machine to get a cup of instant sludge. What she really wanted to do was talk it over with McQueen. He was a good sounding board and could have worked up each of the killers' psychological profiles. Could they be the same person? There was no pattern at all, but could that be a pattern in itself? It was probably too far-fetched, but anything was possible. She went back to her desk and brought up the case notes again and began to read them for the hundredth time.

Eleven

McQueen rolled over and turned on the light, blinked until his eyes adjusted then, lying on his back he took a few deep breaths and tried to calm himself down. His hand on his chest was practically bouncing on his heaving ribcage. He could feel the nobbles of the metal that had been used to bind his sternum together after his open-heart operation. The doctors don't bother to open you up again to take the staples out, they leave them there for eternity. Not for the first time, McQueen wondered if his heaving lungs could burst the metal apart. Unfortunately, his rapid heartbeat was born of fear, not sexual passion. From his past studies, McQueen knew a little about post-traumatic stress disorder. He knew about its various causes, symptoms, and manifestations, but as he had taken the forensic rather than clinical psychology path, it had never really been an area of expertise for him. Not until the nightmares came.

The terrifying dreams had started about six months after a particularly harrowing case in which he'd come very close to being killed by a psychopath. In his recurring nightmare, he was back there again, fighting for his life, but this time he didn't win. When he would wake from these dreams, sweating and panting, his heart thundering beneath his ribs, there was no flood of relief in realising that the world he had been drowning in wasn't real, that there was no water in his lungs, and there was no hand pressing his head down into the waves. The fear was very real and too strong to dissipate easily.

It was the what-if thinking that was hard to shake. What if he hadn't had PC Tracey Bingham there to help him and what if they hadn't managed to escape? It wasn't enough to tell himself he had survived; it didn't ease the anxiety. After waking, he usually sat up in a state of hyperarousal for an hour or so until the terror started to slowly subside. *Physician, heal thyself?* It didn't seem to be possible for him. He knew he should be getting help and, in fact, had casually spoken to a friend, Maggie, who was a trauma therapist, without specifying he was asking for himself. He'd pretended he was enquiring for a client, and whether she believed him or not, she didn't probe further. Maggie dealt with serious trauma victims every day of the week, people whose awful life experiences made McQueen's problems look like a pleasant birthday party, which left him feeling like a fraud.

He had managed to get Maggie to talk about her methods, though, and perhaps she had guessed there was more to his interest than professional curiosity. She had said that as a trauma therapist she taught grounding techniques with the aim of getting people to live in the here and now.

Then she gently explained her approach by using an analogy of a linen cupboard. The linen cupboard of your mind was at the top of the stairs and it was where all the unpleasant memories were stuffed, and the door was forced shut. Sometimes the door burst open, and the memories came spilling out and tumbled down the stairs. One solution was to carefully take all those experiences out, examine them one by one, shake them, fold them, then pack them away neatly. Then you could close a tidy cupboard so the door would stay shut until you wanted to open it. It sounded good in theory, but McQueen couldn't face the careful examination part. He needed someone to help him through it, to guide him as he unpacked the cupboard, but he wasn't ready for the therapist yet. Counselling would feel too much like defeat. It was a stupid resistance based on some kind of misguided macho pride, but even though he knew that, it was how he felt.

Now he was awake, he decided he might as well do some work, so he grabbed his laptop from beside the bed and opened it to check on his emails. According to the general sleep therapy advice he'd read, the combination of strong light and mental stimulation were the worst things to indulge in if you wanted to drop back off to sleep again, but right now, he needed the distraction.

Think of something nice, he told himself, and his mind automatically turned to Emma. The opportunity that Emma Cullen had offered him to break into the world of media was very exciting. There were still a lot of details to be worked out on the contract side, but the basic idea was he would be retained by her production team as an expert consultant on her new show, which was to be called *The Murderous Kind*. To feed his ego, he would also make some appearances on-screen opposite Emma to add credibility to the presentation. It was going to be a history-based show that revisited famous crimes and famous killers. All it needed from him was a massive commitment of time and focus. As an opportunity, it appeared to be exactly what he had been aiming for, but there was something bugging him about it. Perhaps it was the influence of the bad dream that was still clinging to him, but negativity was rearing its head in his thoughts. The show was a seductive offer and could certainly prove to be quite lucrative, but now that it was on the horizon, he couldn't help asking himself if it was really what he wanted to do. Wouldn't it just be a version of the academic world that he had left behind? It would take him away from the investigative work he enjoyed and it would distance him from real people and his current cases. The fame element would be a novelty for a while, but wouldn't it ultimately limit his ability to blend in when he needed to?

There was something else that was troubling him, too, and he was hating himself for letting it get under his skin. A personal relationship had blossomed with Emma, which on its face was a very good thing, but it was still causing him some conflicting emotions. They had been on several dates now and he was feeling very comfortable in her company. She was interesting to be with and seemed to be just as enthralled with him. The relationship was relaxed and relaxing. Not every evening ended in her bed, but some did, and those nights were always wonderful. All in all, it was the most fun he'd had for a long time, but he still had a distant sense of unease humming in his ear. He was trying to convince himself to just enjoy the moment and ignore the rest, but he wasn't made that way.

Emma Cullen was a person who always got what she wanted from life, and a rudimentary glance at her personal history showed there had been some painful casualties along the way. Discarded former colleagues littered Emma's past, some of whom had never recovered. Collateral damage is how people liked to describe it these days, as if we are all involved in a brutal career war. Could it be that all she saw in him was someone who could help to advance her progress, and once she achieved her next set of goals, he would be of less use?

He turned back to the emails. Amongst the messages, there was one that had been forwarded by Lia from the general enquiry inbox she monitored. She'd added the additional comment of, "This looks intriguing?" It was from someone called Olivia, and the subject line was, "Was this murder?" Lia was right, it was an intriguing title anyway, so he opened it.

Dr McQueen, I need your help. You don't know me, but I heard your podcast with Emma Cullen.

She said you are a private investigator and a Doctor of Psychology?

I think you are the right person to investigate a murder that happened on a street near me.

A nice old man who had never hurt anyone was killed, but the police aren't investigating it.

They think he died face down on his pillow, but I don't

believe it.

My husband won't let me talk about it. He thinks I'm mad, so I don't want him to know I contacted you.

I have no money to pay you.

I saw someone near the house on that night.

It was suspicious to me, but the police said because I couldn't give a clear description it was no help.

But the man shouldn't have been there.

He was very tall but that's all I could see. He was wearing black and a balaclava.

Someone should look into this, check the house, especially the back door. Are you interested?

If you are, I will send you his address details.

Thank you. Olivia.

McQueen stared at the message for a very long time. A tingling sensation swept down the back of his neck, and he went into a zone of complete concentration where the rest of the world was blocked out as his mind removed all other distractions. It was like the time the doctor had told him he needed heart surgery and a full minute later he had not heard the nurse asking if he was okay. He reread the email several times. It was a lot more than intriguing. A voice was speaking to him through the black and white words on his screen. It could have just been a time-wasting idiot, a busybody with unfounded accusations to throw around, but he didn't think so. He was pretty sure he knew what he had here and he knew he had to treat it carefully. He took a few deep breaths as if he was about to start a race, then he wrote his reply. He answered from his own email address so the reply wouldn't come into the general enquiry box:

Hello, Olivia. Thank you for contacting me. I have a lot more questions I'd like to ask you about this possible murder, and it would be great to meet up to discuss it.

All investigations hinge on people like you, people who care and who are willing to come forward.

I promise you that no one else needs to know and anything you speak to me about would be in the strictest confidence.

You could either come to my office, or if it would be easier, I could come to your house. Or if that's not possible, we could meet somewhere else if that would suit you better. For now, if you could send me the address you mentioned I can at least start the enquiry.

Hope to hear from you soon.

McQueen.

BTW, you don't need to worry about the money. I take on some cases for the challenge, and this could be interesting.

He could have added, "and for the publicity", but it would have given the wrong emphasis.

The person he desperately wanted to discuss this with was Tracey Bingham, but he knew that would prove difficult at the moment. He didn't want to put her in an awkward position and he knew she would be giving him a wide berth until the Markham case was cleared up. Still, he might have to find a way.

Twelve

Later that day in the office, slightly groggy from lack of sleep, which was catching up on him now he was at his desk, McQueen was hitting the coffee hard. He'd managed to give up alcohol in his life without too much of a struggle, but caffeine still had him in its grip. In contrast, when Lia came striding into his office, she was practically sparking with energy and enthusiasm.

Youth, thought McQueen, not for the first time. *Long gone. Only biochemistry can help me now*. When she asked him what he thought of the mysterious message she'd forwarded from Olivia, he was deliberately vague in his answer. He wasn't ready to share his suspicions. They were too huge and could end up making him look like a fool, so he simply told her he thought it was interesting and that he had replied. He then quickly moved the conversation to the Toby Markham case, and Lia was more than ready to talk about that.

'So this is what I've found out so far,' she said, clearly

pleased with herself, as she opened her large notebook and spread it on McQueen's desk. 'Toby Markham was at his girlfriend's house on the evening of Friday the seventeenth because, as you know, that's where he was living. They had just had dinner, and according to Kerry Smith, the girlfriend, he went outside to his car to get something. Her car was in the garage, and his car was parked right outside the front of the house. Kerry didn't go with him.'

McQueen knew the house very well. He had sat outside in his own car not far down the street, cradling his camera for an hour when he'd been tracking the errant husband. It was on a new-build estate, each a house-builder's idea of country mansion in miniature, where everyone had their own car-sized drive and garage. It wasn't an easy place to hide in your car because in such a small clutch of houses, everyone overlooked everyone else, and a car with an occupant was bound to attract attention. He'd felt conspicuous sitting there and had kept his stay to a minimum. Number eighteen was where the lovebirds had lived, but he had no idea if Kerry knew about Toby's marital status. As soon as they had ventured outside together and McQueen had got the incriminating picture of them, he'd driven away before being spotted.

Lia continued her report.

'While Toby was out at his car, someone came up behind him and bludgeoned him with a blunt object in what the police are calling "a frenzied and sustained attack".'

'Hmm,' said McQueen. '"frenzied" implies anger rather than a cold calculating assassination then.'

'Yes, the police are saying it looks like he was kicked

and his head was stomped on, but they haven't had the coroner's report yet.'

McQueen raised his eyebrows and nodded. 'Sounds like a very angry assailant to me. Carry on.'

'Kerry came out after about ten minutes to see where he'd got to and found him lying there in a real mess.'

'Must have been a horrible sight.' McQueen had seen several gory scenes in his work, and they never ceased to sicken him, so he could imagine how it must be for a partner to have to see it.

'Yep. She tried to resuscitate him, but he was already dead. Then she called the emergency services, and as the recording shows, she was in an understandably hysterical state.'

'You've listened to the recording?' he asked, impressed.

She gave a short nod and raised a perfectly manicured index finger to make her point. 'Now, you've seen the street, and I've travelled down it virtually on street view. The amazing thing is that during this lengthy attack, there must have been a fair amount of noise, right? I mean, surely he cried out? But no one in any of those overlooking houses saw or heard anything.'

'Okay,' said McQueen. 'So either the TVs were all turned up too loud and they genuinely heard nothing, or…?' He left the question hanging and Lia eagerly filled the gap.

'Or they heard and saw plenty and are too scared to say so.'

'That thought did cross my mind.'

'Yes, mine too,' said Lia. 'In the neighbourhood where I

grew up, people don't want to help the police, because nothing good ever comes of it. But these people are different.'

'You mean they are middle-class and white?'

Lia shrugged and nodded. 'Yes, it's not a fear of the police, so it must be a fear of something else.'

'How did you find all this out by the way, Lia?'

She grinned and gave him a playfully coy look. 'Sorry, I can't disclose my sources, and as you are possibly in the frame for this one, it's better you don't know anyway.'

He sighed and nodded in agreement. McQueen was always aware of body language, and Lia's was speaking volumes to him. Her eyes were flashing, and she was giving off an almost visible aura. She was clearly enjoying the task he'd set her, and he recognised the signs. She was experiencing the joy of the chase and the thrill of unlocking of a real-life puzzle.

'And how are you feeling about all this?' asked McQueen. 'Just say if it's more than you want to do.'

She smiled broadly. 'I love it. I feel like I'm actually involved in something exciting here. Like something off the TV. Carl even said to me that I seem to be very keen to get to work these days. You wait 'til I tell him I'm taking him on a stakeout.'

She laughed out loud and McQueen chuckled along. Carl was Lia's boyfriend, and McQueen had seen him briefly a couple of times when Carl had been into the office to pick her up after work. He was a good-looking young guy. Like her, he was very well-dressed, and he had one of those smiles that make you instantly want to be friends with the smiler. She'd said he worked for a financial consultancy in Leeds but she wasn't too sure of the details other than it sounded boring.

No one ever seems to know what their partners actually do, thought McQueen.

'I'm glad you're getting something out of it, Double-O-Seven,' he said. 'And I know you're joking about the stakeout, but let's keep it office based for now.'

'McQueen, you don't need to worry about me.' She sounded almost insulted. 'I can handle myself.'

He had no doubts about that.

'I'm not worried about you,' he said. 'I'm thinking of the insurance. I'm not covered for employees jumping out of helicopters.'

'Okay,' she said, 'no helicopters. But I do want to have a closer look at the girlfriend next.'

'Kerry?'

'Yes, Kerry Smith.'

'I thought your intuition had been alerted in the direction of Marina Markham.'

'Anything is possible, of course, and I'm keeping the options open. From the size of her, I'd say Marina is unlikely to have been able to inflict that damage on a grown man, but you never know. Sure, she could have hired a hit man, but judging by the way the police are treating her, I think she must have a solid alibi. I haven't been able to find out what that is yet, but I'm working on it. In the meantime, Kerry might be worth chasing up for background if nothing else.'

'Yes,' agreed McQueen. 'And something that is slightly

odd is the coincidence of Toby going out to his car at the same time that the murderer happened to be out there. He could have had a message on his phone from someone to meet him outside, but if he did, the police would have a record of it. And if he'd seen someone lurking near his car he'd probably have said something to Kerry on his way out.'

'His phone is missing,' said Lia. 'Looks like whoever killed him might have taken it.'

'I see.' McQueen nodded. 'But the police can still get to his messages if they choose to.'

'Anyway,' said Lia, standing up and tucking her notebook under her arm, 'I think Kerry needs to be spoken to in person.'

McQueen grimaced a little. 'Ah, I'm not sure about that, Lia. Don't get me wrong, I think it's a good idea and I'd like to, but I can't be seen personally interfering while the police have me on their list, no matter how ridiculous their stupid list is. I've spoken to Max, my solicitor, and he assures me I have absolutely nothing to worry about. But being a cautious lawyer, he has also advised me to keep my nose out of it until they find their real culprit.'

'I don't mean spoken to by you, I mean spoken to by me.'

McQueen looked at her and he could tell she meant it.

'Now,' Lia continued, 'you can either say, 'No way, your job is here, and you can't leave the office', in which case I'll stay. But that will only mean I have to go after hours, which will be upsetting for Carl as we've planned a quiet dinner out tonight. Or you can say, 'Go ahead, but watch your back and be careful,' and it will all be good.'

McQueen blew out his cheeks and looked around in mock exasperation. 'I've created a monster.' Though he was actually enjoying Lia's energising commitment. In a strange way, it was an affirmation of the choices he'd made when he'd chosen the life of a private investigator. 'However, what I would suggest is that you ring her first to see if she'll even speak to you. It might save you a wasted journey.'

'Already done it,' said Lia, spinning on her heal and heading out to get her coat from the rack. 'Oh, one more thing.' She turned back to him in her best Columbo style. 'No insurance companies are investigating anything because there was no fraud, because there was no insurance. Toby Markham's life wasn't covered, so when he did a runner, he knew no company would be chasing him. He just didn't know about you.'

McQueen was surprised, both at the information and at how thorough Lia had been.

'No wonder Marina was so keen to find him,' he said. 'She'd been left high and dry. It would certainly fuel some righteous anger.'

Lia had her coat on now and was about to leave. 'Yep, she was angry alright, but whether she was angry enough to kill him is yet to be seen.'

McQueen had got up from behind his desk and was standing in the open doorway.

'Well, from my experience, Lia, angry enough to kill doesn't have to be very angry at all. So to echo what you just said to me, go ahead, but watch your back and be careful. I'll keep my phone next to me. Text me when you get there and again when you leave.'

'You sound like my dad. Don't worry, McQueen, I've got this.' She gave him a thumbs up and was gone.

McQueen wasn't entirely comfortable with Lia going out on her own to interview the traumatised partner of a man who had been stomped to death, but he was fairly sure it wouldn't present any danger to Lia, nothing she couldn't handle anyway. Mainly, he was very keen to get this mess sorted out as soon as possible. Even if it ended up with him having to make a trip to the police station with his solicitor, it would be good to have some evidence and counterarguments behind him.

It was very early days, but McQueen was immensely pleased at how well Lia was working out. She was much more than he had hoped for when he'd advertised for an office administrator, that was for sure. He'd always known it would be useful to have an investigating partner in the office, someone to use as a sounding board and someone to add insights that might have escaped him. It was easy to become blinkered when you were deep into a case, and it was good to have someone to give another perspective. In the past, he'd asked Tracey Bingham if it was a role she might be interested in, but she was far too invested in her police career. Lia didn't have Tracey's police connections or anything like her experience but she was incredibly sharp and alive with enthusiasm. This visit to see Kerry could prove to be a valuable test.

McQueen checked his emails. There had been no answer from Olivia. Maybe it would all come to nothing but it was going to be hard to ignore that first message. He read the words again. "Check the back door", "he was wearing a balaclava", "died in his pillow". He wondered about the merits of him sending another message. Would it frighten her off? He wasn't a patient person, and Lia's whirl of activity was still in the air. His fingers took over and he started typing:

Hi, Olivia. I realise you might have had second thoughts about this case, but I assure you that you don't need to be directly involved.

Please send me the address of the victim so I can check to see if there is anything to investigate. We get a lot of crank messages about things like this, so it would help me to see if you are one of those.

Also, can you think again about the man you saw? Try to picture the scene in your mind's eye and describe what you can see. There may be something that comes back to you now.

Thanks. McQueen.

He was taking a risk because he was directly challenging this person, put up or shut up, but if his instincts were right, whoever Olivia was would be ready to accept the challenge. He hesitated for a second then hit the button and sent the message out into the ether. Then he turned to his other business for the day.

Emma had sent him some paperwork for the new show, *The Murderous Kind*, so that he could, in her words, "have a head start" and "hit the ground running". He couldn't remember which of the clichéd phrases she'd actually used, but it was one of them. Whatever the description was that she'd used, she'd sent him a daunting series of attachments. They were production notes, ideas, and outline scripts for the upcoming programmes. There were a lot of questions annotated on them too, such as, "Is this right?" and "Can we say this?" which he was supposed to answer. His enthusiasm for television, massive digital reach or not, was waning as he skimmed through the pages. His phone pinged. It was a text from Lia.

I'm here, is all it said, and he found himself slightly envious of her position out there in the flow of the game. It made him think again about whether he could ever be satisfied as a desk-bound, behind-the-scenes advisor on a TV show. It had never been his dream. It hadn't even been a vague wish.

He checked his emails. No reply yet, but then his mobile rang, and he immediately thought it could be Lia in some kind of trouble. He grabbed the phone from his desk. But checking the screen, he saw it was Anne Kirkpatrick so he let it ring a few times before answering it.

Anne was a local journalist who had been shadowing McQueen for years. For a while, he'd considered her a friend and a resource until she got wind of a possible scandal and sank her journalistic teeth into his backside. Like any good journo, she only had loyalty to the story she was chasing, and if that meant trashing an old friend, she'd do it. However, she changed with the wind, or the prevailing scoop, so when McQueen had landed a couple of big cases, she'd been the first to ring in pursuit of an exclusive. He braced himself, knowing she wasted very little time on small talk and also that she would be recording him.

'McQueen.' Hers was a voice hardened by years of cigarettes, coffee, and not-so-fine wine. 'I'm sitting on a story here, McQueen, and my editor's keen to run it. I wondered if you were willing to comment.'

'How lovely to hear from you, Anne. How have you been?'

She completely ignored his fake cheerfulness. '"Famous detective questioned in connection with Markham murder". Anything to say? I'd love to hear your side.'

He shook his head, though she couldn't see it. The only source she could have got that information from was the police. The trick was not to be flustered enough to blurt out something you wouldn't want to see in print the next day.

'I mean,' she added, 'I think it's bullshit, but without your side, it is what it is.'

'Anne, all I'd say is you've printed hatchet jobs on me before and then had to backtrack. This will be no different. There is no story. Meanwhile, I have a few things going on that are going to make huge stories and I think you'll want to be in on those.'

'Give me something concrete, McQueen. You know how it works: we want our jam today, not tomorrow.'

'Have you ever heard of the pleasures of delayed gratification, Anne?'

'Sure. In my business, it goes along with the word unemployed.'

McQueen wasn't ready to give any details about the job with Emma or the email from Olivia, both of which would have been of interest to Anne. He knew she couldn't be conned or played and that nothing told to her in secret could possibly stay that way.

'Okay, you have to give me something. How about this then, as a human-interest story. We've been sent a picture — not great quality but good enough to print. It's from a phone in a dark restaurant. It seems to be you, McQueen, and a certain celebrity. Romantic dinner? Do you have any comment on that?'

'Look, Anne, print what you want. You will anyway.'

He ended the call, leaned back in his chair and rubbed his hands over his eyes. It wouldn't make a lot of difference if they printed the 'detective questioned' story, but it was a tiny question raised over his integrity that he could do without. With any luck, Lia's visit to see Kerry Smith would turn up a lead and give them something to work on and put that case to bed. He could hope anyway.

Meanwhile, human interest? Seriously? As in tabloid gossip? What kind of human would be remotely interested in that nonsense, and what kind of warped world was he getting into?

The office was bright today as shafts of hopeful sunlight striped the cheap, grey office carpet. But the sun only served to emphasise how oddly quiet it was without the comforting sounds of Lia rattling away at her keyboard. The dust particles circling aimlessly in the sun transfixed him for a while, and for some reason they brought back memories of boring maths lessons at school. McQueen suddenly had a strong urge to get away from his own desk. There was someone he needed to see. It was completely unrelated to anything else he'd been working on, but now was as good a time as any to speak to an unwanted client called Brian

Davidson. He picked up his phone and spoke briefly to Davidson's secretary before being allowed to speak to the man himself. Busy as Davidson was, he was very keen to find out what McQueen had to say, so he agreed to 'squeeze him in' if he came straight over.

McQueen ended the call and grabbed his jacket from the back of his chair. He wasn't particularly looking forward to the meeting, which was why he'd been avoiding it, but it was never easy to turn your back on money.

Thirteen

McQueen had his principles and he was proud of them. He had left behind academia to become a private detective so that he could "do good". It sounded cheesy and it was a much-maligned phrase, one that brought to mind over-eager, self-righteous volunteers and happy-clappy religious zealots, but it summed up the way he felt. He wanted to use his forensic psychology skills and knowledge to help the wider community, not just other academics, no matter how self-righteous it sounded to others. Some of his ex-colleagues had argued their research was how they helped humanity. They fed into the human knowledge bank. But McQueen wanted a more immediate and tangible pay-off than a mention in an obscure scientific journal.

There were some things that were more important than money to McQueen, and he thought of the cases he made nothing on as being like the pro bono work that lawyers take on for the good of society. But, and there was a big but, his successful jobs that had made the papers had given him a lot of publicity, and he saw nothing wrong in monetising his name with those who could afford it. After all, he had an office to pay for, untold additional expenses around the business, and now an assistant to fund. In short, there were some contracts he took on not for the good of society but for the cash, and the Davidson case was a good example.

Brian Davidson was a financier with money to burn but, like most people with enough currency to make a bonfire, he wanted the biggest flaming beacon in the city. Part of his strategy was to grind his rivals into the dust, and right now the particular rival in his sights was a man called Aaron Patterson. McQueen's brief was simple: he was to dig up as much dirt as possible on Aaron. Although Davidson claimed that anything bad would do, enough to destroy Aaron was his ultimate goal.

It was a horrible job. It was unsavoury and cynical, but McQueen rationalised his task by convincing himself that if he didn't do it, someone else would. He also told himself none of these financial sharks were normal people anyway. Even so, he was painfully aware that this was the same line of reasoning used by many of the criminals he came into contact with. It was how they justified their crimes, and it didn't sit particularly well with his so-called principles. *It's my job*, was the other dubious disclaimer often favoured by lawyers who defended the indefensible, and McQueen was happy to use that one, too. He didn't want to do it, but it was his job.

After agreeing to sell his soul to Davidson, McQueen had arranged to meet an old friend who he hoped could help him with this lucrative muck-raking assignment. Tom was a young man who had acted as a support during McQueen's journey to total sobriety. Tom was well-placed to offer substance abuse advice as he himself was a recovering heroin addict. In fact, that's how their relationship had started. McQueen had worked for Tom's now deceased grandmother, and on numerous occasions had tracked him down and hauled him out of various drug dens. Tom had been clean for several years now, but he still exchanged supportive calls with McQueen from time to time.

As McQueen walked across Park Square, he had a wry smile on his face at the silly thought of him ever renting an office there. The square was obviously for rich clients, not their servants and private investigators.

Before going into Davidson's building, McQueen bolstered his resolve by sitting on one of the benches, closing his eyes and rerunning in his mind the meeting he'd had with Tom a week or so before.

They had arranged to meet in a coffee shop, and as Tom had weaved his way through the rustic pine tables to join him, McQueen couldn't help comparing the handsome, healthy-looking young man with the sad and bedraggled lost soul he'd rescued from some of the grimiest flats and houses around Leeds.

'You look great,' McQueen had said as Tom sat down.

'Thanks. You too, McQueen. Well, maybe not great, but no worse than usual.'

McQueen had laughed at that. It was a fair point. They'd had their coffee and McQueen had eaten a sticky pastry while they caught up on general chitchat before getting to the crux of their meeting.

'So, Tom,' McQueen said, 'recap. As I told you before, I have been given the delicate job of finding some — shall we say colourful? — colourful background on this Aaron Patterson character. I started off thinking I might find the usual evidence of dodgy deals or nasty sexual exploits, but there was nothing. Then as I said, after I'd spoken to a few more people, I started to hear persistent rumours about drugs, and that's when...'

'That's when you came to the only recovering drug addict you know.'

'Yes, exactly. And I hope it wasn't too uncomfortable for you, but you have the contacts I don't have, Tom. If it was too much to ask, then I'm sorry. But did you get anything?'

Across the table, Tom had nodded his head as if to say, *oh it's fine, don't worry* and then he caught the attention of the waitress and ordered two more coffees.

'Okay,' Tom began. 'It wasn't easy, but I asked around some of my old acquaintances and it turns out Aaron's an interesting guy.' He pushed his fringe from his forehead and sighed. 'He moves in some rarefied circles, that fella.'

'As do you,' McQueen said, making Tom smirk.

'Maybe once, but not anymore.' He'd said this without any hint of regret. It was true. Tom's grandmother had been fairly rich, and after he'd been disowned by his parents, she had looked after him. He'd had an expensive education and a circle of impressive friends, most of whom had dropped him like a rotting avocado when his life had begun to spiral downwards.

The fresh coffees arrived fairly quickly, and Tom paused

while the waitress moved away then he spoke very slowly and deliberately. 'Imagine you go to parties with the movers and shakers of this world.'

'Okay, but it would be quite a stretch of the imagination,' McQueen had replied, trying to keep it light, but Tom continued without so much as a smile.

'Suppose there are politicians at these parties, business leaders, all kinds of well-healed power players and glitterati. But they are humans just like you and me, especially me, and they like to let their hair down. Who doesn't? So what do you think they do if they want drugs to help the party swing? Do you think they hustle on street corners like council estate junkies? No, of course not. They have people, people who are perfectly at home at those parties, who fit right in unnoticed but who also have access to what they need. Aaron Patterson is one of those people.'

'Right.' McQueen nodded. 'So you're saying that as well as being a well-respected financier, he's a high-class drug dealer?'

'Yes, but he gets more than money out of it. He keeps dirty secrets for people who don't want to appear in the tabloids. So he gets influence, leverage and protection as well as the money.'

'So he could be a dangerous guy?' McQueen asked.

'Oh, more than that, McQueen. Who do you think he gets his supplies from? They are the serious drug dealers who don't have access to those circles but use people like Aaron to get in there. In the same way that an urban dealer who wants to get into kid's playgrounds recruits other kids to sell the drugs, these people recruit users from the upper echelons to punt their stuff. Money's not a problem for those rich customers, so the profits are bigger. Consequently, Aaron is a valuable asset to the suppliers, and they tend to protect their assets with extreme violence.'

'Could be messy,' McQueen said, 'but have you got any evidence of any of this?'

Tom had almost spluttered his coffee in McQueen's face. 'Are you mad? Do you think we're talking about the type of person who leaves evidence lying around?'

McQueen had taken a beat to think it through and then he'd said, 'Right, so all of this is just gossip and hearsay?' McQueen knew he was sounding slightly disappointed and a touch critical, which wasn't fair on Tom, and seeing the young man's face, he regretted having said it.

'It's what I've been told by very reliable sources, McQueen, but they'd rather cut their own tongues out than testify to anything.'

Tom had been getting agitated, and McQueen didn't think it was down to the excess caffeine. McQueen tried to calm him down and repair the damage of his earlier comment.

'It's okay, Tom. I understand, and you did really well. I mean it. It's a great start. Thank you. Now at least I know what I'm facing.' He hadn't wanted Tom to think he was disappointed in the information, because he knew it must have taken a lot to get it. He'd asked a lot of Tom, who'd worked hard to cut himself off from his old drug contacts and his old life, and McQueen had pushed him back there just to gather some gossip. They sat quietly for a couple of minutes, then Tom had changed the subject.

95

'So anyway, McQueen, how are you doing? Still keeping away from the demon drink?'

'Yes, I'm doing fine, thanks. Life's a bit more boring. Time drags by sometimes and some of the social events I go to are hard to stomach without the help of alcohol. You know what it's like listening to drunks when you're stone cold sober? They're repetitive and dull, and the worst part is they think they're funny. I get the odd craving to join in the fun, but all in all, it's good. I'm busy and that helps.'

'Me too,' Tom had agreed. 'Things are better now that I have plenty of distractions.'

Financially, he didn't need to work, his grandmother had seen to that. But that was a relapse danger in itself, so he worked seven days a week with a charity, using his posh voice and charm to organise the donations for their food banks. He was very busy all the time, which made it even more of a sacrifice that he should give up any of his precious hours to do this research for McQueen.

As they had been preparing to leave, Tom had taken hold of McQueen's forearm and squeezed it to make his point.

'I don't know who you're working for, McQueen, and I don't want to know. But you'd do well to advise them not to get on Aaron Patterson's wrong side. He comes across as a lightweight socialite, but you don't get to his position with those people without having a broad streak of ruthless cruelty running through you. He supplies drugs to his so-called friends, and if their lives implode, he wouldn't give a shit.' It had been personal for Tom, and McQueen could understand the depth of his feeling, but he'd been squeezing his arm very hard. 'And you, McQueen, you be careful and don't get dragged into someone else's fight.'

He'd let go of McQueen's arm and attempted a weak smile. The psychologist in McQueen had surfaced and he'd seen that the mental anguish caused by years of addiction wasn't buried very deep in Tom. They had been through a lot together over the years and their attachment was strong. When Tom had lost his grandmother, he'd lost a great deal of support and now he was trying to be protective of McQueen. In that instant McQueen seriously regretted having asked this favour of his friend. It had been selfish of him and insensitive. He should have known Tom could never refuse, no matter how much trouble it was going to cause him.

For his part, McQueen had decided to take what he had learned back to Davidson and hope it was enough. It was a well-paying job, but not well-paying enough to risk life and limb over and certainly wasn't worth the loss of Tom's friendship. The meeting with Tom had made a deep impression. It had been a sharp reminder that abandoning his principles was never going to be an easy journey.

Sitting now in Davidson's office, McQueen was absorbing the disappointment of a client who was used to getting what he wanted. Davidson was wearing a suit that surely cost more than McQueen's entire wardrobe, and the watch sparkling just under his cuff was certainly worth more than the car McQueen had driven over in. McQueen had carefully explained what Tom had found out. At first, Davidson had been very happy, but when McQueen told him that none of it was provable without evidence, his joy dissipated fast.

'Right, this is what we need to do,' he said, in the tone of a man used to being decisive and commanding. He then suggested that McQueen should set up a sting operation, plant a person with a wiretap, possibly Tom, at one of the parties and get video evidence of Aaron Patterson making a drug deal. It seemed fairly simple to Davidson, as his experience of such things was gained mostly through Hollywood. This was the point in the meeting that McQueen's nasty old principles made an unwelcome appearance.

'Sorry, Mr Davidson,' McQueen said to the rapidly reddening face on the other side of the desk. 'But you can count me out. That's not my style.'

'What do you mean?' Davidson gave a wicked smile. 'Oh, I get it. You want more money. You want to increase your fee?'

'No, that's not it at all. What I mean is I don't want to pursue this case. I'm done. I'm out.'

Davidson looked back at him with such incredulity and lack of understanding that it was as if McQueen had been trying to explain quantum physics in Cantonese.

'But you're a private dick, aren't you?' he said. 'This is what you do. This is your job for Christ's sake. All I'm saying is do your job.'

'Well, yes, I am a private investigator, but I get to choose my jobs and I don't get involved with this kind of blatant entrapment.' McQueen's principles were feeling more fragile by the second. 'There are plenty of firms online that might be able to help you, Mr Davidson, but right now I have my own police concerns, and this level of setup operation very much crosses some legal lines. I'm sorry, but there it is.' He got up and offered his hand to shake, but Davidson didn't take it.

'Fine,' said the still-seated man. 'I'll get someone else. But let me tell you, I don't lose, McQueen. And in a month's time you'll come running back here, begging me to take you on again. You can send me an invoice for your time, but the bonuses we discussed won't come into play as all you gave me was rumour and hearsay, which I already knew. Meanwhile, don't expect to be getting any glowing references from me, McQueen. I have a lot of influential friends, and I can guarantee you won't be seeing any future business from any of them.'

'Thank you,' said McQueen, as pleasantly as he could. 'Good luck with your mission. Oh, and one other thing, Mr Davidson. I'd be remiss if I didn't mention that Tom, my inside contact, wanted me to tell you Aaron Patterson is involved with some very serious players, violent people, and that you should be very careful.'

Davidson snorted. 'It's Patterson who needs to be careful. I'm coming for him, and once I find a private eye with some balls, it's Patterson who'll be in danger.'

McQueen nodded, and without the slightest regret, turned his back on a payday that would have taken care of his office rent for a year.

Fourteen

Lia parked her car, remembered to send the *I'm here* text to McQueen, gathered up her notebook and courage, and got out without pausing. On the face of it, she might have been brimming with self-assured confidence, but not far beneath the surface armour, she had the inevitable jitters of someone doing something for the very first time. Her nervousness was centred on the breakneck speed she was moving on the road to becoming an actual private investigator, a path she'd never dreamed of, let alone planned. It was more than database research and phone calls from the safety of her desk now, it was suddenly becoming very real. She took a deep breath. She didn't want to give herself time to think too much about what the hell she was about to do, because she didn't want any hesitancy to show. With a very tiny shake of her head, she put aside her doubts. After all, she was only going to be talking to another human being. How hard could it be? True, she was a person who could conceivably turn out to be a murderer for all they knew.

Kerry had certainly been there at the time of the crime, but still, that was nothing to worry about, was it?

Lia hadn't told her boyfriend, Carl, about her trip to conduct an actual face-to-face interview, knowing he would have tried to talk her out of it. He'd already expressed his concerns that she was getting too involved with the agency and she was being asked to do way more than she was being paid for. He didn't believe her when she told him she had been the one who had gladly extended her work boundaries. He thought she was being pressured by her new boss, because in Carl's corporate world, that's how things worked. Boss-pressure is what kept him working until ten at night, the fear of falling short and being fired. The difference between Carl's and Lia's overtime was only that he was paid accordingly.

As she walked up the short drive, she looked around for any press photographers who might be lurking but saw none. The story was already growing cold in their eyes. She also checked to see if there were any signs of the crime itself, such as blood stains where the car would have been, but everything had been cleaned away. The blue police forensics tent was long gone, and Lia presumed they had taken the car, too. Before she could raise her hand to the doorbell, the door was opened by a very pretty dark-haired woman whom Lia barely recognised from McQueen's surveillance pictures. Her eyes were puffy, and she'd obviously been crying recently.

'Hello, Kerry Smith?' asked Lia, smiling. 'I'm Sekalyia Campbell.'

The woman looked back at her dead-eyed and didn't

respond.

'I work for the McQueen agency,' Lia added. 'We spoke earlier on the phone. I'd just like to ask you a couple of questions if that's okay?'

Kerry motioned with her chin for Lia to follow her and then went inside. They went through a short hallway into a living room where the curtains were closed and the lights were on, even though it was the middle of the day. Lia didn't need to ask what was going on. It was clearly a strategy to avoid prying eyes and telescopic lenses. Kerry turned to face her but didn't invite her to sit down.

'Why do you want to speak to me?' Kerry's tone was flat and sounded more defeated than aggressive. 'I've told the police everything I can. What do you want?'

Lia smiled her friendliest nonthreatening smile, then let her face fall into what she hoped was sympathetic seriousness. 'First of all, I'd just like to say I'm sorry for your loss. It must have been absolutely terrible for you.' The sympathy didn't soften the atmosphere, and Kerry let the comment drift past her unacknowledged.

'So,' Kerry said, 'you said you work for the guy who tracked Toby down?'

Lia had already decided that honesty was the best policy; you couldn't build lasting trust on easily spotted half-truths. 'Yes, that's right.'

'And he was working for Toby's...' She hesitated and then managed to summon the strength to say, 'for Toby's wife?'

'Yes, he was.'

'Can you tell her something from me?'

Lia hadn't been expecting this and she wasn't sure how to respond. She didn't think they were in a position to communicate with Marina Markham at the moment, not while the investigation was still ongoing, but Kerry didn't wait for her to answer anyway.

'I've seen what they said in the papers,' she said. 'It's all wrong. I'm not a husband stealer. Can you tell her that I had no idea he was married? He told me he was single. I wouldn't have started a relationship with him if I had known.'

Lia opened her notebook and began to write, but it was a bit difficult to juggle the large book.

'Can I sit down?' Lia asked.

Kerry nodded, slightly surprised, as if the thought hadn't even occurred to her.

Balancing the book on her knees, Lia wrote down verbatim what Kerry had said, and then thought she would chance her arm a little. 'And what was he like? Toby?' She asked this in a soft tone, as if they had been friends for years. Lia had taken an armchair, and now Kerry flopped down onto the matching sofa as if she were a puppet with its strings suddenly cut.

'He was really nice to me. He never did anything to hurt me and he always treated me good.' She looked up and saw Lia writing. 'I'm not used to men being nice to me, and it was nice.'

Lia cocked her head to study Kerry. This was a woman who was dealing with a lot. She was broken. Lia closed her book and dropped it on the floor, then with a big smile she said, 'Can I suggest something? How about I go into your kitchen, if that's okay, and make us both a nice cup of tea?'

It could have been a step too far, an intrusion, but Kerry was past caring and only shrugged.

Lia managed to find the tea bags and she washed a couple of the mugs that were sitting at the top of the pile in the sink. Thankfully, in a sparsely populated fridge, there was still a little milk left in a plastic bottle.

'Did you want sugar?' Lia asked as she handed Kerry the hot mug, but the shell-shocked woman shook her head.

Lia sat back down but didn't pick up her book. She wanted this to feel like a chat, not an interrogation.

'He tricked me,' said Kerry, clutching the mug with both hands. 'He said he didn't have a partner. He shouldn'ta done that, and now he's dead.'

'What did you hear?' asked Lia. 'At the time he was being murdered, there must have been some noise. Did you hear anything at all?'

Kerry looked back at her blankly and didn't answer the question.

'He wasn't as bad as my ex,' she said after a pause. 'But he still tricked me, and like an idiot, I believed him. Maybe I am an idiot.'

Something — and Lia couldn't have named what it was — screamed out to her and placed the next question onto her tongue: 'Your ex?'

Almost in a trance, Kerry said in a very quiet voice as if she was only talking to herself, 'Craig. My ex who still thinks he owns me. But then he's a Preston, so what did I expect from that family?'

Lia looked at this woman sitting slouched on her sofa

like a wounded animal curling protectively into itself. She looked at Kerry's face, her eyes and her hand gripping the mug.

'Look, Kerry,' Lia said gently, 'if you're frightened of something, or someone, you can—' But she didn't get to finish her sentence.

'Sorry.' Kerry stood up so quickly that her tea splashed a little onto her top. 'I can't do this. I want you to go now.'

Lia was taken aback by the sudden change of pace, and it forced her to make a quick choice. Kerry was clearly vulnerable and might be ready to talk more, but if Lia pressed on with the questions, that could alienate her forever, and what Lia was aiming at was getting to a place of trust. She was sure there was more to learn, but now didn't seem to be the right time.

'Okay,' she said instantly and put down her mug. 'No problem at all.' She had no business cards, so she wrote her number on a page of her book and tore it out. 'This is my number, Kerry. Any time at all that you want to chat, just give me a call.'

Kerry followed her to the front door. 'You'll tell her, then? The wife? You'll tell her I didn't know?'

'Next time I see her, I promise I'll tell her.' It wasn't exactly a lie, but it omitted the fact that she wouldn't be seeing Marina any time soon. Before Kerry could close the door on her, Lia wanted to plant a seed. She wanted her parting words to leave Kerry with something to mull over.

'The police have to find out who did this terrible murder, Kerry. Without help, they could accuse the wrong person, and that would be another life ruined. So anything,

anything at all you can remember could be saving a life.' She turned away and heard the door close behind her.

Back in her car, Lia was absolutely elated. It was such a buzz of excitement that she couldn't help grinning and she hoped Kerry wasn't watching her private reaction through a crack in the curtains. She had done it. She had spoken to a victim, and it had gone very well. She had learned something and given herself the next lead: Craig Preston, the ex. Lia knew a thing or two about ex-partners. She knew what they were capable of.

She sent the text: *I'm out and on my way back.* She almost put "Don't worry, Dad" at the end but thought better of it.

Fifteen

Several miles away, sitting on his sofa, his laptop balanced on his knees, Ian Bridger checked through his messages. He had a lot of accounts and many inboxes to keep track of. As far as the authorities were concerned, the accounts were all hidden and untraceable, routed back and forth through private servers dotted all over the world. He thought of them as his spinning plates; all they needed was a slight nudge now and then to keep them in the air. He was probably being overcautious but he believed in the mantra that paranoia saves lives, or in his case saves liberty. He found the inbox he wanted, the one in his mother's name, the "Olivia" account. He read the email and smiled. It was following the usual pattern. People were so predictable, even famous psychologists. Two replies within hours of the original message.

He's keen, very keen, Ian thought, *the sharpness of the hook against the softness of the mouth.*

Then he read the second message and bristled a little.

'Crank?' he said, out loud in the echoey room.

McQueen had used the phrase *crank messages*, which implied he thought the message might be from a crank. If McQueen had only known how wrong he was about that. Cranks were pathetic people who had never actually done anything of consequence, and that couldn't be further from the truth in Ian's case. Cranks could be ignored. Is that what McQueen thought, that this message could be ignored?

Ian was breathing heavily but he decided to leave McQueen to stew for a good while before answering. It was best not to rush. The hook always worked better when it had been given time to embed itself into the flesh of the lip. Let the target spend some time with their own imagination, inventing ideas and checking their phones. He would let it resolve before setting the arrogant detective running on his hamster wheel.

He clicked back to the online videos he'd found of Emma Cullen, not the various TV shows she had been in, but the news reports that had featured her over the years. In one, she came out of her own front door to a blinding burst of flashes. Her podcast had just helped to catch a pervert and the press wanted a story. Even though she wasn't in the studio she looked as she always did, like a hideous painted doll. But Ian wasn't interested in her. He was curious about her home. She lived in a town house where the door opened right onto a few steps that then led straight onto the pavement. It looked a bit like 10 Downing Street to Ian. No drive or front garden, nowhere to hide and wait. It would be a case of ringing the doorbell and hoping she answered her own door. Did people like that have a butler or a maid, perhaps?

He picked the gun up from the seat next to him and felt its comforting heaviness in his hand again. He held it with two hands the way actors did in films but he couldn't imagine Emma's face in from of him; his brain didn't work like that. Instead, he pointed the barrel at the frozen screen image of Emma. He knew he needed to be close. He hadn't done much shooting other than with light air-pistols and he didn't want to miss. A head shot was the most likely to kill, but faces are smaller targets than bodies. He didn't know how accurate the gun was. It occurred to him to take the gun out into the woods somewhere and practise on a tree, but if he was caught doing that, it would ruin everything. He wasn't sure how much support he would get from the invisible powers of the universe if he wasn't in the process of actually killing someone. It was death that fed the cosmos, not target practice. No, he decided, he would get as close as possible and rely on surprise. The one thing he was sure of was that he would have no nerves and his hand would be steady. It always was.

Sixteen

When Lia got back to the office, McQueen wasn't there, which was good because it gave her time to think about how she was going to approach this. It was the strangest thing, but she had somehow developed a sense of ownership over the Toby Markham murder. She had found things out and she had an idea about where she wanted to take it. She didn't want to simply hand this case back to McQueen when he came in.

At her desk, in the slatted sunlight that was still falling weakly through the blinds, Lia began checking through police reports and archived press coverage. As she did so, she found herself slowly shaking her head. Surely this guy was the number one police suspect? Taking the half-revealed lead from Kerry, Lia had chased up as much as she could about Kerry's ex-partner, Craig Preston. He hadn't been hard to find. He was a bad man from a notoriously bad family. The Prestons seemed to crop up everywhere in the crime reports: uncles and brothers all equally feared for their close association with casual violence and criminality. As for Craig Preston, there were numerous incidents of violence and antisocial behaviour that centred around his name in particular. There were also several ex-partners who had made claims of harassment and abuse against him. Lia was sure that it must have been a pretty lively scene at Kerry's address, but if there had been anything noisy going on in her street, it seemed that none of the neighbours had ever come forward with any testimony.

It all made sense to Lia. In her notebook, she wrote: "Craig Preston, local small-time criminal and general nasty comes to the house jealous and angry, calls Toby Markham outside and kills him. Any of the neighbours who do hear or see anything are too scared to come forward because they know they can't be protected from the rest of the family. Kerry herself is petrified as she probably has every right to be."

Lia checked the neatly handwritten notes she'd made at the house and then carefully typed everything into a blank document she titled, "Markham Case Notes".

The door opened and a smiling McQueen stepped into the office.

'You're alive,' he said airily upon seeing her, then jokily added, 'only two in ten of the assistants I send out on dangerous missions ever manage to return intact, so you've passed that test.'

'Yeah, funny how you kept that statistic to yourself, McQueen,' she responded, not looking up from her screen. 'Anyway, it's none of my business, but where were you?' She finally lifted her gaze to him. 'I didn't think we scheduled any meetings today?'

'Oh, I had a little appointment to turn down a lot of money. Anyway, let me grab a coffee, and then come in and tell me how you got on.'

When McQueen had settled himself at his desk, Lia came into his office but she didn't have her notes. She explained she had got on very well with Kerry Smith but that she had a few more details she wanted to clarify before she gave him her full report. She said that she was typing it up, but it needed a bit more work before she was happy to hand it over. It was the perfectionist in her, she said. What she was actually doing was trying to buy herself some time. Secretly, she wanted to present McQueen with more than a comprehensive report. She wanted to hand him a solved case. Her case.

She had expected McQueen to demand that she tell him what she had found out and not bother with a full report, but surprisingly, he accepted what she said with a simple nod. Then, as if he had read her mind, he said he thought it would be good if she ran with the Markham case herself. She was amazed. He said he had some other things on his mind, and that as his lawyer had advised him to stay clear of Markham, he was happy for her to work independently on the case. He did say that he was available for guidance and advice if she needed any, but other than that, it could be her baby.

Lia was thrilled. It was exactly what she wanted, and more than that, it bode well for the future. McQueen was turning out to be a very encouraging boss. She'd never been a fan of micromanagement. It smacked of lack of trust to her. But McQueen's style was the opposite. He was trusting her to do what she could with a case that directly impacted on him, and that said a lot. It made her even more determined to solve the murder.

What Lia didn't know was that McQueen was already feeling very confident about the Toby Markham case. The police hadn't come back, his lawyer had told him it was all nonsense and even Anne Kirkpatrick hadn't printed her rumours. Knowing Anne, that meant she had seen where the case was heading. There wasn't much risk involved, so it was a perfect project for Lia to cut her teeth on. If she managed to come up with anything, it would be a bonus, and if she didn't, it wouldn't matter too much. It would be up to the police to do their thing.

Meanwhile, McQueen had the Olivia message to think about. There was so little to go on, but a very strong alarm bell had rung in his head from the moment he'd seen it. Was it instinct, experience, or nothing at all? Was it just a fake feeling produced by too little sleep and too many nightmares? He was basing his guesses on only a few words sent over a cold email, but they had produced a very powerful reaction in whatever part of his brain nurtured his suspicious nature. If he was right, it could prove to be exactly the kind of work he'd always seen himself doing. It could also prove to be a dangerous path.

Seventeen

Sometimes they didn't go out to a restaurant but instead Emma cooked for them at her home or, to be more accurate, she had food sent in by one of her favourite restaurants and then heated it up. She had a fantastic kitchen in which any TV chef would have been happy to film an entire cooking series but she used only a fraction of its capacity. There were tastefully gleaming copper and steel pans hanging all over the place and professional-standard equipment in every cupboard. But the microwave and the oven were about all she ever used, apart from the beautiful matching plates with not a chipped edge anywhere to be seen.

Staying in had the advantage of making it easier to have a proper talk. McQueen had adjusted to the public attention that Emma received, but it was inhibiting to know multiple surrounding ears were tuned in to your conversation and listening for any juicy celebrity chat. So far, they had never been to McQueen's flat. Although he had offered the full tour, Emma said she felt more comfortable in her own surroundings, which he was very glad about. It wasn't that he was ashamed of his place, it was just it didn't come close to the luxury of her lovely home. He did have a cleaner for his flat who came in once a week, and he wasn't a secret hoarder or especially untidy. His flat wasn't even one of those man caves dominated by a huge screen and gaming consoles, but it was a utilitarian place to eat and sleep. He felt it was sadly lacking any wow factor. Furniture shopping was McQueen's idea of hell and that showed in his interior design. One Saturday after he'd moved in, he'd prepared himself for the pain, visited IKEA and tried to replicate the mocked-up rooms they displayed. Not much had happened since in the way of decorative glorification.

In contrast, there was nothing flat-packed about Emma's house, although it did have the slight vibe of an expensive hotel rather than a family home.

Tonight, they were eating a tray-baked salmon dish with green beans, tomatoes, and olives. There were also some tiny and perfectly round new potatoes. It was delicious. McQueen had something he wanted to say but he was waiting for the right time. Emma was drinking wine tonight, a glass of an expensive white, and for the first time in a long time McQueen felt tempted to join her. But the urge was fleeting, and instead he sipped from his sparkling water. As far as alcohol went, it was all or nothing for him. Emma would probably stop after enjoying a glass with her meal, but McQueen knew that one glass could never be the end to his evening's drinking.

Something else he liked about staying over at hers that he hadn't mentioned to Emma because it didn't exactly sound romantic was the absence of nightmares. There was something comforting about being in a bed with another person that kept the lurid dreams at bay for him. He didn't know why that was. Perhaps it was the sense of security. But whatever the reason, it was a relief to not wake up in a cold sweat struggling for breath in an imaginary sea, drowning in non-existent salt water, his hands and feet bound up, when in reality the bindings were just the clinging duvet. He was dreading a morning when it would happen and he'd have to explain his terror, but so far they had both been spared that difficult conversation.

However, when it came to PTSD, McQueen knew how lucky he was. So far, he'd got off lightly. He was well aware for some sufferers, every sleeping *and* waking moment of their lives was a battle against demons. Triggers could be all around that could send them running for cover at any moment. Amongst other things, hyperawareness could mean them seeing danger everywhere, especially in crowded places, and therefore keep them out of society. Thankfully, McQueen felt that his problems were under control, but it was still nice not to have the nightmares.

As he tucked the last forkful of salmon into his mouth, McQueen looked at Emma and wondered if he should broach the subject of her new show, *The Murderous Kind*. As yet, nothing was actually signed apart from a nondisclosure agreement that he'd had to agree to before the scripts had been sent to him. He didn't want to let her down but he was feeling more and more uncomfortable about the setup. If he committed to the job, even though it would be on a freelance basis, in reality he would no longer be his own boss, and it was that loss which rankled most. Ultimately, all the decisions would be Emma's, which was only right as it was her project, but even so it would feel like a backward step. He didn't know if Emma would still want him to do any on-screen guest spots if he pulled out of the production duties of the show, and it was the screen time that he had initially wanted to boost the profile of his detective services.

And there were all the other things he hadn't told her about yet, such as the Toby Markham case and how he was involved, and the email from the mysterious Olivia. He was certain she'd be very interested in that, but as she was a fame-hungry media person, he wasn't sure how much he trusted her to keep a secret.

Then again, the dinner was going so well, and Emma looked lovelier than ever, now that over the weeks she had morphed before his eyes from a static ice-maiden screen image to a very warm and funny person. He was relaxed and enjoying himself and he didn't want to spoil the mood. There was plenty of time to tackle the business stuff during office hours, and right now he was off duty. However, when Emma left the room for a few moments, McQueen couldn't help checking his phone.

When he was with her and in full "dating mode", he tried to keep his mobile out of sight and turned on silent. He knew how annoying it was to have a companion who was only partially present, because he'd sat through other dates when he had merely been an audience for someone interacting with an unseen other. To her credit, Emma stuck to the same no-phone rule, which was just as well because she was in great demand and whenever her phone was turned on, it was pinging and ringing almost constantly.

McQueen looked at the screen and saw he had received an email from Olivia. He could hear Emma coming back down the hallway so he guiltily put the phone back in his pocket like a pupil not wanting to be caught in class. Unfortunately, the damage had already been done to his concentration, and all he could think about was the message from Olivia. He'd seen studies that had suggested a phone only needs only to be within your eye line for it to significantly distract you. His was in his pocket and was still managing to steal his attention.

Emma was talking about her recent trip to Rome, during which she'd been following up a Mafia story, but after a few minutes of only partially hearing any of it, McQueen excused himself to go to the bathroom. Sitting on the closed toilet seat with the door locked behind him, he opened the email. There wasn't much in it.

I'M NO CRANK. The address you want is 111 Albemarle Terrace, LS16. That's where he died. I don't know what you mean about my mind's eye. I don't know what that's meant to mean, but I told you what I remember.

And that was it. It didn't have many words, but it was saying a lot to McQueen. Now he had the address to check up on so he could find out if anything had even happened, but it was the other thing that was intriguing. He flushed the toilet and noisily washed his hands in case Emma could hear and then went to rejoin her.

Emma was too good an interviewer and reader of

people to miss that McQueen's attention was straying, and after a few minutes she asked, 'Is there something on your mind, McQueen?'

There were many answers he could have given to that question, ranging from his doubts about his place on her new show to his current status as a murder suspect in the Markham case to even his latest email from Olivia. He looked at Emma's eager face and recognised the same professional inquisitiveness that he'd seen on Anne the journalist's face more than once. He decided to play it safe.

'Well,' he said, 'if I like someone, I try not to bore them with obscure psychology.'

'Nice to hear that you like me,' she replied, but her curiosity seemed to have been piqued. 'Bore away. I'm always interested in the mind.' She sat forward at the table in a theatrical "I'm listening" pose, her chin resting on her hand. It struck him that he was liking her more and more.

'Okay.' He felt as scrutinised as he used to feel when he was about to deliver a lecture to a roomful of eager students. 'Have you ever heard of a mental phenomenon called aphantasia?'

She shook her head. 'Nope, but I have seen the Disney film, *Fantasia*. Anything to do with that?' She took a sip of her wine, raising her eyebrows in a "go on, then" gesture.

'No, not really. Aphantasia, from the Greek for imagination, of course—'

'Of course,' she interjected playfully.

He wasn't used to being heckled in his lectures but he didn't let it put him off.

'…is a fascinating condition,' he continued. 'Fascinating

119

to me, anyway. It's estimated to affect about two percent of the population and it describes people who don't have the ability to visualise pictures in their heads. They can't close their eyes and see an image of anything. Not their loved ones, not simple things like a round ball, nothing.'

'Really? What do they see?' She didn't seem bored yet.

'Blackness. It's as if they have no mind's eye, or if they do, it's blind.'

Emma then asked the obvious question, the one that had initially occurred to McQueen when he'd first learned of the condition while he was studying for his psychology degree all those years ago.

'So can a person with aphantasia dream?' she asked.

'Not as we think of dreaming, no. At least they report not remembering any visual dreams.'

She was nodding appreciatively, and he felt he'd picked a good topic to bore her with.

'Now, the amazing thing,' said McQueen, warming to his subject, 'is that many of these souls can live all of their lives never knowing they have this condition. They have no way to know what they are experiencing is not what everyone else sees, or to be more accurate, doesn't see. And so from childhood, they play along with the game that they think everyone else is playing. Some finally work it out in later life, but it's a revelation to them.'

'Wow, I've never heard of this,' said Emma. 'It must be horrible for them. Does it limit their lives at all?'

'It doesn't seem to. I mean, they can't miss what they've never had. And in fact, there have been famous artists and animators who have had the condition.'

She sat up a little at this. 'Now you're joking. How would that work? How could you draw a horse, for instance, if you couldn't imagine what one looks like?'

'I think they make it form on the paper in front of them. Perhaps the person knows the details of a horse and they draw it out. I don't really know.'

'Well, I'll give you this one, McQueen. It is interesting, but what made you think of this now?'

McQueen didn't want to admit to sneaking off to the toilet to look at his phone. 'Oh, it was just an email I got earlier today,' he said casually. 'And I could be wrong, but I think I've been speaking to someone online who has the condition.'

'Okay.'

'And it started a train of thought and got me thinking: suppose a person didn't want to draw a picture of a horse. What if they wanted to make an actual scene in front of them?'

'What do you mean?'

'I mean, suppose they wanted to know what a murder looked like, for instance, but they couldn't visualise it, so they made one happen in front of them to see it.'

'Surely they could simply watch films? There's enough murders on TV to keep them amused forever.'

'But they're not real, are they? I mean even if the event itself is real, like the appalling internet clips of beheadings, they are just flat images.'

'So are you saying that anyone with aphantasia is likely to be a murderer? The famous animator you mentioned before, are you telling me he was actually a killer with a pen in his hand? Drawing bunny rabbits by day and drawing blood by night?'

He laughed. 'Of course not. All I'm saying is that if you were a serial killer who happened to have the condition, it could be part of your motivation, that's all.'

Emma had turned back to her wine bottle for a top-up, and McQueen could tell he was losing his audience. It was time to change the subject before he ruined the whole evening. 'Anyway, it's just a silly theory. But you did ask.'

'Not sure if I should be insulted,' she replied, taking a sip from the glass. 'Here I am, doing my best to captivate and impress you, and all you're thinking about is possible motivations for murders.' She was smiling when she said this, but McQueen took the hint and launched his rescue mission.

'Oh, I'm captivated,' he assured her. 'You don't need to worry about that.'

They finished their meal, and sensing it was her turn to take the floor, Emma chatted easily about her early life in media and how she'd had to fight to get to where she was in an incredibly competitive field. There were the inevitable setbacks that she'd faced, which she managed to turn into hilarious asides. She self-effacingly dismissed her main successes as blind luck of the right-time and right-place variety. McQueen liked that. In his experience, it was the people who tried to claim fortunate events as entirely down to their own skill who were to be avoided. He thought of them as the you-make-your-own-luck merchants, the ones born into family wealth and privilege who believed they'd somehow earned it by their brilliance.

He was surprised to find that, like him, Emma was a council estate kid who had worked hard at school and aced every exam she'd ever taken. That part of her life hadn't been covered on Wikipedia. From what she was saying, she'd certainly had some breaks, but McQueen knew it was more than luck that had propelled her upwards through the ranks of wannabe TV stars and kept her there. He let the nagging urge to answer Olivia's email fade away as he began to fully appreciate that what he was seeing here, sitting right in front of him, was a rare individual. Talent was a very hard word to define, but whatever the definition, Emma Cullen had a big dollop of it.

Selfishly, McQueen was also looking forward to a night with Emma's soft body amongst her heavenly cloud-like bedding, a night that had the added bonus of not being interrupted by nightmares.

On the other side of the city, Tom Lewis was just shutting up his office at the back of the charity food bank for the night. As usual, he was the last one to leave. The volunteers had all gone home but they'd be back bright and early the next morning, and he'd made sure everything was ready for them. It had been a busy day, and he'd hardly had a moment to think about anything other than work, which was just the way he liked it. He was glad not to be going out to do any more sleuthing for McQueen. It had been a test to go back to his old haunts and talk to his old acquaintances and he was happy not to do that ever again.

It was quite dark now, but as he locked the front door behind him, he was aware of the large black van parked across the street. He didn't pay much attention to it until the doors opened and two men got out. They came across the road, both wearing black from head to toe: hoodies, jogging bottoms, and boots. Tom had been around the streets long enough to know trouble when he saw it. He thought of running but they were too close now.

'I have no money,' he said, then pointed at the charity office door. 'And there's nothing of value in here.'

'Tom?' asked the first man. 'Are you Tom?'

Eighteen

The dog was called Charlie and he was a solid black Labrador. He saw and recognised McQueen from a distance and left his slobber-covered tennis ball in the grass to come gambolling over to say hello, his sturdy tail wagging so hard as he turned in excited circles it almost knocked McQueen off his feet. In contrast, his owner, when she'd slowly walked across, was less than overjoyed to see McQueen.

'I shouldn't be seen talking to you,' said Detective Tracey Bingham with a heavy sigh. 'And you shouldn't be stalking me.'

It was true McQueen knew what time she was likely to be walking Charlie on the grassy turf of this corner of Roundhay Park. They'd met out there before, and he'd come today especially hoping to catch her. He knew Tracey had a romantic partner these days, a woman called Sophie. He'd never met her, and although he was looking forward to doing that, he'd been hoping that she wouldn't be out walking with Sophie today. He wanted Tracey's full attention.

'An amazing coincidence,' he said brightly. 'I was just out for a walk for my mental health. You know how beneficial the open air can be. And there you were.'

Tracey didn't even grace his jokey lie with a comment.

'How have you been?' he asked, maintaining his cheery tone, but Tracey wasn't prepared to join in the game.

'Before you start,' she said. 'I can't talk to you about the Markham case, McQueen. I know you think you're being persecuted by the police and I certainly can't talk about that either.'

'And I really don't want to talk about that. Obviously, we both know it's utter bullshit and those two numpties should never have even come to my office, but it will all be resolved in time.' He bent to ruffle Charlie's ears. 'No, Tracey, now that I've bumped into you, that's not what I want to talk about. But I do have a favour to ask.'

Tracey knew she should be telling him to leave her alone, but in truth she had missed talking to him. Even though she wasn't going to admit it, it was good to see him. Also, she too had some things she was longing to discuss.

They walked for a while in silence, taking it in turns to kick the ball for Charlie, the unspecified favour hanging heavily in the air, until McQueen began speaking again.

He had followed up on the address Olivia had given him and now outlined the facts for Tracey as he knew them. Importantly, he only referred to Olivia as an anonymous lead. He wasn't ready to give away everything just yet.

He told Tracey the cold facts, that an old man had been

found dead in his own bed at 111 Albemarle Terrace, and it had been dismissed as natural causes. However, he explained that he'd received a tip-off from someone who said they believed it had been a murder. The interesting point was the source had specifically mentioned the back door of the old guy's house and that it should be checked. McQueen said he felt his lead was implying maybe there were signs of a break-in that had been missed by the police. Tracey stopped walking and looked hard at her friend when he said this.

'McQueen,' she said, 'if that's right, and further investigation shows that yes, the door was tampered with, and that yes, the man was killed, then it tells us something interesting about your lead.'

'Yep,' said McQueen, nodding. 'Either she's a nosey neighbour with high-powered binoculars, or she's the murderer. Or she's spoken to the murderer.'

'She?' said Tracey. 'I thought you said the tip-off was anonymous?'

McQueen grinned. He should have remembered who he was dealing with here.

'He, she, they?' he asked. 'Who knows? Personal pronouns are a minefield on the internet. But there's one other thing. The tip-off person told me that she had gone to the police already with a very vague description: a very tall man, wearing all black, in the area on the night of the death. She said the police had said that it was of no help. But there would be a record of that call, wouldn't there?'

'Should be,' said Tracey with a slight shrug.

She was quiet for a while as she likely thought about the

logistics and internal problems of reopening a closed case. She shuddered at the thought of the paperwork to be completed and the arguments to be had. It wouldn't be easy, especially as the request stemmed from an anonymous tip-off of dubious credibility. The lead had not even been received directly by the police, but by someone who was under investigation himself. She was reluctant to get involved, but at the same time, she trusted McQueen's judgement.

McQueen could tell from her silence she was probably writing this off as a waste of time. She was kicking Charlie's tennis ball with a little more venom, and her body language was a little more tensed. Fearing he was about to be brushed off, he tried to make her realise how important he thought this tip-off was.

'Tracey, I understand your resourcing issues, and I know you have plenty of live cases that all need your time, but all I can say is for some reason, from that very first email she sent, I knew it was something I couldn't ignore. I just knew.'

'A good old McQueen hunch, eh?' said Tracey with a humourless smile.

'Yes,' he replied, 'a hunch. A hunch that I'd been messaged by a murderer. Their crime has gone unnoticed, and maybe they want some bragging rights? Maybe they want to do some taunting? You know as we'll as me that's not unheard of. I'd love to be proved wrong, Tracey. I'd love this to turn out to be a busybody neighbour with too much time on their hands and an overactive imagination, but I need your help to find that out.'

They walked on further with Charlie making the only sounds. Having lost his ball somewhere, he was sniffing loudly around in the grass behind them. Eventually, Tracey sighed again in resignation and reluctantly promised she would do whatever she could to find out about the old man's death. She took out her phone and made a note of the address, which McQueen gave her again.

Already moving forward in his mind and trying to see where this might go, McQueen then asked Tracey whether it was possible to trace an email address back to a real person. She said that *if* the evidence proved to be strong enough, and *if* they could get a court order, then *maybe* it was possible, but not necessarily. In normal circumstances, she said, an email source could usually be traced, but not if the sender had the expertise to hide their IP address and use proxy servers in foreign countries. It would mean the kind of international cooperation and resources normally only used to keep tabs on international terrorists, and even then it wasn't always possible. If the person was very clever and they were good with technology, it was nigh on impossible to track them.

'Now it's my turn,' she said. She briefly mapped out the two murders she'd been focusing her efforts on: the man strangled with his scarf and the woman pushed down the stairs. McQueen remembered the grainy video image that had been circulated publicly after the woman had been killed but recalled little else. Tracey filled him in on some of the details and then asked her question, a query she didn't dare float with anyone else for fear of being ridiculed.

'These are the most difficult kind of murders to solve,'

she said. 'Random, motiveless killings. But could that be a connection?'

'Connection? You mean could it be the same person who did it?'

She shrugged. 'You know how it works, McQueen. If murders are sexually motivated, even if the victims aren't sexually assaulted, something links the victims. They are all young women or gay men, for instance. Or there's a murder method that is the same, a stabbing, a strangling, whatever. But as it stands, both of these killings will go unsolved. Both of them will be abandoned and forgotten because they are too difficult. But what if nothing to connect them is their connection? Or am I being crazy?'

'A good old Tracey Bingham hunch?' he said, grinning. 'I like it, and I say run with it. No one has better instincts than you, Tracey, not even me.' To lighten the mood, McQueen added, 'Mind you, I may have found a contender for your crown. I've hired a new assistant called Sekalyia who is going to put us both to shame, I'm certain of it.'

'Oh, so you found someone to take that job you offered me?'

'No, no, you could have been a full partner, Tracey — name on the door, the works. But you turned me down for a car with a flashing light and a pension.'

They exchanged jibes and jokes for a bit longer until they were back at Tracey's car. She opened the hatchback boot, and with a little help from Tracey, Charlie scrambled up onto his blanket.

'Murders aside,' McQueen said. 'It was good to see you again.' He was keeping a slight distance, not wanting to make it too uncomfortable for her as he knew she would be nervous about being seen with him.

'You too.' She fussed on with making sure Charlie was settled before closing the door on him.

'Let me tell you about a real mystery that I can't solve,' she said. 'Last night, I laid out some red wine, cheese, and biscuits on a low table in the living room for Sophie and me to have a relaxing evening watching TV. We were in the kitchen, but when we went back to the living room, the door was ajar, the wine had been knocked over, and the cheese was all gone. Charlie was lying down on the other side of the room, so, y'know, it couldn't possibly have been him, right?'

Charlie was looking sheepishly at Tracey as if he knew what she was talking about.

'The evidence,' she continued, 'points to a greedy dog with a tail that can sweep a bottle from a table if it's wagging.'

McQueen leaned into the car and patted Charlie's head. 'I'll give you the name of my lawyer,' he whispered to the Labrador. 'They've got nothing on you. It's all circumstantial.' Then he straightened up again. 'Well, I kept the deal. I didn't hassle you about the Markham case.'

'True,' she said. 'But are you about to do it now?'

'No need.' He laughed and patted her on the arm rather than engaging in their usual good-bye hug. 'I think Sekalyia is already working on it.'

Tracey was just getting into her car when she checked her phone. She ducked back out of the door. 'McQueen. Make sure your mobile is on. There's been an incident and I think the police want to contact you.'

Nineteen

Here I am again, thought McQueen as the automatic doors swished closed behind him and he stepped into the enveloping warmth of the hospital. *The opposite of summer in Spain, where leaving a building made you walk into a wall of heat.*

He immediately took off his coat to carry it over his arm. In his hand was a sagging clear-plastic bag of grapes. Old-school, but what else are you supposed to take to a patient? For some vague hygiene reasons, most hospitals didn't allow flowers to be brought in anymore, but that was fine with McQueen. He was bad at flowers, always managing to choose the least attractive bunch that would invariably wilt before they left their cellophane wrapper. He looked down at the grapes in the bag, which weren't doing so well either. There were already a couple at the bottom of the bag that were squashed and brown. Bizarrely, it reminded him that according to a scientist he'd recently heard on the radio, squashed grapes were one of the slipperiest substances known to man. Apparently, injuries after slipping on dropped grapes near the fruit and veg section had resulted in more than one lawsuit against supermarkets. Maybe it was the grapes that should have been banned rather than the flowers.

The reception area of the hospital was located inside a huge open-plan, high-ceilinged atrium, like an outdoors that was indoors. It was busy with people in all states of dress, from patients in pyjamas to visitors in overcoats, all milling around or being pushed around in wheelchairs. Most of them were staring at the overhead signage, trying to work out which way to go. There were words up there that you never saw anywhere else, such as "maxillofacial" and "phlebotomy". To the right was a large coffee shop area where patients, visitors, and medical staff intermingled in the queue for their life-saving lattes and cappuccinos. Then taking their recyclable cups, they sat outside, still within the cover of the atrium, at the cluttered tables.

McQueen stood for a second to take it all in. It wasn't a popular opinion, but he liked hospitals. But then he had every reason to. A hospital just like this one had been the place of rebirth for him after his open-heart surgery several years before, and he loved the sense of security he felt every time he stepped inside one. At its most basic, his comfort came from the knowledge that if he collapsed right now, there would be plenty of people on hand with the expertise to rev him back to life. The care he'd received during and after his operation had been exceptional, and he felt nothing but gratitude and warmth when he thought of it. True, the food had been fairly appalling, and another week of it would probably have killed him, but he could never get over the thought that the seven-hour operation which had saved his life would have bankrupted him if he'd lived in the US. The modern approach to recovery after major surgery had you out of your bed the next day if possible. The days of twelve weeks of lying on your back were long gone, and it occurred to McQueen that some of the patients shuffling to the coffee shop may well have been under the knife a matter of hours before.

As far as McQueen was concerned, the wonderful NHS was made up of teams of underpaid genuine do-gooders, and he could even forgive the rude receptionists he sometimes encountered. He was sure he would probably be rude too if he had to deal with the whinging public day after day.

No, all in all, hospitals generally gave him a good feeling. But today was different, and he was wishing with all his battered heart that he didn't have to be there.

He followed the confusing signs, went up in the lift and then eventually found the right ward. He checked in with the nurse in charge at the desk and then made his way to the bed at the end of a row of four. The nurse had warned him Tom would be resting, and he seemed to be asleep, so McQueen quietly put the bag of grapes down on the bedside cabinet and then pulled up a chair next to the bed.

He sat looking at Tom's pale, drawn features and he remembered Tom's grandmother, Grace. She had paid McQueen a retainer to look after Tom. That was the job really, *to pull him out of the odd scrape*, as she called it. What would she be thinking now if she was still alive? What would she think of this scrape? Over the years he had seen

Tom in some bad states, when drugs had robbed him of his vitality and personal cleanliness had been low on his list of priorities. He'd seen him with ratty, dirty hair and the darkest of rings round his reddened eyes. He'd seen the cuts and scabs and dirty fingernails of Tom's addiction, but this was different. He was clean on the surface. His hair had even been combed. But his sleeping face was grey and drained of blood.

Minutes after Tracey had warned him, McQueen had received a telephone message via the police that Tom had been involved in some kind of accident. The officious female voice who had answered McQueen's increasingly emotional questions with all the warmth of an automaton told him Tom had two broken legs but couldn't remember anything at all about how it had happened. He'd been found on a patch of ground near his work and he had been in agony but still conscious when he'd been taken to hospital. On admission to A&E, he'd quickly been taken to an operating theatre where surgeons tried to reassemble his legs, a couple of operations that had required a number of metal pins and screws.

Afterwards, when he'd been asked for a next of kin or personal contact, he'd given McQueen's name and number, hence the call. McQueen came off the phone with the distinct impression that it was going to be a while until Tom was walking again.

Tom was on the police records as an addict who'd been involved in various accident-related incidents in the past, so their sympathy was somewhat lacking but they still seemed to be interested in finding out what had happened.

Whatever the incident had been, at least Tom was still alive, but McQueen had a very bad feeling about this accident and he was dreading the discussion he was about to have.

He watched his sleeping friend for a while, the scene bringing back disjointed memories of his own experience in a hospital bed. For McQueen, his main memory was the first few seconds of groggily waking up after his bypass surgery, the dryness in his mouth and the joy at still being alive. At that point, there had been no pain from the twelve-inch incision that was running down his chest because he was nicely numbed by morphine. It wasn't until later that he'd had to be shown how to cough without damaging himself. A spare pillow had to be hugged against his chest. He remembered that.

As he sat next to Tom, who didn't know he was there, McQueen also remembered having seen a man come to visit the patient in the next bed to his during his own stay. The visitor had sat for a full two hours while the other person slept and then eventually left without speaking to him.

But you were there, McQueen had thought, *you made the effort.*

The personal recollections that were cascading through his mind were hard to avoid, but McQueen reminded himself not to self-reference when Tom finally woke up. It was a classic mistake in the eyes of any therapist to talk about yourself when it's the other person that is in pain. Through force of habit and the addictive nature of modern technology, McQueen took out his phone to check his messages and emails. Nothing more from Olivia. When he looked up, Tom's eyes were open.

'I hope you're not taking pictures,' Tom croaked with a watery smile, looking at the phone in McQueen's hand.

'How are you doing?' McQueen tried to infuse his voice with a lightness he didn't feel, but Tom just shook his head. McQueen continued in the same unreasonably jolly tone. 'The police said something about an accident?'

Tom raised his arm, which had a catheter taped into it that in turn was attached to a drip, and he beckoned for McQueen to come closer. McQueen leaned out of his chair and over the bed.

Tom whispered, 'The kind of accident you have when you ask too many questions about Aaron Patterson.'

It was exactly what McQueen had dreaded hearing. He started to sit back down again, but Tom motioned for him to come closer again.

'I thought I'd been careful and clever,' Tom continued. 'I only spoke to people I thought were safe and I thought I hadn't made it too obvious, but I was wrong.'

'Did you get a good look at the people who did this?'

Seeing where that question was going, Tom's eyes widened. 'Look, I'm saying nothing to the police. Nothing. Some people only threaten to break your legs to scare you, and some people really do it. I told you about his suppliers and associates. They are very serious people.'

McQueen didn't know what to say, but the shame that had been eagerly waiting in the wings burst forward now and engulfed him. There was no escaping it: Tom's predicament was McQueen's fault as surely as if the private eye had taken a sledgehammer and smashed his tibias and fibulas himself. Tom had been doing just fine, making his way in a clean and productive life. He was no part of this mess until McQueen had asked a favour of him, only to see him pay the price in shattered bones. McQueen was aghast at his own blinkered stupidity. It was so obvious now that he thought about it. The junkies Tom had been questioning would always be looking for easy ways to get money for drugs. It wouldn't have taken long for one of them to have realised Tom's interest in Aaron might be information that was worth something to somebody, so it would have passed up the chain pretty quickly.

'God, I'm so sorry,' said McQueen. 'How can I make it up to you?' It was pathetic but it was all he could think of to say.

'By leaving it alone,' hissed Tom. 'Please back off, McQueen. They'll kill you if you carry on, and I don't want to see that.'

It was heart-breaking that even lying in his hospital bed, when he had every right to feel anger and bitterness towards him, Tom's first thought wasn't about himself but to warn McQueen of the dangers of continuing the case. By the look on Tom's haggard face, McQueen could see just how terrified the young man was and all McQueen wanted in that moment was to reassure, comfort and protect him.

Too little, too late, his internal critic screamed in his head.

'It's okay,' McQueen said gently. 'Don't worry, I already quit that job. I told my client that I wasn't interested in chasing Aaron and that I didn't want any part of it. But I suppose Aaron's associates weren't to know that.'

For a split second, an unwelcome, nasty thought snaked its way through McQueen's mind: there was another possibility. But he chose to bite down on it and not to share it with Tom just yet.

The patient attempted a smile but then put his hands on his bedding above his thighs and winced, baring his teeth in pain. McQueen jumped up, glad of the chance to do something, anything.

'I'll get the nurse,' he said.

Tom stopped him with a shake of his head. 'No, don't. I'll be okay.' Then he added, 'Unfortunately, effective pain control is opiate based. Essentially, that's the same as heroin, and I'm a recovering addict. They have a limited and controlled drug plan for me, but I have to stick to the times and dosage. No extras.'

It was on the tip of McQueen's tongue to mention how sleepy and hallucinatory he had found the pain-killing drugs he had been given during his own stay, but he managed to keep that self-reference to himself.

They lapsed into an awkward silence until Tom spoke again.

'Look, there's something you should know, McQueen.' Tears were welling in his eyes. 'I'm no hero. I'm a coward. And when they asked me why I'd been poking around asking questions, I told them. I wanted the pain to stop. I told them your name. I didn't want to, but I did.' He was crying a little when he said this, and McQueen stood up.

'Hey, it's okay,' McQueen said. 'Really. Anyone other than James Bond would have done the same, and he's a fictional character.' Grinning, he touched Tom very gently on the back of his hand to make a physical human connection. 'Don't worry about me. Just get yourself better.'

Even to his own ears, it sounded exactly like the kind of meaningless piffle people say when they are visiting ill people in hospital, but it fitted well with the cliché of the grapes.

'But they wanted to know who your client was, McQueen, who you were working for. But I couldn't tell them, could I? Because I didn't know.' Now Tom really was crying. 'That's when they really hurt me. I wanted to tell them but I couldn't, and they didn't believe me.'

McQueen did the only thing he could do: he put his hand on Tom's heaving shoulder and repeated, 'I'm so sorry, Tom. I really am.'

McQueen was thinking practically now, looking for solutions. He was aware Tom lived alone, still estranged from his parents who had thrown him out years before when the lying, cheating, and stealing that had accompanied his descent into serious drug addiction had got too much for them. The tough love had apparently been advised by some guru or other at the time. That's when Tom had turned to his grandmother, whose soft love, patience, and tolerance were inexhaustible. But Grace was gone now, and mobility was going to be very difficult for Tom over the months of his recovery.

'You might need to come and live with me for a while when you get out,' McQueen said. He hadn't really thought it through, and the practicalities of the arrangement would be difficult, but McQueen was sure he could work it out.

Tom, however, was shaking his head. 'No,' he said quietly. 'I'll manage. I still have money and I can sort out a carer if I need one. I think you and I have reached a point where we need to see less of each other for a while, not more.'

'But I...' McQueen started to say, but stopped when Tom shook his head again.

'I'm not feeling great about you, McQueen. I feel used and I need time away from you to get over that before we can be friends again.'

Ten minutes later, sitting at one of the messy tables of the hospital coffee shop, McQueen was staring into the swirling surface of his flat white. He needed some minutes to compose himself before heading out into traffic again. He had enough awareness to realise it wasn't a good idea to drive while he was so distracted. Guilt had a strong grip on his throat, and he knew he had to get past that before he could focus again.

On his way out of the ward, he'd stopped to ask the nurse about the pain control and the possibility that it could subsequently send Tom into a relapse. She had explained they had a procedure for recovering addicts which was all about keeping the drugs on a completely clinical basis and strict dosage. McQueen already knew that often the euphoric effects of drugs were largely down to the environment and rituals addicts undertake. It made sense by maintaining the clinical coldness of administering medicine, the psychological links could be broken. However, once Tom was out of hospital and in charge of his own pain relief, it might be a different story.

McQueen looked around at some of the sad faces of his fellow visitors who were probably coping with their own versions of bad news. In contrast, the doctors and nurses in their blue uniforms and rubber clogs were generally smiling, happy to be grabbing a few minutes away from their jobs and whatever awful problems they had been dealing with. It was a prerequisite of that career choice, being able to distance yourself from the endless stream of misery you had to encounter daily.

McQueen thought of something his mother always used to say: if people in a room full of strangers were to put all their problems in a pile in the middle of the carpet, once they had seen what others were struggling with, they would probably take back their own.

The sight of Tom so damaged and frightened had shocked and appalled him, but now his thoughts were turning to Lia. What had he been sending her out into and how safe had she been? Sure, she'd got back safely, and it was only an interview with a witness, but had it been irresponsible to allow her to go alone? He was about to call her on his phone to check in on her when a man placed a cup of coffee opposite his, and without asking, joined him at the table. At first, McQueen didn't recognise this bullet-headed lump of a man, but then the penny dropped. It was one of the detectives who'd come to his office to question him about Toby Markham.

'Detective Reed, isn't it?' McQueen asked, forcing a smile.

'Chambers,' replied the detective dryly.

'Oh, that's right. Sorry, Reed was the handsome one.'

The policeman didn't respond to that. 'Been visiting Tom Lewis? I was on my way up to see him myself when I saw you sitting here, looking all lost and lonely, so I thought I'd join you.'

When McQueen didn't answer, Chambers asked, 'He gave you as his main contact, didn't he?'

It was a difficult situation for McQueen. The need for revenge, powered by his own guilt, was burning a hole in his chest. What he most wanted to do was tell the detective everything and then have the animals that had attacked Tom hunted down and thrown in jail. But it was a fantasy. There was very little to go on, so all it would mean is the police would turn up asking questions, and there was a strong chance it would make things worse for Tom, which was one thing McQueen couldn't risk. Tom had already decided to tell the police nothing, and McQueen had to respect that. The reality was there was no protection the police could possibly offer Tom that would actually keep him safe.

'We're old friends,' said McQueen.

'Did he say what happened? Did he fall or was he beaten up? Looks like deliberate injuries to me.' He studied McQueen's face for any reaction and saw none. He took a sip of his coffee, leaving a slight moustache of foam on his upper lip he wiped away with the back of his hand. 'Did he have drug debts or something? He must be in a lot of pain, poor guy.' The detective had taken on an unconvincingly friendly stance, hoping the chatty approach and a blizzard of questions would open McQueen up.

'He doesn't remember.' McQueen had resigned himself to saying as little as possible.

Stony faced, all pretence of friendliness gone, the

policeman nodded and made a note in his book. 'Well, turns out there was some CCTV footage from that area set up to monitor drug activity, so we'll be looking into it. Let's hope you don't turn up on it, eh, McQueen?' When he got no response, the detective pressed on. 'You're a bit of a curse, aren't you, McQueen?' He dropped the pal act and picked up his coffee. 'Old friends who get beaten up and a client's husband who ends up dead. We haven't forgotten about that, by the way.' He stood up. 'Inquiries are still under way, and you are still very much in the picture.'

'Max Goodson,' said McQueen. 'That's the name of my solicitor. If you need any more help from me, he's the guy to contact.'

'Oh, we know all about Mr Goodson. Mr Technicality. Friend and protector to low-life scum. Well, let's go and see if young Tom can remember anything else now he's had time to reflect on things.'

McQueen had kept quiet so long his jaw was aching. It just wasn't his style. Some of the bitterness and frustration of the day so far came bubbling up.

'What is your problem?' McQueen said to the detective who was towering over his table. 'With me, I mean? In general, what is it that bugs you so much? Is it because I've solved a couple of cases you guys had given up on? I know I've made you look stupid and incompetent from time to time. Is that it? Or is it because I get all the media attention while you get nightshifts and zero respect?'

McQueen could see the anger rising in Chambers, and Chambers was clearly struggling to keep himself from overturning the table. But he managed to look around and compute how bad it would look for a policeman to make a scene outside a hospital coffee shop. He made the right choice, said nothing and turned away.

McQueen watched the bulky detective ease off into the crowd and smiled. It was a big, confusing hospital, and the policeman was heading in the wrong direction. *Typical*, thought McQueen.

Twenty

There was an uneasy quiet in Sekalyia's house as she got ready for work. The mood was dominated by the argument she and Carl had had the night before. After the raised voices, it had ended in silence and not so much as a *goodnight* when the lights had been turned out. There had been no cuddling in bed, no comforting spooning, and they'd each kept very much to their own sides of the mattress.

The next morning, Carl had finished shaving and he looked immaculate in his dark blue suit and white shirt, but Lia only glimpsed him as he skipped breakfast and slammed the door on his way out without saying goodbye. It was upsetting for her, but she wasn't going to back down, and as for Carl, she wasn't sure if he had the word sorry in his vocabulary. She'd end up having to make the peace but she was prepared to hold out for a while longer. It was a matter of principle. She wasn't about to let him start telling her how she should be living her work life. She'd had controlling boyfriends before and she wasn't going to go through that again.

The argument had started over dinner when Lia had said she intended to go back to visit Kerry Smith again this morning. Carl had said she shouldn't go and then he became very angry when she said it was her job, her life, and she was going to go no matter what he said. He had pushed his half-eaten dinner to one side and began carefully pointing out — illustrating with hard taps on the table with his index finger — all the reasons why he thought she was being stupid. The possible danger involved and the lack of extra pay were his two main points. It all sounded very patronising to Lia, and with her arms folded and eyes narrowed, she said so. Then she pointed out that she never told him not to work late or spoil their weekends fussing over corporate presentations. Carl had that it wasn't the same thing at all and then finished by saying he knew more about life than her and that he was saying don't do it. To Lia, it had sounded a lot like an order and had been pretty much the last straw.

His final shout with his finger pointing aggressively in her direction was, 'You're obsessed, Lia.'

Her defences kicked in. She shut up shop, and he started sulking.

What she'd wanted from Carl was support and encouragement in her new career direction. She'd wanted him to be as excited as she was, but it clearly wasn't going to happen. The thing was that in many ways she knew he was right. There were a lot of reasons why she should stay clear of Kerry and her domestic murder scene, but she couldn't let it go. Maybe she *was* obsessed.

Lia was convinced that now that Kerry had had time to mull it over, she might be ready to say more. She was hoping to leverage the trust atmosphere she had tried to produce the last time they'd met. To her, it was clear: Craig Preston had probably killed Toby Markham in an if-I-can't-have-you-no-one-can fit of jealousy. Lia had seen it before. She had once been out at a bar with a new boyfriend when an ex approached them and started threatening her date. It had been nasty. Fortunately, it hadn't ended in violence, but the new boyfriend had never returned her calls after that.

Lia felt certain that Kerry must have seen something of the murder. After all, it had been a long, noisy sustained attack right outside her window. The key to it all was breaking through Kerry's fear and getting her to admit what she'd seen or at least what she knew. Perhaps then some of the neighbours might come forward with evidence of their own. Lia hadn't discussed any of her suspicions with McQueen. He'd been busy, and she'd been keeping things to herself, determined to impress him with how much she had achieved.

She picked up her notebook and thought about phoning ahead, but she didn't want to give Kerry the chance to turn her down. It was risky, but it would be better to turn up unannounced and hope to catch her off guard.

Lia parked a little bit further away so Kerry wouldn't see her car, then walked down the street towards her house. This time, there was no soul-searching or doubt in Lia's mind about what she was doing. The argument with Carl had motivated and empowered her to prove him wrong.

As she was passing the neighbour's house only two doors away from Kerry's drive, she saw an older man standing in his front window watching her.

Nosey neighbour, she thought, *perfect.* On an impulse, she waved and smiled, changed her route, and approached his door instead. When he answered her ring, she introduced herself, explained that no, she wasn't with the police, but she was a private investigator. She said she was investigating the unfortunate incident that had happened further down the road.

'The brutal murder, you mean?' said the man, who looked to be in his seventies. He seemed like a very happy man. He was smiling away, his slightly yellowed teeth displayed beneath his dry lips. He was one of those wiry individuals who looked like he could still run a marathon if he wanted to. The subject matter hadn't ruffled him at all. He continued amiably, 'Yes, it was terrible, but I don't know anything about it. I was asleep when it happened.'

Lia looked up at the front upstairs windows, which overlooked the murder scene.

'It must have made a lot of noise,' she said. 'It didn't wake you?'

'Nope,' he said with the sweetest smile. 'As I told the police, I saw nothing, heard nothing. Sorry I can't help.'

She nodded, made a note and then asked his name.

'You don't need my name,' he said pleasantly, still with the same fixed smile. She sighed and began to turn away. It wouldn't be difficult to find out his name, but he wasn't going to be much help.

Her disappointment must have stirred some sympathy

in him because he said, 'Let me ask you something, young lady.'

She turned back expectantly to face him.

'Have you ever had a breeze block thrown through your front window at two in the morning?'

She couldn't hide her shock at this sudden change in his tack, even though the sweet smile was still plastered on his face.

'Because I have,' he said. 'There's no police patrols round here at two in the morning, I can tell you that. It was the last time I made a complaint.' And then he closed the door.

Lia left the old man and carried on to Kerry's house, more convinced than ever she knew what had been going on. The downstairs curtains were still drawn. Lia rang the doorbell and waited, then she rang it again, then again. She thought she saw the curtains move, and standing very close to the door, she heard voices inside although she couldn't swear that she hadn't imagined it. Lia bent over and opened the letter box.

'Kerry?' she shouted. 'It's Lia. I spoke to you before. Are you okay in there? Are you safe?' There was no answer so she shouted again, 'I'm worried about you, Kerry. Do you need me to call the police to come and check up on you?'

Lia thought she heard the bumble of voices again, then the door opened a little way, but Kerry stood in the gap. From what Lia could see, she looked the same as before, eyes puffy, maybe even the same clothes. She was still the image of a woman suffering.

'I'm fine,' she said. 'There's no need for any police.

What do you want?'

'Can I come in?' asked Lia, smiling as if she was on a Sunday visit to a best friend.

'No.' Kerry stole a glance over her shoulder. 'I'm busy.'

Lia wasn't sure how to proceed, it wasn't the tearful confession scene she had hoped for. She had imagined that in a warm, friendly conversation, she would have been able to convince Kerry her only option was to come forward. But now she had no choice but to crudely push on with her blunt statements.

'It's about Craig Preston,' Lia said. 'Look, if you're frightened, the police can give you protection. If Craig killed Toby, he'll go inside for a long time, but you have to tell the truth, Kerry.'

'You're wrong. Craig didn't kill Toby.' Kerry stepped aside to slam the door.

As Kerry moved to one side, Lia could see past her and down the hall, where a youngish man was standing near the kitchen. He was wearing dark jogging bottoms and a plain black T-shirt that fitted tightly over his muscled upper body. With short-cut brown hair that was shaved on the sides, he was looking straight at her, and from the mugshots she'd seen online, he looked a lot like Craig Preston. He made no attempt to hide and turned to face Lia directly. He stared hard at her with a mocking smirk playing on the corners of his lips, and for the first time since she'd started this case, she felt the icy tingle of fear touch her heart. It all happened in the seconds that it took for Kerry to close the door, but his face was imprinted on Lia's memory.

After turning away, she walked quickly, and although

she didn't look around, she was listening for any following footsteps. In his window, the old man watched her go, the smile still on his face.

Back in the safety of her car, Lia's hands were shaking slightly, but she opened her notebook and found the number she wanted. She rang and then waited a few seconds before a gruff voice answered.

'Detective Chambers?' she asked, her voice still steady. 'This is Sekalyia Campbell. I work with McQueen and I got your number from the card you left at the office.'

'Right. How can I help you, Miss Campbell?' Chambers was in his friendly guise. Normally she'd have corrected him that she was a Ms, but she let it go this time. He carried on: 'Have you got some information about your boss that you want to tell us, Sekalyia? Are you looking to do the right thing? It would all be in strictest confidence.'

'No, but I wanted to ask you why you haven't detained Craig Preston. He's Kerry Smith's ex-boyfriend and he's got a list of convictions for violence. He had a motive to kill Toby Markham, one of the oldest in the book: jealousy. So why haven't you been hounding him instead of McQueen?'

There was a long laugh at the other end of the line, and then Chambers spoke but this time without the friendliness.

'Is that it?' he asked. 'That's your bid to get your boss off the hook, is it? How stupid do you and McQueen think we are?'

'Craig's holding the whole street in a grip of terror. That's why no one will come forward with witness statements. McQueen doesn't even know I'm here, but I'm outside Kerry's house and I saw him. He's here now.'

Chambers laughed again and then he dropped his bomb.

'Is that right?' His tone was dripping with sarcasm. 'You amateurs make me laugh. Well, you're not much of an investigator, are you, Sekalyia? Because Craig Preston's been in prison for the last three months and he's not due out for another five weeks. That's probably why we haven't made him our number one suspect. Meanwhile, Sekalyia, if you have anything at all that you'd like to share with us about your boss, he need never know. Think about it.'

After the call, Lia sat in her car surveying the street before her. Nice houses. Who could have guessed what went on inside them? She threw her notebook down onto the passenger seat and held her phone in her hand. She rotated its cold weight in her fingers. It was comforting. She looked at the shiny blank screen and thought, distracted, how she really had to get a protective case for it before it got even more scratched. She didn't like phone cases. Carl said it showed she was a risk taker, but there was something about the phone's thin sleekness that she loved. At her touch, the screen saver burst into life, an image of a grinning Carl with his arm around her. It was a selfie she'd taken when they'd been at the open-air ice rink at Christmas, a lovely day, and for a second she felt like crying. She desperately wanted to call him, but he was always in meetings and he never answered personal calls to anyone during the day. Suddenly the glass and metal comforter in her hand rang, making her jump. Seeing the name flash up, she answered immediately.

Before she could tell Carl how much she had wanted to

speak to him, he had already apologised for the previous night's argument. He said sorry for not supporting her and then added his whole overreaction had been because he worried so much about her.

When they'd finished making up and saying how much they loved each other, Carl asked, 'So how did it go? Your meeting with this Kerry woman?'

'Not great,' said Lia. 'Not great at all.'

'Okay, let's talk about it when you get home. Maybe we can come up with a plan.'

She ended the call and dropped the phone into her bag.

'More like it, Carl,' she said to herself with a smile. 'Much more like it.'

Twenty-one

Ian was listening once again to the recorded podcast about grooming where he had first been alerted to the threat of McQueen. As before, it was the middle of the night, and he was sitting up in bed because it was exactly the same time and place he'd been when he'd first heard that episode. It was important. He had to be in those time and space coordinates because that's what would maximise his power. Had he read that or seen it in a film? He couldn't remember and he didn't know how it worked, but it didn't matter. All he knew was it was what the universe which spun around him required.

He listened as McQueen described the tricks that groomers use, as if he were talking about a vague group of people, but Ian knew he was really saying these are the tricks that Ian Bridger uses. The playing on vulnerabilities, the use of words that would make a person feel special, the turning of flattery and praise into a weapon. McQueen was right, giving worthless people a sense of worth was such a strong weapon.

'Manipulators cleverly make themselves the only escape route for people who think they are trapped,' McQueen said from the podcast.

Ian listened to the voice; he listened to the way McQueen phrased his sentences. He wanted to know McQueen. Ian wanted to know them both, McQueen and Cullen. Usually his victims were total strangers, and there was immense power in that, but this time they wouldn't be unknown to him although he would be a deadly stranger to them. It was a new power.

Emma Cullen was easy. She was all over the internet. But McQueen was more difficult to find. They were formidable, those two, and together they made a very strong threat.

Ian had read on a tabloid news site they had been seen out at a restaurant together, and he had scrutinised that photograph very, very closely until he believed he could hear what they were saying. What were they talking about? About him, of course.

He'd also seen a report Emma was rumoured to be getting a new TV show. Well, it was obvious, but what would her first show be about? It would be about Ian Bridger. It would be about tracking him down. What else could it be about?

He opened up the "Olivia" email account. His mother's name held no emotional value to him. It was just a name he used, and she had just been a woman. He'd seen children at school who had cried about things their mothers had said to them, and he'd found it bizarre. Why would they care? Why would something someone said to anyone make them cry?

He wanted to dangle more things in front of McQueen but he had to be careful. He liked this game because McQueen thought he knew about manipulators, but here McQueen was falling for the trap just like everyone else. It showed if the cosmos was on your side, if you respected and followed its rules, the rules that the universe showed to you, you could never lose.

He had told McQueen about the back door, but maybe he should tell him about the stupid dog. Or about the way the man's arms were trapped inside his bed clothes. He could remember all of it, but none of it came with mental pictures.

The more he listened to McQueen's voice captured for eternity on the podcast, so authoritative and soothing, so knowledgeable and assured, the more Ian was filled with a need to share special information with him, to tell him things that only Ian could know. And that's what McQueen wanted. He didn't want love like some of the other internet morons. He wanted nuggets of information. That was the hook. And Ian's need was to make a link with a man who wanted to catch him. He had never felt this before, but it excited him. There was a risk, of course, but perhaps that was why it was thrilling, like standing on the edge of a cliff so close to the edge your legs start to tremble.

Sharing dangerous secrets with someone else would be like the time he made a complete backup of his computers on an external hard drive. He'd marvelled at the thin, flat black lump of metal and plastic no more than fifteen centimetres long that contained all his secrets in one place.

Enough information to convict him many times over. He had held it right there in his hand and then thrown it onto the kitchen floor and smashed it to pieces with a hammer. That was powerful, a sacrifice of incriminating information, and the universe had seen it and rewarded him with good fortune for his gesture. If he let McQueen into some secrets, let him think he had learned special things, and then killed him while that knowledge was in his head, that would double the power. Cullen was a distraction. She was no more than a performing puppet. She could die first.

Twenty-two

Tracey had the report spread out in front of her, but it had come at the huge cost of her having to practically beg to see it, and she didn't do begging. Searching questions had been asked of her and she didn't really have a solid response for them. A case that was closed and forgotten which had never actually been a case at all, an old man called Harold Kaylor died alone in his house. So what? All she had to go on was an anonymous tip-off and she'd had to keep quiet about the fact it had come second hand through McQueen.

From a distance, she'd been watching Chambers and Reed as well as the way the Toby Markham murder case was unfolding. She knew it was nonsense for them to include McQueen as a suspect, but her opinion hadn't been canvased. She didn't think the detectives themselves even believed it was credible McQueen had been involved, but they were sticking to the standard line of "We're ruling out nothing at this stage of the enquiries" as their justification to keep McQueen's name pinned to their incident board.

Since receiving the email alert when she was with McQueen, Tracey had also picked up on the murmurs around the station regarding Tom Lewis and the suspicious injuries he'd sustained. She'd never actually met Tom, but she knew all about him and knew he was a friend of McQueen's. The young man had helped out in one of the cases they had both worked on. To Tracey, two broken legs looked like serious intimidation or punishment rather than an accident, and although she was concerned and curious, she knew she had to keep out of it. Maybe McQueen was getting mixed up in something he shouldn't, but he couldn't rely on any special favours or backup from her. She tried to put Tom out of her mind; she couldn't afford to have too many visible links to McQueen. It could be that the wisdom of the crowd was right and she should stay clear of private investigators. Was she being manipulated by McQueen? She didn't think so, but at the same time, she didn't need to be dragged into more trouble than she already had.

Everyone at the station knew how close she had been to McQueen in the past. If Tracey hadn't been openly gay, the rampant rumour mill would probably have made even more of their relationship. In fact, knowing how nasty gossipmongers could be, those stupid rumours probably existed anyway. For some very valid reasons of self-protection, the police force could be a closed shop, so outside friendships with private investigators who weren't ex-coppers themselves weren't popular. She was sure the unfortunate result of their closeness was some of the heat that McQueen was currently taking was an indirect hit at her.

Tracey hadn't made a lot of friends in the force, but it didn't bother her. She had joined to make a difference, not find buddies. That's why her partner, Sophie, was so important to her life. She gave her another view that wasn't dominated by criminals.

Sophie was a vet, and they had met on one of Charlie's yearly vaccination visits. Sophie had zero interest in hearing about police work and she'd made that clear from the start, but it hadn't put Tracey off. In fact, she saw it as a bonus. Sophie seemed to have been born with a huge dose of empathy running through her veins. She was so sensitive to hearing about the pain of others that she never wanted to be told about any of the gruesome details of Tracey's job. She wasn't exactly squeamish; how could she be as a vet? But she saw operating on animals as something very different to the blood and guts the world was dishing out all around her.

Sophie was the kind of person who would turn off a nature documentary if a lion was about to kill its prey and she didn't watch any fictional drama that featured violence, especially when it was directed towards women. Unfortunately, there was a lot of that on TV these days, so there were many nights when the TV remote was kept busy.

Tracey loved that contrast in their relationship and she wasn't looking for someone to dump all her work worries onto anyway, so it worked out fine. She liked being able to leave the stresses of her job behind and not be quizzed or judged by Sophie, but it didn't mean she took her police work any less seriously, far from it. The distance allowed her to approach it with fresh, unjaded eyes every morning.

McQueen might have had his principles, but so too did Tracey, and working for the police was the best way to serve those ideals as far as she could see. The organisation wasn't perfect, nothing ever was, but they did some good work. And no one on the outside like McQueen had the power and resources that she could tap into.

But here it was again. She had trusted McQueen's judgement, and here was the report from the investigating officer in black and white. There it was on page two: yes, there had been indications of a possible break-in at the back door, fresh marks that had been noticed by the officer but had not been given much attention. No prints had been taken and there were no photographs. The coroner's report said death by natural causes, and the body had not been sent for a postmortem. They had decided the old man had died in his sleep, face down on his pillow. There was a line in the report which read, "A dog was sleeping in the kitchen who would have barked if there had been an intruder". The report had all the hallmarks of a case that had been kicked into touch because the old guy had no family or friends to stir up a fuss. A box had been ticked which led to another bigger box being sent off to the crematorium.

Tracey also checked the message logs to the station, and there was no report of any calls whatsoever regarding the death at Albemarle Terrace, let alone a vague description of a suspicious man in the area. True, it wouldn't be the first time a tip-off had slipped through the net, but that usually happened on very large investigations dealing with hundreds of calls, not on cases like this.

Tracey looked over the sparse report again. Sure,

it *was* possible someone had smothered the old man, but why? As far as the officers could see, there was nothing suspicious about the death and there seemed to be nothing taken from the house. The TV was still there, and the man's wallet was still on the bedside table with a small amount of cash in it.

There wasn't much to go on, and she couldn't see how she could make much headway with it, but if McQueen had the email link to someone who knew more than they should, it might just be something. She picked up her phone and thought for only a few seconds before finding McQueen's number to text him. It had been a little while since she'd been in regular contact with him, but she owed him this much. She didn't bother with any introductions or preamble; he'd have been waiting for this text.

Yes, she typed. *It does look like the back door could have been broken into, and someone would have needed to be inside to know that. There's no record of anyone calling in either. Sorry, McQueen, but that's as far as it goes for me. I can't do anything with this unless you get me more information. If you do, can you pass it through the normal channels?*

She hoped it didn't sound too harsh, but she'd done her bit. Her career had to be bigger than the things she'd achieved with McQueen, and she needed to focus on her own cases now. She had two unsolved murders that were stagnant. She'd made no progress, and McQueen's dead old man had been a distraction. McQueen's email tip-off would probably come to nothing, and she hoped the whole thing would disappear. That's what she was thinking as she tried to convince herself to forget McQueen and his dead old man. But there was always a part of her that could never let things go. Her tenacious approach and her dog-with-a-bone attitude had served her well in the past but it had also driven her to distraction too.

She checked the address again on the map. Albemarle Terrace. It was near a route she sometimes took with Charlie on his walk towards the park. It sparked a thought: if she was out there anyway, it wouldn't hurt to make a little detour, would it? It might even help her to put the case to bed in her mind if she saw the house and especially the back door. If she felt nothing, she might be able to cross it off her current list of things that were bugging her.

She wouldn't be able to get inside the house, but sometimes feelings and insights could happen just by being close to a scene.

Twenty-three

In the calming tones of their softly lit living room, they sat together on the sofa, close enough for their legs to be touching, and Lia told Carl everything that had happened at Kerry's house. She went on to mention the subsequently fruitless call to the police and how stupid it had made her feel. He'd listened quietly without interrupting or questioning, and when she'd finished, he didn't launch into the I-told-you-so criticism she'd half expected.

'Okay,' he'd said kindly. 'What's your plan?'

It was a complete turnaround from his aggressive attitude of the night before, and when she asked why he'd changed his stance so suddenly, he held up his hands in surrender.

'I went to work and sat at my desk, he said, 'and when I turned on my computer and looked at the screen full of boring numbers, two things hit me. One, that you are the most important thing in my world and way more important than any stupid argument.'

Lia took his hand and squeezed it tightly. 'And two?' she asked, unable to stop the smile spreading across her face.

'And two, that maybe I had been a little tiny bit unreasonable.'

'Maybe?'

'Yeah. I mean, I still stick by what I said and I don't want you to do anything dangerous, but arguments are never really about what they seem to be about, are they?'

'How do you mean?'

'I mean that when I really thought about it, perhaps my reaction was based on me being a little bit jealous of all the attention you've been giving to that new job.'

'Really? That's pretty silly, Carl. You do know that, right? You're not in competition with my job.'

'Yeah, I know,' he said. 'It's childish and more than silly. It's batshit crazy. I should be glad you've got a job that's not draining your will to live, and there are plenty of those out there. Believe it or not, I want you to be happy. I want you to come home smiling, in a good mood, even if it means I have to worry about you sometimes.'

Carl's transformation was turning out to be the best thing that had happened to Lia all day. After driving back from Kerry's house, she had returned to the office, but McQueen hadn't come in. He'd left a message that he had to visit someone in hospital and then another a little later on saying he would be working from home the rest of the day. It allowed Lia to catch up on some of her admin work she'd been neglecting, but she kept returning to the Markham case.

What she had really been banking on was forging some kind of bond with Kerry and then getting privileged inside information that was out of reach for McQueen and the police. She was sure Kerry held the key to it all but was keeping everyone at arm's length, probably through fear. It had been a blow to get such a frosty reception at the door, but it had also been frustrating when her theory about Craig Preston had evaporated. So who was the man in Kerry's house?

Lia was also struggling to see where to go next. She still wanted to solve the case and hand it gift wrapped to McQueen. She wanted to see his look of surprise when she handed him the solution. She'd imagined and visualised the moment, certain it would open another chapter for her career. It was an ambitious goal for someone so new to the business, but in the past, she'd always set her sights high and achieved them. She didn't want to admit failure now but she was finally having to face up to some of her limitations. She'd made an error. She should have known Craig was already in prison. It was something she could have easily found out, but she hadn't been looking properly. She had decided on a hunch that she had cracked it and she'd looked for the evidence to support her view. Classic confirmation bias. She'd seen what she wanted to see.

'Okay, do you want my advice?' Carl asked.

She nodded. Even if she wasn't going to take it, she wanted to hear what he had to say.

'Not long after I started at work, I was doing a big presentation for the board on a new acquisition.' Carl had already been working at the financial consultancy firm

FinCan when they had met, and Lia hadn't heard this story before. 'It was a big deal, and I was new and wanted to impress everyone, especially my boss. It was hard, and I didn't want them to think that I couldn't handle it, so I spent hours and hours on it night after night, and frankly I got myself into a right mess. I didn't have the experience. I had spreadsheet after spreadsheet, information everywhere, and I couldn't see the wood for the trees. A few days before the thing was due, I thought either I could wing it and hope for the best, a risky strategy that could have seen me humiliated in front of the board, or I could bite the bullet and humbly ask for help. So what did I do? I went to my boss, feeling like I'd failed at the first hurdle, told him I was struggling and asked for his help.'

'I know this has a happy ending,' said Lia, grinning, 'because you're still there.'

Carl carried on as if she hadn't chipped in. 'And you know something? Turns out that's exactly what he wanted me to do. He wanted to see that I was the kind of person who could work in a team, take advice when it was needed and wasn't too self-absorbed to wreck a project for the sake of my pride.'

'Hell of a speech,' said Lia. 'Which I guess is supposed to show me that I should go to McQueen, show him what I've found and ask for his help?'

Carl didn't say anything but he didn't have to. His point had been made.

Twenty-four

It had not been a good night for McQueen. After visiting the hospital, even though he'd wanted to see how Lia was getting on, he hadn't gone back into the office. He was still struggling that morning to process the guilt he felt over Tom. It was mixed up with an idea that had first come to him in the hospital but had started to take root in the night. Its scariness had been enhanced by the nightmare that had woken him. In his dream, once again, he was fighting to make it up from the bottom of the ocean. His lungs were bursting, and panic was shaking his heart. No matter how much he kicked his legs and swam upwards, he couldn't reach the surface. Something was holding him down, and he couldn't breathe. When he woke, he gasped in relief, but the image of the sea was very real and he had to turn on the light to try to expunge it.

He knew he was being too harsh on himself about Tom and the first rule of self-help was to be kind to yourself, but he couldn't shake the doubt that had been stirred up inside him. He had asked Tom to get involved, and that had been a mistake. Sometimes when McQueen examined his own thought processes, he was left baffled. How could something that had seemed like such a good idea at the time be so obviously stupid a matter of days later? As a psychologist, how was he supposed to give insight into the thoughts of others if he couldn't even explain his own irrational decisions?

Tom had said he had been very careful about who he'd spoken to when he was asking around about Aaron Patterson, and McQueen believed him. That's what was bugging him. McQueen got out of bed and started making notes. Like a personal brainstorm, he jotted down anything that came into his mind, and then later, standing at the kitchen sink with a cup of tea in his hand, he watched the pale sun rise over the horizon.

On the previous day, he'd received the text from Tracey saying that the back door of the old man's house showed signs of a break-in, and he was still weighing up how to respond to Olivia. The information she had given him had been too specific. If it had only been some shady character she'd seen skulking around, he could have written it off as imagination, but she had given him a fact that was still etched into the doorframe. It was a piece of evidence the police had overlooked and that a person would have to be inside the kitchen to see. Also, there was the lie Olivia had told: according to their records, she hadn't been to the police with her suspicions or her description of someone nearby.

He fetched his laptop from the hallway and sat at the kitchen table, still in the shorts and T-shirt he'd worn to bed.

As soon as his computer sprang into life, it opened on the news story he'd been looking at the night before. Anne Kirkpatrick had used the grainy phone picture on her paper's website along with some innuendo about a romantic dinner for him and Emma. Now it had been picked up by other gossip sites and embellished at every retelling. He hoped Emma wasn't too upset. Anne hadn't gone with the story of him being questioned by the police yet, but she was probably keeping that for later. It was textbook journalism: build them up to then knock them down. He couldn't help squinting at the image, and even at that resolution Emma looked good. Him, not so much. He started to think about Emma, their relationship and the job she was starting to pressure him to commit to. It was yet another thing pressing on him.

He lifted his face from the screen and took in his surroundings. His kitchen was a long way from the tasteful magnificence of Emma's. He surveyed the plain-fronted cupboards and the dark and granite-look-alike worktop. Gleaming pans were not swinging elegantly from any hooks above his cooker. His simple white electric kettle was perched in the corner of the worktop next to the microwave, and they were probably the most used appliances in the whole room. Actually, McQueen could handle basic cooking. He'd learned to survive on a budget as a student, and that had meant trying to enliven rice and pasta with creative sauces. As long as he had a recipe or a YouTube video to follow, he could manage, but he didn't enjoy the whole messy faff of it all. It seemed wasteful of his time to spend an hour or more chopping and cooking for the results to be gone in less than five minutes, leaving him with a mountain of washing up. Mostly, these days, he grabbed takeaways or ready meals, which probably accounted for his growing waistline.

He looked back down at his laptop. It was easy to get drawn into endless cyber rabbit warrens online, especially when his own name kept cropping up, but he managed to close all the open tabs and opened his emails instead. He wrote,

Olivia, thank you so much. You were right! There were some signs of tampering at the back door. Unfortunately, the police have little to go on. The man choked, but how that happened isn't known. I would really like to meet up with you to see if we can come up with something together. Maybe you'll be able to remember more about the man you saw. I have some theories that I'd love to go through with you, but it would have to be in person. You have already been very helpful, and anything you can add would be amazing.

He didn't ask how she could have known about the back door. He didn't want to scare her off. Whoever Olivia was, McQueen had to keep her interested.

He sent the email and then got ready to go into the office. In the mirror, he looked exactly like a man who hadn't slept properly, his face puffy and grey. It reminded him of some of the ghastly morning mirror shocks he'd had when he was still drinking. He also had the same slightly disembodied feeling that a hangover could bring, but fortunately, he didn't have the headache or the clinging reek of alcohol. So on balance, it was all good.

In the office, Lia was already at her desk, and as soon as McQueen stepped inside the door, she pointed a long finger at him and said, 'I need to talk to you.'

It sounded serious, so McQueen beckoned for her to follow him to his desk and threw his bag down onto the floor next to his chair.

'Absolutely,' he said. 'So what's on your mind?'

Taking Carl's advice on stressing upfront she needed help, Lia began to do just that. Over the next few minutes, she explained step by step everything that had happened with Kerry Smith, about how she'd gone back to the house certain that Craig Preston was the culprit, how she'd talked to the neighbour, how she'd seen the young man in her hallway and finally how she'd called the police only to be told by Detective Chambers how wrong she'd been. That was the part she was most nervous about sharing with McQueen because she realised that because she worked for him, it opened him up to accusations of meddling in the case and maybe even witness intimidation. With the main facts out of the way, and feeling lighter with every word, she found herself opening up more than she'd intended. She told McQueen about Carl, how the visit had impacted on their relationship and then how he'd helped her to get things in perspective.

Nowhere in the telling of her story did she try to use any excuses or make any apologies. What did she have to be sorry about? As a final flourish, she told McQueen how she'd been driven by a desire to solve the case herself but now she'd seen that she needed his help.

When he was certain she'd finished, McQueen didn't say anything other than requesting that she wait while he made them both a drink. When he returned and sat back down, it was Lia who spoke first.

'So? What do you think? Am I out of work?'

He shook his head. 'Of course not. First of all, Lia, let me say that I think you are absolutely amazing. Truly. Talk about above and beyond, you are on another level. You have done a fantastic, thorough job on this. It was a case I dumped on you because I was distracted, and with zero experience you've been running with it. I'm seriously, seriously impressed.'

'But?' asked Lia.

'But, bearing all that in mind, I want to agree 100 percent with Carl. He sounds like a smart guy, and I'm sorry if this caused a problem for you both. Let me make it very clear: I do not want you in any kind of situation that could ever be dangerous.'

'Oh, come on, McQueen. I was only asking a few questions.'

McQueen's mind flashed to Tom and where a few innocent questions had got him. He wondered if he should share the details of Tom's experience to enforce his point but decided against it. There was no need to overly frighten her.

'It's the new rule,' he said. 'You're a trainee private detective, and if you go out to question anyone at all, I come too. That's non-negotiable, by the way. The good news is that your new position comes with a pay rise. After all, I'm sure Carl's been telling you you're not getting paid what your work is worth.'

'How did you know that?' she asked, looking a bit shocked, not having mentioned Carl's reservations surrounding her salary. For a second, she had the horrifying thought that perhaps her boyfriend had contacted McQueen directly.

'Because he sounds clever,' he said. 'Because he obviously cares about you and because you told me he works in financial consultancy. I'm guessing judging the value of labour is part of his job.'

McQueen told her not to worry about Detective Chambers and that the Markham case against him was going nowhere. It wasn't the entire truth, but her involvement with Kerry would be something for his solicitor, Max, to worry about if it ever came up. Then he asked her if she thought the man she'd glimpsed in the hallway could have been one of Craig's brothers. Lia had already searched all over the internet, including social media sites, for images of Preston's brothers and cousins, but so far she hadn't recognised any of them as the man she'd seen.

It was while McQueen was working with Lia through the things they knew and the players involved when his inbox pinged, and he saw he had a reply from Olivia. He asked Lia to go to her desk and to continue to put down on paper everything she was feeling about this case, the fear in the street, the reaction of Kerry Smith and even her original feelings about Marina Markham.

'Marina is still in this,' he said. 'She has a motive and she's the one who tried to shift the attention to me.'

As Lia was going, he reminded her it wasn't their case to solve; the police were working on it. It was the police's responsibility and they had more resources at their disposal. He pointed out that all he and Lia were doing was making sure they could head off any miscarriage of justice if it came hurtling in McQueen's direction.

He added, 'I just need a mass of evidence to defend me should the need arise.'

When Lia had gone back to her desk, McQueen opened Olivia's message.

We can't meet. My husband wouldn't like it. I have remembered something though, but I'm not sure if I should say yet. It might get someone into trouble.

If you could catch this murderer, Dr McQueen, you would be very famous. You would be in all the papers. Emma Cullen would have you back on the podcast.

McQueen had to smile in appreciation when he read it. The message was a perfect tease. It offered possible new information to spike his curiosity and keep him interested, and it sweetened the deal with a list of the benefits to him from cracking the case. He had a choice. He could play along with the game, plead to know what Olivia had remembered and hope she didn't string him along too much. If there was more to know, perhaps it would give something away that could be followed up. On the other hand, Olivia was holding all the cards and was controlling the conversation. She could get bored at any moment, and he would never hear from her again. At this point, he didn't even know that Olivia really was a female. McQueen had to find a way to try to break her out of the loop. He needed a curveball, a message that might take Olivia off guard and open things up. He'd noted she hadn't liked the insinuation she might be a crank. By the block capitals in her answer, it had got to her somehow. Maybe there was a chance to break through.

Olivia, as you know, I'm a psychologist. You said in one of your emails you didn't understand what I meant by 'mind's eye'. Do you mean that if you close your eyes and try to visualise an image, you can't? You can't see actual pictures or mental videos? If that's true, if that's what happens for you, did you know that you are very rare? Only 2% of the population can't make mental images. Did you know that? When you were at school and the teacher asked you to close your eyes and imagine a beach, did you wonder what they were talking about? So that the other kids wouldn't realise, did you play along and say that you could see it too? Have you always thought that things like 'mental image' were things people say that didn't really mean anything? It's called 'aphantasia'.

He left it at that and sent the email, with no mention of the old man's murder and no begging to know what else she could tell him about it. It was a gamble based on one short line in the email didn't know what he meant by *mind's eye*. From that, he'd made the huge leap to a whole diagnosis. He could be completely wrong but he was trying to provoke an unguarded reaction. Was it yet another move he'd regret

178

in the morning? He wasn't sure about anything at the moment, but as it stood, he didn't think he had a lot to lose. If nothing else, it was a way to move the conversation on.

With the email sent, he turned his attention back to Lia, but suddenly his nightmare from the night before bubbled to the surface and he felt the panic of being underwater again. He began breathing heavily, but by concentrating on the air that was filling and leaving his lungs, he managed to stave off what he was sure was going to be a panic attack. He'd never experienced one before but he'd spoken to enough people who had to recognise the signs. He'd also never had a waking flashback, and it seemed to be a new development in his PTSD symptoms. He thought perhaps it was the stress of seeing Tom in hospital, but whatever it was, it wasn't good. Maybe it was time to visit his friend, the therapist.

Meanwhile, this had been churning over in his mind long enough now, and he knew there was someone he needed to talk to. You can only do the things that are within your own control, and there was something he could do to alleviate his own stress. As he passed through Lia's outer office, she looked up from her computer.

'Are we going somewhere?' she asked.

'Sorry Lia,' he said, straightening his collar. 'The new rule for joint meetings only works one way, and this is one that for your own safety you absolutely can't come to.'

Twenty-five

McQueen didn't know much about finance or financiers, and that probably explained why he wasn't rich. As far as he knew, Brian Davidson managed large amounts of money for other people, companies, maybe even governments, and somehow as that big ball of money rolled around, some of it got stuck to Davidson's fingers. But how exactly do you go about managing a massive ball of money? Was it about putting people who needed money in touch with the people who had it? Surely the internet could do that. McQueen had no idea. All he knew was that where there was money, there were rivals and deals, and that was obviously what had sparked Davidson's interest in Aaron Patterson. If Patterson, with his high-class connections and his low-class drug supplying leverage, was in some way keeping Davidson from getting access to the best deals, then maybe that was why he wanted to destroy him. McQueen had seen people get pretty intense over a game of monopoly, so he could only imagine how it could be if the money was real.

McQueen was sitting in a very tasteful waiting area outside Davidson's office. It was a place that must have played host to many important people, and McQueen couldn't help wondering how many millionaire buttocks had warmed the very sofa he was now perched on. Opposite him, the receptionist was sitting at her desk, clattering away at her computer keyboard. He had declined the coffee she had offered him on the grounds that he might not be there very long. He didn't have an appointment and the last time he'd been there to tell Davidson he didn't want his job, he hadn't left on the best of terms. In fact, he wouldn't have been surprised if he'd been escorted off the premises by a couple of security guards, except that he had an inkling Davidson would actually be very pleased to see him, and he might even have been expecting his visit.

Eventually the receptionist, a beauty with a face as expressive as an automaton, answered her phone and then told McQueen that Davidson would see him in five minutes. Twenty-five minutes later, McQueen was regretting having turned down the coffee, but he knew the game. It was called "make them wait so they can see how important you are". It was a very childish game played by rock groups and businessmen alike. McQueen was just about to ask if he could change his mind about the coffee when the woman took another call, pointed at Davidson's door and nodded for him to go in.

Behind his desk, Davidson was grinning, but it wasn't a pleasant grin. It was more like the grin of a torturer who enjoys his work.

'I knew you'd come crawling back,' he said.

'And how did you know that?' asked McQueen evenly.

'Because I never lose,' said Davidson. 'And I need you to nail Aaron Patterson's arse to the wall for me, so it had to happen. You're right, the internet is full of private dicks, but I need someone very smart and very subtle to do this kind of inside job. I always go to the top man when I hire people, and you're the one who's been in the papers, so that's you.'

'Right, I'm the lucky winner.'

'Now, I heard about your associate Tom Lewis and about the injuries that Patterson's friends did to him, so I'm sure you're as keen as me to take revenge on Patterson now. It should add some extra focus to your job now it's personal.'

The thought that had first crept into McQueen's consciousness and then been hammered into shape by his sleepless night had brought him here to Davidson's office. He had wanted to see if his theory might be true, and now, seeing the man again, he was certain he was right.

'Oh, also, I do my research and I saw this online you're seeing that woman off the telly, Emma Cullen? Nice one. I would myself. Maybe you could introduce us? You're punching a bit above your weight there, I'd say, McQueen. She's way out of your league.' This was Davidson's stumbling attempt at belittling banter.

Why was it that people who were so good with money were often so bad with people?

Davidson clearly thought with McQueen simply coming back and sitting there in the guest's chair, he was showing he was beaten, like a dog rolling on its back to show submission. That was why, like a classic bully, Davidson

182

thought it was time for some fun and ridicule, to underline his superiority. Like kicking the dog.

'How do you know it was Patterson's friends?' asked McQueen quietly. 'How do you know it was anyone to do with Aaron Patterson who broke Tom's legs and left him lying there in agony on a patch of waste ground?'

Davidson looked a little taken aback, and wave passed over his face that McQueen could only describe as suspicion.

'Well, it's obvious, isn't it?' he said. 'You told me Tom was asking questions around all the junkies about Patterson, and then he gets nobbled by Patterson's men. That's why you're here, isn't it?'

'But what if it wasn't Patterson?' asked McQueen. It was the idea that had been eating at him since he'd seen his friend suffering in his hospital bed, and he had to voice it. That's why he'd come to see Davidson. 'What if it wasn't Patterson's people? What if it was you, for instance, who ordered the beating? What if you wanted me to come crawling back as you call it, with a strong motive to destroy Aaron Patterson myself? What if this is how you did it? It's much easier to hire thugs than decent investigators, isn't it?'

In his capacity as a forensic psychologist, McQueen had spent a lot of time studying lie detection and the interview techniques, especially as used by US law enforcement agencies. He'd learned early on that lie detector machines were notoriously unreliable, and that's why they were given more credence by tabloid TV shows than by the courts. However, body language could tell you a lot of things when someone was faced with a difficult question and they were under close scrutiny. It was why police forces often allowed family suspects in missing persons cases to do TV appeals. The pressure of the public eye could force suspects to give away much more than they realised. A verbal slap in the face with a hard question they weren't expecting was a good way to put someone under that pressure. Sometimes when a person is caught out in something that they thought they'd got away with, they bluster, obfuscate and talk too much. They protest too much, as Shakespeare had observed four hundred years before lie detectors had even been invented. But sometimes liars do the opposite, they clam right up in an attempt to protect themselves. Not many people are able to act naturally when they are psychologically squeezed, and as successful as he was, Davidson was no exception. In McQueen's judgement, the pressured financier was not acting at all naturally.

Davidson was not saying anything but he had sat forward in his chair, his shoulders were shrugged almost up to his ears and his arms were stretched out rigid in front of him, straining, as if he were pushing McQueen away or holding his heavy desk to the floor. His eyes had narrowed, and his pupils had gone jet black as he stared hard across the space at McQueen. Sitting back in his own chair, his face impassive, McQueen could almost feel the force of Davidson's personality bearing down on him and could imagine what an irresistible financial negotiator he must be. But this wasn't finance, and McQueen had faced some forceful spirits before.

'The police are still looking into the incident,' McQueen said. 'I was talking to the detective in charge only yesterday.

I don't know if they'll catch anyone, but in my experience, those kinds of hired meatheads make mistakes.' McQueen stood up to leave.

Davidson rallied enough to bluster. 'I have no idea what you're talking about, and you should be very careful what you say.'

'Or what?' McQueen smiled and stood up to lean over Davidson's desk. He was sure Davidson would have been on negotiation courses that had told him to take the highest chair in the room. To be above your opponent is a subtle psychological advantage. 'Or you'll have my legs broken? I came here to test a theory, Mr Davidson, and thank you, your reaction has been very illuminating. Oh, nice touch, by the way. Before the thugs shattered Tom's legs they made a really big deal of asking who I was working for. As if they really wanted to stress they didn't know your name. They kind of underlined the point with their hammer. A little bit too much maybe?'

McQueen left, and behind him, he could still hear Davidson and his threats.

Twenty-six

Ian read McQueen's email reply to "Olivia" and was filled with disgust at the sheer stupidity of it. It was such a clumsy, transparent attempt to make Olivia, and therefore Ian, feel small and inferior. McQueen was trying to tell him there was something wrong with his brain and that he was crazy. He was criticising a mind that was so in tune with everything the universe was saying and so linked to its waves and motions that it could never be understood by someone like McQueen. Psychologist? That was a meaningless title and McQueen had proved it. Labels, labels, labels. That's what psychologists were: labellers. They put a made-up label on someone, then that's what the person is for life. They'd tried it when Ian was at school. There was a child psychologist who the teachers had brought in specially to talk to him. Tests and questions and labels.

Ian had briefly looked online to see if there was even such a thing as aphantasia, but the revelation that it did exist had made no impression on him whatsoever. The descriptions of the condition had made no sense to him. It was just nonsense made up by online pseudo-medical idiots. So what if he had no capacity to see mental images? What did that mean? What were mental images anyway, and what earthly difference did it make? Ian could remember the tiniest details from all of the murders he'd committed. It was how he'd stayed undetected, his exhaustive attention to detail.

He ran through some of the catalogue of facts that were stored in his head: The colour of the scarf the man had worn that Ian had used to strangle him, a dark green. He didn't need to visualise that to remember it. The number of stairs the previous owner of his house had hit before she'd broken her neck. Eight. On the eighth stair from the top, her life had ended. There were so many details from so many years. The shoes they'd worn, the colour of their hair, the things his victims had said when he'd allowed them that last chance. The number plates of the cars, the feel of the initial resistance and then the ease of the knife going in, the awful smell of the cheap aftershave that had been overpowered by the bowel evacuation of a choking man.

McQueen simply did not understand the person he was talking to, the man who would kill him. He typed his email response.

McQueen, I know so many things, and not just about the old man in his house. What I remember is that he was a nosey old git, always poking his nose into people's lives, gossiping, complaining, so he must have had enemies. I think that's probably why someone killed him. You should look for his enemies. But there is crime everywhere, a lot for you to solve, I think. I saw that a woman was pushed down some stairs near a carpark in Leeds. That was terrible. I saw the video the police put out. It might have been the same man I saw outside the old man's house.

I have a lot more I could help you with, and it could make you very, very famous. I read Emma Cullen is your girlfriend now. I've seen your picture. You are a very attractive man. You could certainly do better than her. Be careful, she wants to steal your fame. She's trouble. If you disrupt the balance of the universe, bad things can happen. My husband doesn't want me to talk to you anymore. I must go.

He hit the button to send the email and then snapped the lid shut on his laptop.

The exchange had left him feeling unsettled. He could feel the unseen waves, the ripples of disturbance in the invisible fabric of existence. He needed to do something to calm the energy. Once when he was a child, he had lost something he really liked. It was a coloured marble, clear with streaks of blue where he could see the universe suspended in the pitted glass. He'd looked everywhere for it and couldn't find it, so even then, all those years ago, he knew what he had to do. He went to his drawer and took out a broken watch he'd found on the way home from school months before. With a clear purpose, he squeezed the sharp edges of the watch in his hand and whispered that he was willing to swap a watch for a marble. Walking fast, he took the cracked timepiece back to the grassy slope where he'd found it and then without ceremony he dropped it. It wasn't superstition, it was how things worked, and he alone knew that. When he got home, his mother handed him his marble. It had been in the pocket of his school trousers, and she'd found it rattling around in the washing machine. He wasn't surprised or overly happy at getting it back because he knew he would. The next day, he crossed the slope again on his way to school and the broken watch was gone. It was the way things worked. Everything was connected, and no gesture went unnoticed.

After he sent the email to McQueen, Ian put his coat on and then left the house to retrace the same route he'd taken when he'd followed the old man and his dog. He walked through the quiet streets until he reached Albemarle Terrace. He had come to look at the house, to see the door where the man had gone in. He walked past the house and turned down the alley that behind. As he approached the address, he suddenly noticed a young woman who had been walking her dog but had stopped outside number 111. She was blonde with her mid-length hair pulled back into a ponytail. She was taking a good long look beyond the gate, at the back door of the house. He'd grabbed ponytails before; they were convenient. The dog was quite big, a black Labrador, and he was on a lead at her side. He would be heavy, but Labradors weren't particularly vicious. Ian slowed right down, but the woman hadn't noticed him. He could hear she was talking to the dog, just as the old man had talked to his.

'This is the place, Charlie, isn't it?' she said. 'I just

wanted to get a feel of it.'

As Ian got nearer to her, the dog saw him and in a friendly way started to move towards him, but the woman pulled back on his lead.

'He gets a bit boisterous sometimes,' she said, looking at Ian for the first time. 'You don't want him to get mud on you.'

She was smiling, but Ian didn't answer. He moved out of the way and then past them both. Her life hung suspended like the blue swirls in the marble, and she didn't even know it.

As he walked to the end of the alley, he knew he had done what the celestial forces had required and now the waves could settle again. He had been sent a woman with a dog outside the house where he'd killed a man who'd had a dog, and Ian hadn't killed her. He had spared her. It was an offering made with life. But the next sacrifice had to be death, maybe two.

As Tracey watched the man slowly walk away, she wondered for a second why he was cutting through like that. He hadn't come from any of the houses and he wasn't going into any of the back gates. The alley wasn't really a shortcut so why was he there? She turned and looked again at the backdoor of number 111. She had the feeling something could have happened here. She wouldn't have been able to articulate it in a black and white report or explain it to a sceptical colleague, but McQueen would have understood. A hunch.

When Charlie, bored with standing still, had tugged her

away from the house and they reached the end of the alley, she looked both ways out of curiosity but the man was gone. She tried to remember what he'd looked like but couldn't recall anything about him at all. She smiled at the thought of how many eyewitnesses she had inwardly criticised and silently berated when they weren't able to remember the tiniest of details. Charlie meanwhile knew the only detail he needed, the way to the park, and he was keen to show Tracey, who had obviously forgotten.

Twenty-seven

Lia had been set some mundane admin tasks by McQueen, presumably to distract her from the Markham case. He'd given her a list of invoices and report documents that needed to be sent out to clients. As he explained, in a failed attempt to motivate her, it was an important job that lay at the very core of what the agency did. Using documents, maps, diagrams, photographs, and graphs, the reports spelled out exactly what the results of the investigations had been, and the invoices asked for the money that kept the agency's lights on. There couldn't have been a more fundamentally existential office function, she understood that. But as far as keeping her mind off Toby Markham's murder, it wasn't working. She couldn't go for more than a few minutes without her mind straying back to the real-life puzzle she hadn't solved. She'd once read those musical earworms that drive you insane with some endlessly repeated tune, a song you don't even like, were in fact just your mind trying to solve a musical conundrum. In recent times, internet app developers had latched onto the mind's need to solve riddles with annoyingly addictive phone games. But this wasn't a game, and Lia was hooked. Instead of attending to the tasks she'd been asked to complete, she was endlessly poring over the various sheets of information she had compiled, but she didn't seem to be making any headway.

McQueen had said she should write up everything she had found out and then leave it alone for a while to give herself some distance and perspective. Lia had felt slightly patronised by his advice. His reasoning was that the police would soon solve the murder anyway, and if none of her efforts would be needed, he didn't want her to feel she had wasted her time. But for high-achieving Lia, that wasn't the point at all. She had willingly taken on the challenge and she had failed. It wasn't in her makeup to let that lie.

When she glanced over her neatly written lists, she could see she hadn't found out anything useful at all. All she'd done was make a quickly formed assumption that Craig Preston was the culprit based on her own prejudices, then she'd put all her focus onto him and had been spectacularly wrong.

At the same time, the trust-based relationship she'd tried to instigate with Kerry Smith had amounted to nothing. Kerry wouldn't even open the door to her now and she hadn't answered any of the messages Lia had been sending.

On the other branch of her notes, Lia didn't need to be told that she also wasn't allowed to speak to — or contact in any way — Marina Markham, the other main person of interest. Even in her eagerness, Lia could see that, in the eyes of the police, it would be a very bad idea to engage with McQueen's accuser.

So what did she actually have that could support McQueen if the police turned up the heat on him? Nothing. Sure, the neighbours in the street were scared, but that was completely understandable. They'd had a violent murder happen right under their noses. Yes, Kerry had acted strangely at the door, but her partner had been savagely killed right outside that very door, so she had every right to be wary. There had been the mystery man in her hallway, the guy Lia had assumed was Craig Preston, but so what? The man could have been anyone. He might have been from Kerry's own family, a brother for instance. Lia was jotting these thoughts down on her ever-expanding sheet, but this one made her stop.

Brothers can be pretty protective, she thought. While it was still fresh in her mind, she turned to her screen and back to Kerry's social media accounts, which Lia had already browsed numerous times. She'd been blinkered by looking for family members of the ex, Craig Preston, and hadn't thought to search for Kerry's own family. After following some links to other relatives, Lia found him, Kerry's brother, the man from the hallway.

In itself, it meant nothing. Why shouldn't a brother be comforting his grieving sister? But the picture she'd found had an interesting element that sent her spinning off in another direction. Graham, as she discovered the brother was called, had his arm around the neck of Craig Preston as they grinned drunkenly into the camera. But judging by the caption, this was a picture from several years before. With some more searching back through the timelines, she pieced together that the two young men must have been friends before Kerry had even started appearing in the pictures. Maybe that's how she'd met Craig, through her brother.

Now that she was online, Lia tried to do some similar research on Marina Markham but hit a brick wall. Her entire family's social media presence had been completely locked down, and there was nothing to see.

As Lia was starting to think that she really should get on with her job and send out some of the waiting invoices, her phone rang, and her heart skipped a beat when she saw the name that came up.

'Hi, Kerry,' she said quickly. 'Are you okay?' There was a pause at the other end of the line leaving Lia holding her breath.

'Can we meet?' asked Kerry's small-sounding voice. The request was more than Lia could possibly have hoped for. All caution was cast to the wind and McQueen's new rule was instantly forgotten, or more accurately, remembered but ignored.

'Sure,' said Lia. 'Do you want me to come round to the house?'

'No, not here,' said Kerry quickly. 'Do you know the Hot Choc café in town?'

'Of course,' Lia lied. She had never been to the place but she was sure she'd be able to find it online and she didn't want to introduce the slightest hint of resistance to the meeting.

'Three o'clock,' Kerry said and then hung up.

'Wow,' shouted Lia into the empty office. 'Wow.' She immediately started searching the internet and soon located the café. It was near the city centre and quite near to where Carl worked. Now that she thought about it, she remembered him mentioning it as a place where his team sometimes held informal work meetings. Lia was barely able to contain her excitement. Perhaps her attempts to get through to Kerry on a personal level to show she could be trusted had finally worked, and now away from the house and her brother, she might be able to talk. Lia could see nothing dangerous about meeting another woman in a busy city-centre café, so she felt sure that McQueen would understand that this was an exception to his rule.

Parking in Leeds was never easy, but she'd managed to find an on-street space not too far from the café and paid through the online app. It wasn't going to be a cheap meeting, and she made a note to herself she had to ask McQueen how she could claim expenses. She smiled to herself, thinking she was going to be asking his agency to pay her to break the only rule he'd ever given her. While she had her phone in her hand, she typed out quite a long text to Carl before getting out of the car.

As she approached the café, she scanned the outside tables looking for Kerry but couldn't see her. She headed for the door to check inside but didn't get as far as that. A strong hand took her by the elbow and started to steer her away. She turned to see the man she'd last seen glaring at her from the end of Kerry's hallway.

'Walk,' he said.

Lia looked to see if he had a knife or another kind of

weapon. His other hand was in the pocket of his jacket, which was bulging with something, and she couldn't be sure what was inside. She reluctantly started to walk.

'Graham, isn't it?' she asked, keeping her voice calm and friendly. 'Kerry's brother?' Maybe he'd only come to tell her Kerry was delayed but she was still on her way. That thought was soon dashed.

'Been busy snooping, have we? I know you, you're not the police. You're nothing. And I'm telling you now, you have to stop coming round to her house and you have to stop sending her messages.'

They were heading towards an alley that Lia knew led behind the shops to a carpark. It would be quieter there, and she didn't want to be away from the crowd. She stopped walking, and he tugged at her arm more viciously.

'You've made your point,' she said firmly, 'and I'm not going anywhere with you.'

'Yeah?' he sneered, putting his face very close to hers. 'I'm her brother and I'm the one looking after her now.' He made a gesture with his pocketed hand. 'You need a lesson in manners.' He yanked again at her arm and gave it a twist.

Lia was about to go to her next move, which would have been to scream and make a scene while there were still enough people around to help her, but thankfully it didn't come to that.

'Everything alright, babe?' asked a welcome voice from behind Graham, who immediately let go of Lia's arm.

He turned to see Carl, who was in his smart work suit but was still an imposing figure from his size and bearing. Graham looked at Carl's stonily aggressive gaze, which was aimed directly at him, and seemed to be making some fast self-preservation calculations. Carl resembled a nightclub bouncer who was about to throw out a drunk.

Lia took her chance to try to head off any physical confrontation.

'There's CCTV scanning every inch of this area,' she said loudly. She knew Carl could handle himself but she didn't trust whatever was hidden in Graham's jacket.

Graham looked up at the surrounding buildings, checking for cameras, then pulled his hand from his pocket. For a heart stopping moment, Lia saw something glint in his fist before she recognised it as a phone.

Knowing full well what Lia had been dreading, Graham put on a huge sickly smile. 'Lovely to see you again. Let's make it the last time, eh?' Then he sauntered away, down the path to the carpark without looking at or acknowledging Carl.

'Do you want me to go after him?' Carl asked, but Lia shook her head.

'No, let him go,' she said. 'You know I would have been fine, don't you? *But* I'm still really glad you got my text and you found a window in your schedule for me. Thank you.' She put her arms around Carl's bulky shoulders and gave him a hug, feeling more than a little relieved.

'You were lucky. My meeting had just finished, so I was able to step out.' He grinned. 'I was just arriving when I saw you moving away with that bloke. I didn't want to interfere in case you were in the middle of some work thing or other, but you didn't look too happy, and I didn't like the look of him.'

'He was Kerry Smith's brother and he was trying to scare me off,' she said as they walked back towards the café. 'He said he was protecting his sister. But I guess the question is, how far would he go to do that? Would protection include killing a new boyfriend he thought was taking advantage of his sister? Or maybe he was keeping the field clear for his best mate while he's in prison?'

Lia wasn't feeling scared or shaken by the meeting but she was massively disappointed it hadn't been Kerry who'd turned up. Once again, she'd felt she was close to getting a break only for it to be snatched away. Had Graham forced Kerry to make the call, or was it her idea? Why had they chosen such a public place if all he wanted to do was intimidate her? Perhaps it was so that, with Lia feeling safe, her guard would be down?

It had been another disastrous day, but some of Carl's concern and McQueen's rulemaking must have sunk in and that was why she'd messaged her boyfriend to meet her if he could. She'd asked for backup and she'd got it.

'You want some hot chocolate?' Carl asked as they passed the café.

'Sorry, I can't,' she said. 'I've got a bunch of invoices and reports to send out waiting for me back at the office.'

'Yeah, and I've got a presentation I should be working on.' He pointed at an empty table. 'But I think there's always time for chocolate with someone you care about, right?'

Lia sighed and let the tension she had been holding in her stomach for the last few minutes seep away.

'You know what?' she said, moving towards the table,

'when you're right, you're right.'

Twenty-eight

It was time for McQueen to make some decisions. He'd let things ride along for too long now and it wasn't good for his nightmares. The pressure had been slowly building, and like so many destructive forces that stay hidden from view, the stress had to show its face somewhere. The burning lava of terror bubbled to the surface in his dreams. Too many issues were competing for his mental energy, and some of that was his own fault.

Emma wasn't a woman to stand still, and the work on her new show was progressing at pace, driven by her endless enthusiasm. Now she needed a contractual commitment from McQueen, "mere paperwork for the pen pushers" as she dismissively described it. The problem was she had assumed McQueen's commitment was already in the bag because McQueen had kept his numerous doubts to himself so far. That was his fault. He didn't want to jeopardise the relationship that had given him the biggest personal boost he'd had since his divorce but he was still increasingly uncomfortable with the idea of letting his agency take a back seat to Emma's ambitions. He'd lost his marriage to the glamour of being a private detective, so it would be a bitter irony to lose the agency to a relationship that may or may not last past series one.

He'd been looking for a suitable compromise, but there didn't seem to be one. He didn't want to divide his attention and make a half-arsed attempt at either of the roles, and there was only so much time in the day. He had seen how Emma dealt with other members of her production team, and it could best be summed up as unforgiving. At the end of the day, that's all he would be, a member of the team, a cog in a programme-making machine. But he was used to making all the decisions in his work life, good or bad. It was weird, really, because for so long he had idly imagined that a break into the media psychology circuit would be the answer to his prayers. But now he'd seen that behind the curtain there was no glitter. What good would free advertising for the McQueen agency be if he didn't have the time to follow it up? Lia was great, but she wasn't ready to take on the bulk of the work. One thing she had done, though, is inspire him. Her dedication to hunting for the truth had reminded him of a younger version of himself, and he wasn't ready to let that energy go.

Adding to his personal turmoil was the response from Olivia. His plan of shaking her up with a curveball email had worked, but he wasn't sure whether he'd got the response he'd wanted or where to take it now. He seemed to have offended her, and he was worried it would be the last he'd hear from her. She'd finished by saying her husband didn't want her to talk to him anymore, but did that mean never again? And there was intriguing new information in the email. The most interesting part was the reference to the woman who had been pushed down the stairs of the carpark. He remembered that case with its indistinguishable video image and he also recalled talking to Tracey about it when they'd met at the park. It was one of the two cases she'd said she'd been working on. It could have been that Olivia was randomly mentioning crimes she'd seen on the news, but it was still something he knew he should go to Tracey with.

As for Olivia's warnings about Emma, he wasn't sure what that was about. It sounded a little like jealousy. Was it to reinforce the idea she was a woman and maybe play on some of the knee-jerk temptation instincts that were so alive on the internet? Whatever it was, it was a pretty crude attempt to form a wedge between him and Emma, but why? The line about him being an attractive man was clearly to flatter him. Was it meant to mess with his mind and weaken him in some way? It was almost the polar opposite of the remark Davidson had made about him not being worthy of Emma, but both lines came from the same place: an attempt to strike at his heart.

McQueen arrived at Emma's house clear in his mind that he needed to be honest with her about the production job. On the drive over, he had finally made up his mind that he didn't want the role, and even if it cost him a nightmare-free night in the softness of Emma's duvet, he was ready to tell her tonight. Many would have thought it stupid to throw away a golden opportunity to be semi-famous, let alone risk his romance with Emma just to spend his days chasing criminals. In many ways, it was the same decision he'd made when he left behind the security of academia, and to give in now for an easier life would have felt like a betrayal of himself. It was those nasty old principles rearing their heads again.

Emma looked more beautiful than ever when she opened the door to him, and her first words were to make fun of how the news sites had decided they were a couple. He had worried she might think it was bad for her image, but she laughed the whole thing off.

'What a terrible picture though,' she said. 'I look awful. If they'd contacted my publicist, she would have come up with something a bit sexier.' She threw back her head and guffawed, showing it was all a joke to her, and McQueen joined in.

Emma was in a really good mood throughout dinner, and it transpired she'd just received confirmation that a much-respected set designer had agreed to come onboard to mastermind the look of her show. There was no aspect of her work she left to others. She was a perfectionist and she wanted everything to be right, even the colour of the onscreen desk.

Over drinks, McQueen on tea and Emma on white wine, they talked a little bit about the programme, and it led naturally to McQueen's chance to say his piece. He was reluctant to ruin the mood. He was enjoying her company so much, but it was time.

'Emma,' he said. 'Err, about the show.'

'Yes?' she said, noticing his tone had become serious.

'What about it?'

'Well, it's your generous offer to put me in the production team.'

'Put you at the top of the production team,' she corrected. 'For you to be the guiding light and expert technical consultant of the team.'

'Yes, well, I'm really flattered. It's a wonderful opportunity, and I know I'm going to really regret saying this, but...' He paused to sip his tea, and Emma picked up the flow.

'But you don't want to do it?' she interrupted.

Relief washed over him to finally get it said. 'I don't think it's right for me, and I don't think it's right for your show. I have no experience in media production, and all in all, in the final analysis, I have other things I want to do with my time.'

Emma had cocked her head to one side as she listened, but McQueen could see no anger or upset surfacing, so he pressed on.

'I've been thinking about it a lot,' he continued, 'and I wanted to give you enough time to find someone else, but what I really hope is that it won't affect me and you. I hope this relationship can continue to grow because I've been having a fantastic time with you. I really have and I don't want to lose that.'

There was silence, and Emma's face was maintaining the same calm exterior as she thought it through.

'First of all, McQueen, believe it or not, I'm not an idiot. If I think you are right for the show, then it's based on experience, and I know what I'm saying. I wouldn't have offered it to you otherwise. It is a great opportunity, and you are a fool to let it go. But secondly, how shallow do you think I am? Did you think I was only sleeping with you to get you to do the show?'

'No, I didn't think that,' assured McQueen, even though it had crossed his mind. 'But I thought if I turned down your offer, it might make it awkward between us.'

'Why should it?' she asked, a smile returning to her lips. 'Maybe it's better. Maybe working together would have been too much anyway.'

'So you're okay with this? Me quitting before I've even started?'

'It's fine, really. I would have preferred it if you had taken the job, because I think you could have added a lot. But I'm not going to try to convince you if you've made your decision. I will respect that.' She shrugged.

McQueen hadn't been entirely sure how it was going to pan out, but it had gone better than he'd expected.

'Come on,' said Emma. 'Let's not say another thing about it and just enjoy our evening.'

She brought over a board that had some very inviting cheese lined up on it, and not for the first time, McQueen wished he was still able to add a glass of red wine to the mix. Surely one small glass in a calm, non-party setting like this wouldn't make any difference. He was just about to ask Emma what reds she had in the rack behind her when the doorbell rang. They both looked at each other, slightly surprised. It was only nine in the evening, but Emma didn't usually get visitors.

'Ah,' she said snapping her fingers. 'Must be the courier.

I asked for some papers that need to be signed to be sent over from the office. Your contract in fact, but I guess we won't be needing that.'

She got up from the island stool, and McQueen heard the tip-tap of her heels moving down the long hall to the front door, which he then heard open. As he got up himself to go over to examine the bottles in the wine rack, he heard Emma's voice though he couldn't make out what she was saying. Then he heard a loud noise, which was followed by a scraping sound that echoed down the hall to reach him.

'Emma?' he shouted. He moved quickly through the kitchen door and could see her lying in the doorway.

'Emma?' he shouted again. When he reached her slumped body he rolled her over onto her back to start some rudimentary first aid, but as he did so, he saw that she had a bullet hole in her cheek and there was blood all over her face. Her eyes were open but they were vacant. He felt for her pulse but couldn't find one. Should he try CPR? Uselessly, he shook her, and he heard his voice as if it was someone else's, screaming her name over and over again.

He tried to focus, to take some breaths. He was in a complete panic, and his reasoning had deserted him. He fumbled for his phone to call for an ambulance, knowing that it was already too late. He couldn't open the phone. It wasn't recognising his face in the gloom of the hall, so he began punching in the passcode. He started to dial, but then the realisation she had been shot and that someone must have done it kicked in. He stood up and stepped over her body to run into the street. He looked both ways up and down the road, but it was completely empty of people.

'Come back!' he screamed into the street. He didn't know why. It was the most useless thing he'd ever done or said in his whole life.

He went back to Emma and then finally managed to dial for an ambulance and the police.

Twenty-nine

It had been very easy, just as Ian knew it would be. She had come to the door and had been surprised to see him there. She had been friendly and she'd said something like, "Are you a courier?" so he pulled the gun out of his pocket and pointed it at her, about a metre from her face. She looked at it, as if she was trying to make sense of what she was seeing but didn't seem to understand. She seemed totally confused, and her confusion had frozen her. He'd seen that before in other victims, usually caused by fear, one of the natural responses of fight, flight, freeze, or fawn. He'd read that freezing was a form of playing dead to protect yourself. Playing dead before you became dead. That was funny.

He didn't say anything at all to her, this woman from the telly who was planning to track him down with her podcast who, along with her boyfriend, McQueen, was a threat to his way of life. He squeezed the trigger.

He'd watched some YouTube videos about how to fire a gun. He'd made sure the safety catch was off and he'd squeezed, not pulled at the trigger. Pulling too hard tipped the gun slightly, making your shot less accurate, or so an American had said on camera. The baseball hatted instructor had also said smaller guns often have louder bangs than larger ones because of the small area that the force has to travel through. He'd also said they often have more forceful kickbacks. Sure enough, small as it was the gun still jumped in his hand and made a surprisingly loud sound rather than the pop that Ian had been expecting. He watched as she dropped to the floor and then he'd heard a man's voice call her name from down the hall, so he'd turned and walked quickly away. As he strode along the street, he could hear from behind him someone shouting that name over and over again. He turned at the end of the line of houses, crossed the road and was now a shadow amongst the parked cars. He had wanted to stay to see if she was properly dead but he couldn't take that risk, especially when he heard the shouting.

He walked into the night towards the city, passing one or two figures who would never remember him. It was a blessing that everyone these days walked with their faces lit by their phones. They barely saw busy roads, let alone the people on the pavements.

Ian eventually met one of the bridges that crosses the slow-moving River Aire as it winds its way through the centre of Leeds. He knew the water passed the Royal Armouries Museum on its journey, which made it a very fitting final destination for the disposal of his own firearm. In the past, he'd thrown knives from this bridge, and once a screwdriver. Even if one day a police diver ever found the exact spot in that huge body of water and retrieved it, there was no way the gun could ever be traced back to him. He liked the gun and he really didn't want to do it, but in any endeavour of merit sacrifices have to be made.

Making sure there was no one following him and that any approaching car headlights had passed, he pulled back his arm to throw the weapon that fitted so snugly in the palm of his hand. But at the last second, he changed his mind. This was the gun that should kill McQueen. Both of the threats that had come to him through the podcast had to die in the same way. It was only natural, how it should be. He put the gun back in his pocket. He wasn't worried about the dead weight of it swinging in his coat. He wouldn't be stopped, he wouldn't be searched. He never was.

There was an excited nervousness in his mind when he thought about whether Emma Cullen was actually dead. A shot in the head should have been enough, but people had survived those before. It was like an exhilarating gamble. Even if she was still alive, there was a good chance she'd have brain damage. And what would she remember anyway of the nondescript man at her door?

Back in the quiet darkness of his house, in the very early hours of the new morning, Ian didn't have to wait long before the news reports started breaking the story online. There was no TV in his house; the old lady didn't have one and Ian lived his life through the internet. Emma Cullen, much loved TV presenter and crime podcaster, had been shot dead outside her £1.5 million town house, and although the police weren't prepared to speculate at this stage about who could have killed her, the online news sites were more than prepared to advance their speculative theories.

Gangland execution was their favoured guess at this stage. One of the papers had listed the cases that listeners of Emma's podcast had managed to solve by mobilising an army of online busybodies and amateur sleuths. Fingers were being pointed, and it was very exciting for Ian to know he was the only person in the whole world who really knew what had happened. He had valuable knowledge no one else could possibly know, and that was powerful.

Ian kept checking the updated story as tributes and memories and, most of all, images of the photogenic presenter started to flood in. People did seem to love her, which was strange, this person they'd never met, a face on the TV, a voice over the internet. They thought they knew her, however weird that was. He knew her better than any of them because she was inextricably linked to him forever, the man who had put a final end to her life story.

He watched all the coverage as it became more frantic and exited with every passing hour and he noted the desperation in the eyes of the reporters who were so hungry for something new to say. It was the most fuss there had ever been over anyone he'd killed, and he was fascinated by the clamour he'd unleashed. He felt like an impassionate scientist coolly observing the results of an experiment.

And then, amongst the rehashed chatter, some new information emerged that led to a newly invigorated feeding frenzy. Emma Cullen had not been alone in the house, which was something Ian already knew. But what he hadn't known was that it was McQueen whose voice Ian had heard shouting her name. McQueen wasn't anywhere near as famous as Cullen, but he had been in the papers for his investigative successes, and that was enough for the media to decide he was newsworthy. They began recounting his impressive academic credentials, the psychology degree, the MSc in forensic psychology and the PhD in criminology. Then they showed some of the tabloid headlines he'd generated as a private investigator when he'd cracked a difficult murder case. Finally, they showed the image from the web of him sitting in a restaurant with Emma Cullen.

Ian closed his eyes and noticed he was breathing heavily. It was rare for any external information to cause an emotional reaction in him. He judged everything he saw and heard in the physical world as a flat tableau devoid of emotional content. Nothing usually touched him. But now, his hands had balled into fists.

It was that name, McQueen. Had the universe given Ian the opportunity to kill them both at the same time, to totally eradicate the threat forever, and he had missed it? Had he been too quick to leave? He should have known whose voice it was. He should have guessed McQueen would be there. If Ian had waited another minute, McQueen would have come out to see what had happened, and Ian could have shot him too.

It was a lost opportunity, which had never happened to Ian before. Every time he had ever been presented with a chance by the unseen forces that carefully guided him, he had taken it. His deadly reliability was the source of so much of his power. He had never defaulted on his celestial responsibilities. He could be trusted to make the maximum use of everything he was given. Would that trust be gone now?

He stood up and began pacing around the living room. This was not the same as the offering he'd made by sparing the life of the woman in the alley, because this time had not been his conscious decision. He had not deliberately allowed McQueen to live; Ian hadn't realised he was there. The gesture had no power.

He went to his front window and looked at the morning's lightening sky. It was the first sunrise in thirty-something years that Emma Cullen would not see, but McQueen would see the day. The satisfaction of shooting Cullen had faded. It was tainted now.

Someone passed his front gate. There would be other people out there, people walking around the streets on their own. Perhaps they provided a way for Ian to balance the account with another killing? It would be easy, but he knew it wasn't enough.

He opened his computer to check his accounts. There had been no more money deposited, and one of his fish had sent a message saying she was not going to send anything until she met him. That threat didn't trouble him; he was impossible to trace. But Ian was right: the universe wasn't pleased.

Thirty

Lia often woke in the night, and tonight like so many other recent nights, she was lying awake next to a gently snoring Carl. She could pick out his outline in the half-light as he lay motionless and radiating heat beside her. She didn't resent it but she was envious of his ability to sleep through the slowly passing hours while the red numbers of the digital clock ticked by. She usually tried to avoid picking up her phone, knowing its screen light and the clickbait content were stimulations that would probably see her stay awake until morning. But sometimes she wasn't able to resist the magnetic charms of her mobile, and tonight was one of those nights. As soon as she opened her phone and saw the news alert with the familiar name Emma Cullen, she sat up. Then quietly, so as not to wake Carl, she swung her legs out from beneath the covers and got out of bed. She crept downstairs and making sure the volume was turned right down, she found the twenty-four-hour news channel on TV.

Cullen was big news. Lia watched the harshly floodlit

reporter who was standing at the end of a cordoned-off road. Behind him, a pale blue police tent was being erected at the door of one of the town houses.

Open-mouthed with incredulity and making tiny rhythmical shakes to her head, Lia was taking it all in. She had her legs curled underneath her on the sofa and she absently pulled her dressing gown over her toes to keep her feet warm. She and Carl never kept the heating on at night, so the air was a little bit chilly in the room.

She knew that Emma Cullen was a friend of McQueen's and they had recorded a podcast together, because Lia had listened to it a couple of times. She'd never met Emma, but McQueen had mentioned her a lot recently. Lia had also seen the online story about them dating, which she hadn't discussed with her boss on the grounds it probably wasn't true, and it was none of her business anyway.

Watching now, she was transfixed by the images flashing before her on the painfully bright TV screen. She began to wonder if McQueen had seen the news yet. The overpowering need to share bad news was a strange human compulsion she was struggling to fight. She thought of texting him, then talked herself out of it. She was sure he would know by now and she didn't want to come across as a ghoul.

The reporter kept looking over his shoulder at the scene behind him and he didn't seem to know very much yet other than the bare fact Emma Cullen had been shot in her doorway. After about an hour of repetitive coverage interlaced with montage packages showing some of Emma's key televisual moments, Lia was thinking of trying to sleep again. She was about to turn the TV off when she thought she heard the name McQueen mentioned. She turned the volume up in time to hear the description of the forensic psychologist and private investigator who was being questioned by the police. On screen, they showed the picture that had been all over the internet of the couple in the dark restaurant, then a publicity shot of McQueen taken from his website.

'Christ,' Lia said.

'What's happened?' asked Carl from the doorway, where he was standing in his T-shirt and boxers. Lia was so engrossed she hadn't heard him come in at all.

'I don't know, but it looks like McQueen's being questioned by the police over the death of Emma Cullen, the TV presenter.'

'Christ,' Carl said and then came to sit beside her on the sofa. Together they watched the rolling news as it rolled over them in fifteen-minute cycles of mind-blowing repetition.

Thirty-one

It had taken several hours for McQueen's lawyer to arrive at the police station and, in the meantime, McQueen had refused to answer any questions. Now under the watchful gaze of Max Goodson, McQueen recounted his story to Detectives Reed and Chambers. Not that there was much to recount, but he was very aware they were in an official interview room and his answers were being recorded. He explained in detail exactly what had happened, but at the same time he was battling a rising tide of grief. His mind kept flip-flopping between the image of Emma smiling at him over a glass of wine and the sight of the bullet hole in her cheek. He knew he was vulnerable, which was why he'd insisted on Max being there. He didn't mind giving the statement. In fact, a big part of him was desperate to get it off his chest, but he didn't want his fragmented thinking to trap him into saying something foolish. He hadn't slept yet and fatigue was starting to catch up with him.

In as calm a voice as he could manage, he told the

officers about the doorbell that Emma had thought was a courier. He explained he hadn't gone to answer it himself as it wasn't his house and she had been keen to go. Then he told them about her muffled voice and how he couldn't hear what she'd said. Then there were the other noises, the bang sound followed by the muffled clatter that must have been Emma falling. Finally, he reached the part about him running down to find Emma, and that's when he began to choke up. Ignoring his distress, Detective Chambers pushed him as to why he hadn't gone out looking for the shooter straight away, but McQueen told him he was trying to see if Emma could be saved.

'And then after that, after you had looked in the street and seen nothing, you called 999?' asked Detective Reed. 'Why didn't you do that sooner?'

'I don't know really,' McQueen said. 'I was in shock and I wasn't thinking straight.' He glanced at Max, who was taking notes and hadn't looked up.

When McQueen had finished his statement, Detective Reed went out for a few minutes and came back with a lukewarm cup of coffee for him. McQueen thought it was over, but then they asked him to go over his whole story again. He knew what they were doing. By making him retell his ordeal, they were looking for inconsistences to see if he would change his story or any alternative versions would spill out.

There were some other more general questions they asked too: What had his relationship with Emma Cullen been like? Had they been arguing at all? Had he ever owned a gun?

'You're treating me like a suspect,' said McQueen, starting to get emotional. 'My friend and colleague has been murdered, and you are treating me like the culprit.' At this point Max looked up from his pad and butted in.

'Gentlemen,' he said to the detectives, 'my client has been enormously helpful so far but he's had an emotionally devastating experience, and given the hour, he's very tired. I think it's time we called an end to these proceedings. Otherwise, it starts to feel a lot like coercion, which could invalidate anything that is achieved for you here.'

Once they were out of the station and travelling back in Max's car, the magnitude of the evening's events started to sink in. At a personal level, Max was very sympathetic and understanding. They had known each other for a long time, since their student days in fact, and although they weren't close friends, Max had always been McQueen's solicitor.

In his professional rather than personal capacity, Max reassured McQueen he had absolutely nothing to worry about. He said McQueen was a cooperative, valuable witness in this case, nothing more, and he shouldn't be troubled by the police any further. The police were just doing their job, Max said. McQueen had been at the scene of the crime, so it was only natural they had wanted to talk to him.

McQueen was feeling numb as Max's calming voice washed over him, but as they started to approach McQueen's flat, he spoke more sharply to make a point.

'Don't talk to the press,' he said, 'and especially not that viper Anne Kirkpatrick. No comment, no comment, no comment. Do you understand?' He said it as if he were talking to a child, and McQueen realised he must have been visibly zoning out during their journey.

'Got it,' he answered. 'And thanks, Max. Thanks for coming out so late at night.'

'Not at all,' replied his lawyer. 'All part of the service as you'll see on the invoice.'

Max dropped McQueen outside his flat, and as he got out of the car, a reporter appeared from nowhere with a voice recorder in hand. McQueen pushed past him without comment under a hail of questions and camera flashes and went inside the shared front door of the flats. The silence of the lift was comforting.

A cramped box, he thought, *like a prison cell or a coffin.*

At last in his own room, he slumped onto the sofa and put his head in his hands. His despair was nothing to do with the police and their suspicions. Those were the last of his worries. His thoughts were on Emma. Who could have wanted to kill her and why? The shadow of what had happened to Tom was hanging over his head. Could this also be something he had brought into Emma's life? Had he been to blame in some way for bringing that precious life to an end?

McQueen needed a drink, but there was no alcohol in the flat, a deliberate strategy he'd put in place for times such as this. It wouldn't be difficult to get a bottle of wine, but not having any at home in a cupboard was the extra hurdle he'd arranged that gave him pause to reconsider. Him drinking wouldn't help. It could only make things worse, and the short-term comfort of alcoholic oblivion would lead to worsening guilt and long-term pain. Instead, although he felt like sitting still on the couch for a thousand years, he forced himself up off the sofa and went into the kitchen to make a cup of tea.

He knew the mental mechanics of what he should be doing. He'd read about it often enough. He had academic friends who had written self-help books. In fact, he kept some of them on his shelf in his office, and he had old colleagues who had led grief counselling sessions. He was well aware of the famous Swiss-American psychiatrist Dr Kubler-Ross and how she'd described the five stages of grief as denial, anger, bargaining, depression, and acceptance. The problem was that there was a murderer out there to be caught, and McQueen had to find a way to fast-track himself past the first four stages to acceptance so he could do something about it.

At university, clinical psychology wasn't the area that had captured his interest. He'd always been drawn to criminology. But now he found himself at the crossroads where those two branches collided. Criminal behaviour had led to grief. Now it was time to make the monumental effort of putting into practise some of the techniques he'd heard about.

There was nothing he could do to bring Emma back. He had no control over that, but there were some things he could control.

It starts simply with your arms and legs, he told himself. *It starts with doing what you can, no matter how small or how much you don't want to do it.*

He heard the kettle boil and robotically made himself a milky tea. Who on earth could have wanted to kill Emma?

Someone who had a personal reason, like an ex-partner? Or maybe someone who'd had business dealings with her that had gone sour?

When it comes to her career, she's a forceful, determined person, he thought with a slight smile, then the smile dropped from his face and he immediately corrected himself to the past tense: when it *came* to her career, she *was* a forceful person.

There was another possibility regarding Emma's murder that couldn't be ignored. She was a minor celebrity, and famous faces had a nasty way of sometimes attracting the wrong kind of attention. John Lennon and Gianni Versace were the two who immediately sprang to McQueen's mind, and although Emma hadn't been on that superstar level of fame, it only took one lonely soul with an obsession to shoot a gun.

McQueen was very tired. He didn't know if he would sleep, but he thought he should at least give it a try. He stretched out on the sofa, but as he did, his phone rang. Wearily, he dug it out of his pocket and looked to see that it was Lia calling. He'd forgotten about her, but of course she would be wondering what the hell was going on. He almost rejected the call but didn't want to add to the stress she must have been feeling. He knew she would bombard him with questions and he could understand that. Her own future was in the balance, after all, and the press coverage that she'd seen would no doubt have been lurid.

'Hello Lia,' he said, and braced himself.

'McQueen, how are you?' Her voice was warm and genuinely caring, in what felt like a hug sent down the phone.

'I'm not sure. It hasn't sunk in yet.'

'You poor thing,' she said. 'It must have been absolutely awful for you, and I'm so sorry for your loss. Anything I can do, anything at all, let me know.'

It wasn't what he had expected. He thought she would be relentlessly quizzing him and badgering him for answers, but all she was offering was unconditional support and sympathy. After a tiring night of tragedy, it almost made him cry.

'Thank you, Lia. I appreciate that. You must have a lot of questions, but I'm really tired and —'

'Listen,' she said, cutting him off. 'Take some time away, McQueen. I'll go into the office and —'

But then he interrupted her interruption, and like a ruptured bag of rubbish, it all came spilling out: 'I was in her kitchen, Lia. We'd had a nice dinner. We'd discussed some things to do with her new show, and it was all going really well. We were getting on great. Then the doorbell rang. I let her go to answer it, and someone shot her. I ran down the hall, but she was already dead.'

'I'm so sorry, McQueen,' she said again softly.

'Thing is, I was useless, Lia, absolutely useless. I didn't do anything. And on top of that, I'm left wondering if I caused her murder. Did I put her in danger in some way?'

'You're making a big leap of assumption there,' she said. 'And from my recent experience with Craig Preston, I know where that can get you.'

But McQueen was on a confessional roll and he didn't want to stop. 'Something I didn't tell you: I asked my friend

Tom to do me a favour, to find some information for me, and it ended with him being badly beaten up. That's why you need to be so careful, Lia. Maybe Detective Chambers is right, maybe I'm cursed.'

Lia let him finish and then said, 'Sounds to me like you don't need anyone else to do it. You're doing a pretty good job of finding ways to beat yourself up, McQueen. That's really not going to help anyone, least of all you. Give yourself a break, man. Treat yourself with the same kindness you would treat a good friend.' Then she laughed. 'Yes, that's right, I've read the same self-help books that are on the shelf in your office.'

For the second time, McQueen allowed himself a smile.

'Get some sleep,' Lia said. 'Don't worry about the office, and we'll talk tomorrow.'

McQueen ended the call and closed his eyes. Lia was right; him wallowing in self-pity wasn't going to help anyone. He believed in science, not superstition. He didn't believe in karma. There were too many evil people who lived long, successful lives for that to be true. He didn't believe in the concept of people making their own luck, either. There were too many totally innocent victims of life's random misfortunes for that to have any substance. And he certainly didn't believe in curses. On the other hand, he did believe self-care was important, and that's why he was glad there was no alcohol around. Hopefully, by the afternoon, the police would have arrested someone for Emma's murder. McQueen just had to hope it wasn't him.

Thirty-two

It was a big, messy, open-plan room crammed full of desks, computers, and filing cabinets. As a work space, it didn't lend itself to open, honest discussion amongst colleagues. Someone was always listening. Private meeting rooms were a precious commodity at the police station, and the system for booking them was somewhat unreliable, but Detectives Reed and Chambers had managed to find somewhere to talk with Tracey.

The three of them were sitting at a desk, Chambers and Reed on one side, Tracey on the other, and she had the distinct impression she was about to be grilled like a suspect. However, she wasn't fazed by the setup. She was ready, and all she could think was, *bring it on, boys*.

On the face of it, they were all colleagues of the same rank, but Tracey wasn't sure the two men saw it quite like that. They had been giving her a wide berth around the office, and there was a particular theme she felt had to be avoided at all costs. But today, they surprisingly wanted a meeting specifically focused on that taboo subject, McQueen.

The two men were trying their best to be friendly, and Tracey was prepared to play along with that for as long as it lasted. The three of them went through the usual formalities of "How's it going?" and "How was your weekend?" before they got to the question in hand.

'Okay,' said Reed. 'Now, it's no secret. Everyone in this station knows you have prior personal history with McQueen.' And then for unneeded clarity, he added, 'the private investigator.'

'Personal history?' she asked, sweetly. 'You mean we solved a murder, caught a murderer, and in a him-or-us situation, nearly lost our lives out at sea?'

Reed was nodding. 'Exactly, that's why we need your input on this. You know him better than anyone. Let's show you where we're coming from.' He pointed at Chambers who spread some sheets of A4 on the desk.

'Number one, we've got Toby Markham,' said Chambers, putting the victim's picture down on the desk. 'McQueen spent weeks tracking him down for his wife, found him, and then Markham was killed. Obviously, amongst other people, Marina Markham is a suspect, but she has a cast-iron alibi. And when we questioned her, the name she came up with was McQueen.'

'She said he seemed to take it personally,' chipped in Reed, 'and he talked to her about her taking revenge. McQueen says he has an alibi but he hasn't given it to us yet.'

'Meanwhile,' continued Chambers, 'McQueen's new

assistant, one Sekalyia Campbell, has been hanging around at the scene of the crime and hassling Kerry Smith, the bereaved partner of Toby Markham.'

'Interesting,' Tracey said. 'How do you know that?'

'Because Sekalyia rang me from outside Kerry's house and tried to take the heat off McQueen by putting an ex-boyfriend of Kerry's in the frame for the murder, not realising that he's actually in prison already.'

Both officers grinned at this, taking some pleasure at Lia's mistake.

'So that's Markham,' said Reed. 'Then we've got number two, Tom Lewis. He's a known addict and associate of McQueen's. Poor old Tom is still in hospital after being badly beaten up but won't tell us anything about the attack.'

It was easy to see the two detectives had worked together a lot, as they were bouncing off each other like a well-rehearsed double act at an end-of-pier show.

Now Chambers came back in again. 'On the morning when I went over to speak to Tom, who should I see in the hospital coffee shop but McQueen? The visitors' log showed that he'd just been in to visit Tom, who had funnily enough decided to be uncooperative. Now, we do have a lead on this. It looks like there's some CCTV footage that may be helpful, and the lab boys are working to clean it up to see if we can identify some faces. We'll have to see how that develops.'

Tracey wasn't making any comment, but she was taking notes. Most of what they were telling her was information she already knew, but she was interested to see where this was heading.

'Okay,' said Reed. 'Now we reach number three: the tragic events of the other night. McQueen's girlfriend shot on her doorstep. Not only was McQueen in the house, but according to him, he was just down the hall and yet he saw nothing of the shooter. There was a delay in calling 999, which means there was no chance to save Miss Cullen, and any assassin is long gone by the time help arrives.'

Chambers said, 'And he refused to give a witness statement until his brief arrived, Max 'Technicality' Goodson.'

'And finally, number four,' said Reed with a flourish. 'Today, on the back of the press coverage that McQueen has been getting, we got a call from an influential businessman named Brian Davidson. He says he hired McQueen, but when he sacked him for lack of results, McQueen became abusive and has been making unsubstantiated accusations about him.'

'Abusive?' asked Tracey. 'McQueen?'

The two men crossed their arms as if they had just delivered the death blow in a hand-to-hand battle.

Tracey crossed her own arms and looked back at them. 'So, what are you saying? That you think McQueen is a one-man crime wave?'

'All we're saying,' said Reed calmly, 'is that his name keeps cropping up. It could be coincidence or just bad luck, but you know him pretty well, so it would be interesting to get your view.'

'Any insights you might have that might help with our investigations,' added Chambers. 'You know his weaknesses. Is there anything we can use? We're all on the same team after all, aren't we?'

There was an edge to this final observation, as if they were questioning whether Tracey was on their side. She could have been angry at the insult but decided not to rise to it.

The two men were sitting expectantly, waiting. There were a lot of things that Tracey wanted to say about this team Chambers was so proud of. She could have pointed to the subtle bullying, sexism, and underlying homophobia she had faced on a daily basis ever since she had joined and how she had learned to ignore it. Tracey's success on difficult cases had earned her some respect amongst her colleagues, as well as visibility and protection, but not much. This particular station wasn't as bad as some, but it was only her strength of purpose and her desire to do the job that had sustained her through some tough moments. Sophie thought she was crazy to put up with it, but Sophie hadn't wanted to be a detective since she was a little girl. So of all the things Tracey could have said about the team, she said none of them. It was part of the art of preservation: don't let them see that they've hurt you.

'First of all, thanks for including me in this,' started Tracey, glancing over her notes. 'I always appreciate it when team members reach out to me. My honest view is you should continue with your investigations, and I think you'll find you've been barking up the wrong tree. I predict you'll find four unrelated incidents that just happen to have touched McQueen.'

'That's it?' asked Reed.

'You've asked me, and I'm saying that, in my opinion,

McQueen isn't the person you are looking for in any of these cases.'

'How can you be so sure?' asked Reed.

'Because I know him,' Tracey said, although she was aware of how weak that sounded. Almost every single day of police life, someone was shocked by the actions of someone they thought they knew.

'And if he is involved?' asked Chambers. 'How would you deal with that?'

'I'd be the first to put the cuffs on him,' she said. 'But it won't come to that, and I'd stake my reputation on it.'

Chambers stood up and gathered all the papers together. 'You already have.'

Thirty-three

As she pulled into the carpark, Lia was surprised to see McQueen's car in its usual spot. She hadn't expected to see him back at the office for a few more days. He'd understandably missed the previous day, which meant that after fighting her way through the scrum at the door, she'd spent most of her time batting away enquiries from various press outlets, including some international calls. It seemed the whole world had wanted to talk to McQueen, but Lia's measured response had been a consistent *We have no comment at this time.*

The pushiest journalist by far was a woman called Anne Kirkpatrick, who seemed to think she had some kind of legal right to speak to McQueen. She'd whined and cajoled. She'd tried, *McQueen and I are old friends,* and when that didn't work, *Lia, honey, you are risking losing your job by not putting me through.* Fortunately, Lia had been warned by McQueen about Anne and the media hatchet jobs she was capable of, so Lia was unmoved by the journalist's pleas and threats. She could also have added that using the term "honey" was not the best way to ingratiate herself.

Apart from the disruption of calls, Lia had decided to try to put Emma Cullen's murder out of her mind until she'd had a chance to speak to McQueen. She didn't know anything about the circumstances, or at least no more than the sketchy story that McQueen had told her on the phone. She deliberately avoided the tabloids, knowing that all they could do was make her angry. So it was a waste of time to dwell on the details. She'd talked it over with Carl and asked herself the difficult question of whether there was any way McQueen could have had something to do with the murder. In short, was it possible she was working for a killer? As Carl pointed out in his mathematically logical way, anything was possible, but on balance he didn't think so. Lia went further; she trusted her own judgement and she was certain that there was no chance of McQueen's guilt. Mind made up. She didn't want to entertain that possibility any further.

Instead, as the previous day unfolded with her alone in the office, she had turned back to the Markham murder, which had still been niggling at her like a toothache. She had gone over it a thousand times without moving forward, but there was a slight loose end she was starting to think might be worth exploration. The neighbour she had spoken to might well have seen something, but her unprepared chat with him had been unfruitful. Perhaps if she spent a little time doing some research and found a way to get closer to him, she might be able to find some clues. For a start, there was the breeze block through his window that he'd mentioned. Surely there was something to be found out about that. She'd gone to the databases and used the specialist search tools the agency had. She knew the neighbour's address, so she began to dig. She soon found his name, the name he hadn't wanted to give her. After a few dead ends, she had found a couple of things buried in the web that surprised her and gave her something to ponder on.

That had been the pattern of the day. Her concentration was constantly broken by the phone ringing, and the rest of the time she was absorbed in her research. The time had raced, and before she knew what had happened, it was getting dark, and she decided to call it a day.

She'd been determined to get home before Carl so she could be there when he got in. She'd made another promise to herself too, to not mention one word about Markham, Cullen, or McQueen for the whole night. He'd been trying hard to show interest in her work, but she didn't want to push her luck. It must have been getting boring for him to listen to stories about her obsession. Everything comes down to investment in the end, she told herself, and she was ready to invest in this relationship. She was going to try not to bore him anymore with her findings.

When she'd left the office and passed through the dwindling number of reporters outside, she hadn't thought she would see McQueen for a few more days. Hence her mild shock the following morning at seeing his car parked against the backdrop of poplar trees.

McQueen had got in early and the first thing he'd done was

forward to Detective Tracey Bingham the emails he'd received from Olivia. It was time to trust and share. There was the line about the woman killed at the city carpark that he wanted her to see, but he also wanted Tracey to understand the general flow of the messages. Olivia had made some aggressive comments about Emma that seemed poignant now, and he was keen to have Tracey's opinion.

He read the important lines over again. *I saw that a woman was pushed down some stairs near a carpark in Leeds.* He slowly shook his head. Why mention that particular crime? Of all the criminality that had occurred in the city in the past year, why pick that one?

I read that Emma Cullen is your girlfriend now… Be careful, she wants to steal your fame. Steal your fame? Was that supposed to strike at his desires? Had Olivia decided he was fame-hungry and so that line would get under his skin?

She's trouble. If you disrupt the balance of the universe, bad things can happen. Bad things? Like what? Like murder?

In his forwarding message to Tracey, he deliberately didn't mention the events surrounding Emma's death. He knew the police would be consumed by such a high-profile crime, and she would be in a difficult position. But the reference was there in the message from Olivia, and Tracey would see it. What he did say was,

Tracey, here are all the messages from Olivia, the anonymous tip-off that told us about the back door in the old man's house. You'll also be able to see all my replies. I feel sure there's something in this.

Any thoughts that strayed towards Emma were painful to handle, but if he was going to do anything to help catch her murderer, he had to push himself through that wall.

It was time to message Olivia again. Although his suspicions were, at best, tenuous, Olivia was all he had that gave him any link at all to Emma's murder. He was going to treat this like the scientist he was. In science, the way you test a hypothesis is by trying to disprove it. If Olivia was nothing more than a person with too much time on their hands, then he had to rule her out. He put his head in his hands to think. He needed to turn the heat up. What were the things Olivia hadn't liked? She hadn't liked being called a crank, and she didn't like being asked about her aphantasia. Both seen as weaknesses, perhaps. This was a good sign because it showed she could be affected by the words he typed. There were cracks in the armour. He read her email again. He had two options. The first was to attack and try to flush out an angry reaction that might make her give something away. It was risky because it might mean she would cut off all lines of communication, and he wanted to keep those open.

His other possible approach was to let her think her strategy had worked. She thought he wanted fame and she'd tried to flatter him because she thought that was what men wanted to hear. If Olivia was actually a man, it was still true that buttons were being pushed to produce a certain response. Even though every word was going to be painful to type, McQueen decided to give the reaction Olivia had aimed at.

Olivia, it's nice of you to say I'm handsome. You've given me a bright spot in a bad couple of days. Does your husband know how lucky he is? You were right, something bad did happen. I'm sure you've seen the news. Emma Cullen was shot. You have helped me already with the old man in his house, but do you think there is anything I should be doing to find Emma's killer? You seem to have a good instinct for these things. I really need to find the killer. Not only have I lost a friend, but my career hangs in the balance. Who's going to hire a private detective who can't find his own friend's killer? Can you help?

He was sure he had gauged it right and this would at least start a conversation. He was hoping Olivia would try to manipulate him by seeding him with small pieces of information and give something away that would lead to a breakthrough.

As he finished the email, Lia came in through the outer office door.

'If I'd known you were coming in today,' she said with a big smile, brandishing her bought latte, 'I'd have brought you in a proper coffee too.'

'That's fine,' he said, smiling back. 'I've had a caffeine overload anyway.'

Lia went to her desk to carry on as normal, but McQueen knew nothing was normal.

'Thank you, Lia,' he said, walking over to her desk. 'Thank you for the support yesterday and thank you for coming in to keep the office open.'

She shrugged in a 'it's nothing' gesture. 'The phone was

ringing off the hook, but other than that, it was pretty productive for me.'

'Yeah, I had to turn my mobile off for a few hours too.' Then to get the subject out there, he said, 'I know it must have crossed your mind, especially if you've been reading the papers, so I'll say it up front: I didn't kill her.'

She laughed. 'I know that. Although yes, I have to admit it was a thought for about a millisecond.'

'You wouldn't be human if it hadn't been. So,' he added, clapping his hands to indicate they were moving on, 'you've been badly neglected, Lia. Show me everything you've been working on with the Markham case. It may be more important than ever now because I was with Emma the night of that murder, and now she's gone.'

He didn't put it into words as it might have sounded too cynical, but Lia understood that Emma must have been his alibi for the Markham murder, and now he didn't have one. He took the spare chair in front of her and turned his full attention to what she was saying.

Lia showed McQueen the notes and diagrams she'd made of the Markham killing and told him about her latest angle. She went through the things she'd been researching the day before and the discovery she'd made.

'So the neighbour, a guy called Ross Bailey it turns out, told me this story about getting a breeze block put through his window. I thought that would be an incident which would show up somewhere in the local press or in court reports or something.'

'And?' asked McQueen, knowing there was something coming.

'And there was a breeze-block-verses-window-glass story from about two years ago, in the same street. *But* it wasn't dear old Mr Bailey's window. It was Kerry Smith's window. She'd had a noisy barbeque in the back garden, and someone had smashed in her front window as a protest or something. The police didn't catch anyone for it.'

McQueen was sitting back in the chair with his eyes closed and his fingertips gently rubbing his temples. He was repeating over and over, 'Ross Bailey, Ross Bailey.'

Lia watched him for a few seconds, thinking that he must have a headache after a hard night but eventually asked, 'You okay, McQueen?'

'That name,' he said. 'Ross Bailey. How old is he?'

'I don't know. Seventy, maybe?'

'Okay, have another look through the databases for a Ross 'Bailey' James.'

McQueen stayed in his eyes-closed pose while Lia tapped away at her keyboard until he heard her say, 'Wow.'

McQueen sat up. 'Old time gangster, right? You're probably too young to remember him, but Ross James, nicknamed 'Bailey' after his many appearances at the Old Bailey. He did a long stretch for armed robbery and moved up north, I believe. Looks like he might have ended up in Leeds to me. He was taunting you with that breeze block story. That would be his style.'

Lia was getting excited as her lead seemed to be developing right before her eyes.

'So do you think we should go back and speak to him again? Both of us, I mean?'

'With no more than suspicion? No, I absolutely don't.

First, we need to know for sure that it is actually him. If it is, he's not going to admit anything, and all we could do is make him wary. You said he was practically laughing in your face when you spoke to him on his doorstep. Besides, we'd need more than that to take to the police.'

'Yes,' Lia said. 'As you know, I made that very uncomfortable mistake with that whole Craig Preston debacle.'

Lia's excitement was slightly deflated at the memory, but McQueen wasn't about to let the mood drop.

'You're on to something here, Lia. It could be that he did see what happened on the night of the murder, but he's not going to grass on anyone because of who he is. Or the more interesting theory is that old habits die hard, and he deals with noisy barbeques by throwing bricks through windows and he deals with neighbours he doesn't like by hurting them.'

'Meanwhile,' she said, 'he's the old codger with a history of violence that keeps the whole street in the grip of fear rather than Craig Preston.'

'Right,' said McQueen, trying to keep the mood on an upswing. 'You've done great work here, so dig around some more on Ross James, and let's see what pops up.'

Thirty-four

Sitting on his couch, the curtains in his living room drawn, Ian hadn't eaten or slept properly in two days. He saw the email from McQueen come in and deleted it without even clicking to open it. He didn't care what the private investigator had to say. The man's fate was already sealed. Everything was out of balance now until McQueen was dead. Ian was bored with McQueen and bored with the email game. He had only started the thread because he wanted to mess with him, but that had been foolish and selfishly indulgent, then events had taken over. McQueen was the balancer now. Things had unravelled since Ian had missed the golden opportunity to kill him and Cullen together. He should have known that the voice he'd heard shouting from the hall was McQueen. Why hadn't he known?

Something had been flipped, and suddenly Ian saw everything around him that was going badly as a consequence of his own failings. He no longer felt in complete control. Even small things took on great significance. The milk had gone off in the fridge, the light bulb in the bathroom had blown and meanwhile his head wouldn't stop aching. They were all signs of the displeasure that was circulating in the atmosphere around him. They were all due to the imbalance he had caused.

Even his revenue stream was drying up. The fish on the ends of his lines were suffering from the lack of time he had been investing in them. Cynthia, a woman who had been madly in love with one of his many pseudonyms was proving to be a problem. Ian had invented "Sebastian", a handsome but lonely pilot, and the images he had sent her were compelling. This was a man who was craving the understanding and support of a good woman. You only had to look at his clear green eyes to see that. Of course, it was the financial support that interested Ian. He didn't spend much on his everyday living but he was building an emergency fund that would allow him to disappear and resurface anywhere in the world if he needed to.

After several messages, when Cynthia believed that Sebastian had hit some bad luck and got into difficulties, she had sent him a total of £15,000 in various amounts. Ian had come to rely on the regular money, but now she was saying she was having trouble with the bank account and she couldn't send any more. He'd told her one of his lies about how he owed money to gangsters and that they would hurt him if he didn't find another £5,000, but she said she would only give him the cash if she could finally meet him. He told her he was abroad and it wouldn't be possible, but she was insistent and said she was desperate to. She seemed more abrupt than before and also wanted to start using a messaging app on her phone rather than emails. Of course, Ian had an untraceable burner phone, but that wasn't the point. He was being taken in a direction that he hadn't chosen, and it didn't feel good. He didn't like to let a fish go, but Cynthia was one that might have to be cut loose.

It all came down to McQueen now. The press interest in Emma Cullen's death had been overwhelming in the first few days as the media mourned and wailed over one of their own, but as time passed, even that had started to fade. After all, she hadn't been *that* famous, and many people seemed to believe she had been playing with fire in her podcasts. She had rattled the cages of serious criminals, and that's why she'd been killed. On the edges of the internet, Ian had followed some of the online conspiracy theories that had grown up around the case and he'd found that others were getting the credit for his kill. For the general public, there were always new enticing stories, and interest in Cullen was already withering. Once McQueen was dead and the police worked out that he was killed by the same gun, the power would be reignited.

Ian had printed off the grainy picture from the web, the one that haunted him, of McQueen and Cullen together in the restaurant, the power couple. He'd laid it next to his laptop on the kitchen table. With a black marker, he'd put an 'X' through Emma's face, knowing the world wouldn't be balanced until there was a similar mark on McQueen's outline. He put a circle around McQueen's face. Circles were powerful. They concentrated energy. He took a quartz crystal from his pocket that he'd carried with him for months. Crystals were made by the forces beneath the surface of the earth and they could also harness energy. He'd read that somewhere. He couldn't remember where, but he believed it. He placed the transparent rock formed in the belly of the planet inside the circle that he'd drawn around McQueen's face.

As ever, there was no one to warn Ian that his psyche was fragmenting, or that his logic had dissolved. Ideas and theories were raining down on him now, and his reasoning was spinning uncontrollably. Each new insight was treated as a magnificent revelation. Crystals were something he had dismissed in the past as pathetic hippy shit, but that was forgotten, and now he saw them as yet another message passed to him through the ages.

Ian knew where McQueen worked and he knew how he would kill McQueen. Now all Ian was waiting for was a sign that the celestial alignment was right. The course of things could still be corrected, but timing was everything.

Thirty-five

Tracey had been reading and rereading the Olivia emails that McQueen had sent over, but she snapped the lid closed on her laptop when Sophie came in from the kitchen. Sophie had had a bad day; a very sick cat had been brought in, but there had been nothing they could do for him. The owner had been distraught, and underneath her professional exterior, Sophie was hurting just as much. It was a horrible part of the job. Of course, not all sick animals could be saved, but job or no job, that didn't stop Sophie from feeling the pain. The ones she helped to survive gave her the joy that kept her in the game.

Tracey had debated long and hard with herself before opening the emails from McQueen. She had thought of forwarding them unopened to Reed and Chambers, but in the end, her curiosity had got the better of her. And besides, she didn't trust them to read between the lines. Once she'd skimmed the content and seen what they were about, she couldn't pull herself away from the messages.

Sophie had suggested they watch a film after dinner as a distraction from the pressures of the day, but Tracey wasn't sure she'd be able to concentrate now. To her credit, Sophie had picked up on that vibe and pointed at the laptop.

'Work, right?'

They had an understanding that Tracey didn't discuss police work at home.

'Yeah, sorry. Some interesting emails that I'm really not sure about, that's all.'

'Look,' said Sophie. 'I unloaded my day on you, and it really helped, so let's make an exception tonight. You can tell me about it if you want to, as long as you leave out the gory bits.'

Such was her need to read the emails again that this was the only invitation Tracey needed. She was aware she shouldn't be sharing the information with anyone else, but this technically wasn't police intelligence. These were emails from McQueen, an old friend. Gratefully, she opened the laptop. She explained briefly what the messages were, who Olivia was, and why McQueen had forwarded them to her. She also admitted they were both making a massive assumption that whoever had sent the emails had more than a passing interest in the murder of the old man in the house. On very little evidence, they were assuming that the emails had been sent by someone who had been in the house when the man had died.

'You mean,' Sophie asked, wide-eyed, 'you think it could be a bragging message from the murderer?'

Tracey nodded. 'But it's this line about the woman killed on the carpark steps that's interesting.' She pointed to the screen. 'That's a different case, one I'm working on. And it's just odd she should mention it.'

Sophie read through the emails. 'I don't think Olivia is a woman. This letter just doesn't sound like a woman to me. There's that bit about McQueen being a handsome man. To me, that sounds like a man trying to sound like a woman.'

'I think you're right. Whoever it was, though, they were right about the back door, so we have to take it seriously.'

Tracey was focusing on the later information in the email, the mention of Emma Cullen, because that was the most aggressive part, although there were no direct threats. Sophie was still reading about the old man.

'This bit,' Sophie said, then read out a line: '"…he was a nosey old git, always poking his nose into people's lives, gossiping, complaining, so he must have had enemies".'

'What about it?' asked Tracey.

'You know his name, don't you? The old man?'

'Yes, Harold Kaylor.' Tracey wasn't sure what Sophie was getting at, but she was desperate for any kind of help.

'Well,' Sophie continued, 'we get a lot of older people in the surgery, and from what I can tell, they aren't shy about making complaints to the police. If your Harold Kaylor made some complaints, you might have a record of them, and that might tell you something.'

Tracey put the computer down on the couch next to them and circled her arms around Sophie's neck.

'It must be true that opposites attract,' Tracey said, 'because I'm an idiot and you're a genius.' She then hugged Sophie as tightly as possible and kissed her.

Thirty-six

The detectives had made an appointment, so when they arrived at Davidson's office, they were ushered through to see him quite quickly by his receptionist. He didn't want them waiting around in reception, possibly talking to clients. It was bad for the reputation of a financier to have police visitors. But they had been insistent, and he did have an outstanding complaint with them.

The two policemen couldn't stop their heads from swivelling as they took in the impressive corporate surroundings they found themselves in. It was a sharp contrast to the cramped office space of the station. A huge antique globe dominated one corner of the room, in front of a bookcase of leather-bound editions. It was a modern building, but Davidson had gone for the reassuringly comforting style of the kinds of places for people who know how to take good care of money. It was all about confidence. Long-standing financial stability was the vibe he'd been going for. Web agencies could have their neon signs and pool tables, but he wanted his office to exude seriousness, not creative fun.

'I would offer you coffee,' said Davidson, 'but we're all busy men.' It was a *hurry up*.

'No problem,' said Detective Reed.

'Have you arrested McQueen for the murder of his girlfriend yet?' Davidson asked. 'From what I was reading online, the arrest is imminent.'

'We couldn't possibly comment on an ongoing case, sir,' said Chambers. 'But rest assured, we are leaving no stone unturned in our pursuit of the culprit.'

'You made a complaint against Dr McQueen?' asked Reed.

'It's taken a while for you to get round to it, but yes, I did. I'd like you to warn him off.'

Reed was reading from his notes. 'You made a statement once you had dispensed with his services, he was abusive and that he made unfounded accusations against you. Can you tell us why you'd hired him? What had you asked him to do?'

'Well, that's between him and me. It's a private matter I'd rather not discuss.'

'Alright,' answered Reed. 'But you didn't specify what the accusations were. It would be hard for us to warn Dr McQueen without knowing what we're warning him about.'

'Oh, it doesn't matter what they were, and I may not even press charges. But I would like him warned.'

Chambers took over again. 'Yes, so you said. But we would like to know the substance of the accusations.'

Davidson looked slightly flummoxed and looked down

at his desk, as if the answer was there.

'Would it have been about the grievous bodily harm that was inflicted on a Mr Tom Lewis? Or the two broken legs that were sustained by Mr Lewis in that attack?'

Davidson assumed they had spoken to McQueen already, so he couldn't make up his mind whether to deny it or not. 'Er, yes. I think it was.'

'And did Dr McQueen suggest perhaps you might have been involved in some way with those injuries?'

It was too much. Davidson snapped. He saw the police as no more than civil servants, 'servants' being the operative word. They were there to protect and help people like him, and he didn't like the way this conversation was developing.

'Look,' he said, in a voice only a few decibels short of a full shout. 'I made a complaint. I have already sent a very strong solicitor's letter to him and now all I'm asking you to do is your job. Go down there to whatever hovel he operates out of and shake him up a little. He can't go around making accusations and damaging my reputation in public, and your job is to make sure he doesn't.'

Neither of the officers showed the slightest flicker of emotion. Davidson may have believed that he had given them both barrels of a verbal onslaught, but it didn't come close to some of the things they had faced in their professional careers.

'Well,' said Chambers, 'as you said, we're all busy men. So let's crack on. We'd like to update you on that Lewis case we mentioned.'

'We got a breakthrough,' said Reed, as if chatting to a

pal. 'Doesn't often happen, but when it does, we're grateful. The street where Mr Lewis was attacked had CCTV that had been installed by one of the shops on the other side of the road. We managed to secure the recordings and were able to watch the horrific attack.'

Davidson was slightly uncomfortable. He'd expected the policemen to scuttle away to do his bidding, but instead they seemed to be leading up to something else.

'Brutal.' Chambers shook his head. 'I've seen some bad footage in my time, but this was awful.'

'Very nasty,' added Reed. 'And that's when we got our break. Luckily, my colleague here, Detective Chambers, recognised one of the assailants.'

'Yes, turns out I nicked him a couple of years back. So we found out where he was living now and went down there with a team and raided his place. Get this: he still had the hammer he'd used on Mr Lewis' legs. Blood, DNA, everything.'

Detective Reed had a look of playful incredulity on his face, as if he was inviting Davidson to join him in his amazement at the turn of events. But Davidson was not looking amazed. He was looking stressed.

'Why are you telling me this?' he asked, in a much smaller voice than the one he'd used to try to browbeat them earlier.

'This is where it gets interesting, Mr Davidson,' continued Reed. 'Now you may have heard the phrase 'honour amongst thieves'. Obviously, you don't have the experience we've got, so you wouldn't know, but I'm here to tell you it's bullshit. It's a myth. If a criminal is facing a long, long sentence based on previous crimes and he also happens to be carrying a suspended sentence, there's not much he won't tell us to save his own skin. He's hoping his cooperation will go down well with the sentencing judge and maybe he'll be able to knock a few years off the prison time.'

There was an ominous silence in the room while two of the men stared unflinchingly at the third. At that point, Davidson's office door opened and his PA popped her head into the room. She'd been told by her boss that if the meeting should go on for longer than ten minutes, she was to come in and remind him about a fictitious appointment so he could get rid of the police.

'Mr Davidson,' she said. 'Your three o'clock is —' But she didn't get to finish her bogus warning that Davidson's next appointment was waiting.

He rocked back in his leather chair and screamed, 'Out!'

The PA quickly shut the door. Even with the outburst, the police detectives still showed no reaction, but they exchanged a look that said, *we've got him*. Then Chambers resumed in his steady, unhurried voice.

'What we have, Mr Davidson,' he said, 'is a signed statement saying you hired two men to attack and injure Mr Lewis as some way of getting back at Dr McQueen. Another thing you might not be aware of, not having the experience in this field, is that hiring someone to do a crime is prosecuted as if you did that crime yourself.'

'Or as we would say,' said Detective Reed, 'anyone who aids, abets, or incites another to commit assault occasioning grievous bodily harm with intent will be charged with the principal offence. That's you, Mr Davidson. You're under arrest for said principal offence. If you'd like to come with us, sir?'

'Now?' asked Davidson, blinking with disbelief. 'But what about my three o'clock meeting?'

'Oh, don't worry about that,' said Chambers, standing. 'You've still got a meeting, Mr Davidson, but it's down at the station.'

Thirty-seven

Tracey had hardly been able to wait to get into the station and back to her desk. She didn't even go for her customary kick-start coffee from the machine. Coat still on, she immediately bashed her password into the computer to access the files she wanted. She started to search through the logged reports and complaints from the public. Unfortunately, it was an antiquated legacy IT system, long overdue for an upgrade, and the search function was rudimentary. She could search for exact matches on names, but if someone had stored the name with a slightly different spelling, there was no facility for close matches. There was no Harold Kaylor listed, but that didn't discourage her too much. While it could mean the old man had never contacted the police, which was highly probable, it might also be because the name had been wrongly listed. She began trying variations.

She was so engrossed that she didn't notice Detective Chambers come in, but a few minutes later, he passed by her desk and put a cup of coffee next to her. She lifted her head from the screen and frowned quizzically.

'We've crossed two off the list,' he said.

'What are you talking about?' She was genuinely mystified, partly by his statement and also because he had never given her a cup of coffee before.

'Your mate McQueen,' he explained. 'He had a list of four question marks against his name, but number two and four have gone now. The Tom Lewis thing wasn't down to him, although it seems he was unknowingly part of it. At the same time, we cleared up that accusation of abusive behaviour against McQueen from businessman Brian Davidson. That turned out to be a malicious slur. Kicking a man he thought was down.'

Tracey looked at the coffee. She suddenly recognised it as a peace offering. Maybe Chambers was coming around to her point of view. She'd heard the buzz in the station about the CCTV footage but she wasn't about to take the I-told-you-so route. She wasn't in a position to turn away any gestures of friendship.

'Thank you,' she said pointing at the cup.

He nodded and said airily, 'But it's not over yet for McQueen. He's still got two outstanding issues, as they say, and they're the biggies: the Toby Markham and Emma Cullen murders,' he added, in case she might have forgotten.

'C'mon Detective Chambers. Even you don't really believe he did either of those, do you?'

'At this stage, we are leaving all avenues of investigation open,' he said, but he was smiling broadly, leading Tracey to think that his confidence in pinning anything on McQueen was waning.

He moved past her desk to head to his own. She sipped the coffee, which was cold, but she was grateful anyway, and continued to search. There weren't any guarantees the old man had made a complaint at all. It was only Sophie's guess based on a rambling email from an anonymous source, but right now it was all Tracey had. Good police work often came down to monotonous data-crunching, but Tracey had decided to go back no more than a year in the records before giving up. She was about halfway through the task when she saw the name 'H. Kayler'. She closed her eyes and took three deep breaths to calm her excitement. It had been entered into the system as the name of a man who had phoned in about a neighbour. This absolutely had to be him. She tried to steady herself down and almost rang Sophie to share the find. After a couple of seconds, she read through the complaint.

The man had reported that every day, he walked his dog on the same route and he always waved to a woman in the window at 16 Gresham Street. Then one day, the woman had disappeared, and a new man was now living at the address. He'd asked around and been told that the woman had died after falling down her stairs. He'd also learned the new occupant was not the woman's son. In his report of suspicious behaviour, H. Kayler had asked for the police to go to the house to question the man as he thought it was so strange.

Amazingly, given the gossipy nature of the complaint, a uniformed officer had actually been dispatched to speak to the new occupant. All Tracey could imagine was that it must have been a quiet crime day. The officer had simply ascertained that, yes the man was the legal owner of the property, and that had been that. There were no other entries for the inquiry. It was true people made complaints all the time, and the police had barely enough resources to visit the actively warring neighbours, let alone chase up the reports where no perceivable crime had been committed.

It was probably nothing at all, but she knew she would not be able to rest until she had at least looked into it further. She began to search again and also to make some phone calls.

It took Tracey most of the day to unravel the basic facts. The house at 16 Gresham Street was owned by a Mr Ian Bridger, a man who appeared to have a limited digital footprint other than his legal right to own the house. The property had been left to him by its previous owner, who had indeed fallen down her stairs. She'd had no other kin, her son having recently died in a car crash. Ian Bridger had been added as the beneficiary in the will only weeks before she had died. That raised Tracey's eyebrows a little.

With every piece of information that emerged, Tracey was sure of one thing: it was high time that Mr Harold Kaylor's report of suspicious activity at 16 Gresham Street was followed up properly. She was just about to close her computer when she saw something else that seemed to shine out from the screen. She had managed to stumble on some personal details and records from the childhood of Ian Bridger. There were on-record reports of petty criminality from the age of thirteen. He was accused of killing a neighbour's cat, and although it couldn't be proved, he had been warned. But that wasn't the detail which had struck Tracey. The report gave his mother's name, Olivia Bridger. With mounting excitement, Tracey ran a check. Olivia Bridger had died of natural causes fifteen years before. He was using his mother's name on the emails. Sophie had been right, Olivia was a man.

Tracey stood up quickly from her desk and looked across at Chambers. She was about to ask him to accompany her right then to go and question Ian Bridger, but watching the detective frowning at his screen, she thought again and sat back down.

Chambers would have some sensible and searching questions for her before he would agree to leave the office, and she wasn't sure she had any sensible answers.

What did she actually have to go on? A few flaky emails from who she thought was a man calling himself Olivia, stitched together in a tapestry of suspicion by Tracey's creative imagination. She was making a lot of links in her mind, but they didn't stand up to harsh scrutiny. She tried to think it through. Harold Kaylor made a report against Ian Bridger, and then Kaylor died. So what? There was nothing to prove it was a murder. Then Ian, calling himself Olivia, emailed McQueen with a clue that only someone in the house could have known. So what? In his emails he made mention of the carpark murder, but that had been in the media. He made veiled threats about Emma Cullen, and then she got shot. By rights, with the vague possibility of a gun being present, Tracey should have been requesting a full SWAT team, but she knew her chances of mobilising

258

one on the strength of her suspicions was negligible. No, there was only one person who would treat her theories with any kind of credibility, and unfortunately McQueen was out of bounds.

Thirty-eight

Lia was alone in the office again. McQueen hadn't got in yet. He'd messaged to say he hadn't slept well and he would be in later. She didn't think it was surprising after what he'd been through. She didn't know about his nightmares, but she could tell by the dark rings around his eyes he'd been lacking sleep lately.

She was just settling at her desk when the downstairs door buzzed. For security reasons, McQueen had had a video entrance system fitted. In their line of work, not all visitors were welcome, so it was good to be able to see them first. She looked at the video display and almost jolted with shock.

'Hello, is Lia there?' came the slightly distorted but still familiar voice.

'Kerry?' said Lia, not quite able to believe what she was seeing. Before she released the door, she had a good look at the small screen to see the carpark behind Kerry. 'Are you alone?'

'Yes,' answered Kerry. 'Don't worry. My brother isn't here.' From the safety of the office, Lia watched her come in and double-checked that the door had closed behind her. She wasn't sure how McQueen's rule of not interviewing people on her own worked when they came to her, but she didn't want to take any chances either way.

The first thing Kerry did once she had taken the lift up to the office was apologise for her brother. She explained he'd made her call Lia and arrange the meeting in town and that all he was trying to do was protect his sister. He'd gone about it all wrong, she admitted, but that was how big brothers were, she said.

Lia told her it didn't matter and not to worry about it, though that wasn't exactly what she was feeling, and showed Kerry into McQueen's room, where Lia sat her down with a cup of tea. She was being careful not to let Kerry feel in any way pressured. There was still a chance that she would change her mind and leave, but the woman had made the trip to the office, so she must have more to say than sorry. Kerry looked different away from her house. She'd made some effort to tidy her hair and apply a little makeup but she looked smaller and frailer, and even though her brother wasn't at her shoulder, she still looked terrified. Lia assumed her softest and most sympathetic voice to try to coax her to say whatever it was she'd come to say.

'Are you okay, Kerry?' she asked gently. 'Can I help?'

At the sound of sympathy, the other woman lost control. She broke down sobbing, but between the tears, she managed to say, 'I can't keep living like this, Lia. I don't know what to do. There's no way out. I've got no one to turn to. You're the only one I could think of.'

Lia was feeling very sorry for Kerry. All she wanted to do was hug her and tell her that it was going to be okay. But this was an opportunity that may never return so she had to keep her professional head in the game.

'I'm going to make a guess, Kerry, okay?' she said. 'Now, I may be way wrong, but it's not Craig Preston or his family making you feel like this, is it? And it's not your brother, either.'

Face in hands, Kerry was shaking her head. Lia took a deep breath herself. She was about to make a big step but she had to try.

'I know,' Lia said, 'because it's your neighbour. The old guy you know as Ross Bailey.' Lia didn't phrase it as a question because she didn't want Kerry to think she was still fishing, although that's exactly what she was doing.

The effect was dramatic. Kerry stopped crying and lifted her tear-stained face from her palms. The eye makeup she'd put on to help her face the world had run a little.

Lia handed her a tissue.

'How did you know?' Kerry asked, the shock taking over from the distress on her features.

'We know all about Ross 'Bailey' James, Kerry. That's his full name. Since he put that breeze block through your window, he's been holding the whole street to ransom, hasn't he?'

Kerry was nodding now.

'So what actually happened with Toby Markham?' Lia asked gently.

'It was stupid, so stupid,' said Kerry, crying again. 'All

Toby did was park in front of Bailey's drive. That was it, but the old bloke went absolutely mental. Toby just laughed at him, and that made it worse. I've never seen anyone so angry. Bailey rang on the door, he dragged Toby out of the house at knife point and then he battered him to death. You'd think he'd be too old to do it, but he was like a madman. He kept shouting, 'do you know who you're dealing with?' and he had the knife. Toby was no fighter and Bailey was wild. I was screaming at him to stop, but then he turned and threatened to kill me, too.'

'Why didn't you tell the police all this?' asked Lia, although she already knew the answer.

'He told me exactly who he was, a gangster. And he said if I went to the police, his mates would burn my house down with me inside it, and I believed him. He's evil. I saw how evil he is. I was terrified.'

Lia clasped Kerry's shaking hand. 'It's okay. It's going to be alright. You did the right thing, coming here. But what made you come to see me now?'

'He's started asking for money.' She was crying again. 'I don't have any money, but he knows how scared I am and he's saying my brother will be next if I don't come up with the cash. It's never going to stop.' She was breaking down again.

'You're right, it's not going to get any better until you go to the police,' said Lia firmly. 'It's time. I'll come with you. They'll protect you. You're a star witness, and he's a serious criminal who needs to be taken off the streets.'

Kerry didn't respond but she hadn't stormed out either.

'It's all down to you, Kerry. But I can tell you this: if you don't do something, it's only going to be a matter of time before he decides that you are too big a risk to be left alive as a witness.'

It was a harsh shot but it must have been something that had crossed her own mind, because Kerry was nodding again.

'For a little while, I was happy with Toby.' She was staring into the still-full teacup she was clasping with both hands. 'He said he was going to buy us a house away from here. He had big dreams, and he was so nice to me that I went along with it, but he was a wrong 'un too. He was a lying cheat with a wife. But he still didn't deserve to be killed like that. I just want it all over. Will you help me?'

'Every step of the way.' Lia leaned forward and gently squeezed Kerry's shoulder. 'And the first stop is the police station.'

Thirty-nine

The nightmares had been worse — a lot worse — since Emma's death and they had started to spill over into McQueen's waking moments. If he found himself drifting slightly, losing concentration on what he was doing, the images came crashing in: Emma lying dead at his feet, the blood and the sheer lifelessness of this vibrant, wonderful woman. Along with the image came the huge feeling of utter powerlessness that engulfed him. He had started to recognise triggers too, innocent sights and sounds that could jump-start the memory. There was no point denying it any longer. He needed professional help. He needed to put aside his feelings of defeat and accept even he couldn't fight this battle alone. The trouble was he knew enough about the mechanics of trauma therapy to know what it would entail, and that was partly what was holding him back.

For the therapy to work, at some point he was going to have to come face-to-face with his own traumatic experiences. He was going to have to relive his worst memories and scrutinise them in minute detail so that he could fold them away neatly in the linen cupboard of his mind. He still wasn't sure he was up to it but felt he had to do something to avert the slide into constant fear.

He looked at the phone in his hand for a long time before he eventually called his old friend, Maggie. Amongst other things, she was a professional trauma therapist and, without giving himself time to lose his nerve or get sidetracked, he asked if he could set up a session with her. It was almost as if she'd been expecting his call and although she was always very busy, she kindly said she'd make a space for him. She had guessed from his previous "I'm asking for a friend" questions he had been struggling and she praised him for making the effort that was so difficult for a man in his position. He was admitting that he wasn't infallible.

'It can get better,' she reassured him. 'And you've taken the first step, so the healing has begun.'

With the appointment booked, McQueen felt a slight weight come off his shoulders and he turned to the second difficult call he needed to make. It had been on his mind a lot that Tom would soon be coming out of hospital and how difficult it would be for the guy. He felt an enormous responsibility towards him but at the same time he knew he had to respect Tom's request for him to stay away for a while. Tom would know by now that his injuries had come as a direct result of McQueen's meeting with Davidson. He had every right to be angry, but there was something else McQueen could do, something that might make things a lot worse, but also had the potential to provide a new start for

Tom.

Tom's parents had disowned him when his drug-addicted, petty criminal, teenage behaviour had become too much for them. They didn't understand what had happened. As far as they could see, they had lost their darling boy who had been replaced by a person they didn't like. There had been a lot of hurt on both sides of the chasm that had opened up between them, but the result was a parting of the ways. That's when Tom's grandmother had taken over as his whole family unit until her death. Perhaps his parents had known he would be okay with Grace, but Tom and his parents still hadn't spoken, not even at Grace's funeral, all of them entrenched in their own pain. It wasn't McQueen's place to interfere; he had absolutely no right to get involved, it could be a disaster, but he was going to do it anyway.

McQueen rang Tom's mother. As he suspected, she hadn't heard about Tom's injuries and she was horrified when McQueen told her. Then he spent a long time explaining how far Tom had come in life, how much he was doing in his charity work and what a changed man he was. He didn't ask her to do anything and he didn't make any suggestions, but he said he wanted Tom's parents to at least be aware that the Tom they had known and feared was not the man who was lying in a hospital bed now.

His mother didn't say a lot, but she didn't put the phone down either, and McQueen at one point thought he heard a quiet sob.

McQueen finished the call by saying Tom was about to come out of hospital and that it wouldn't be easy for him.

He left it at that. Very formally, Tom's mother thanked him for passing on the information but she didn't commit to anything and McQueen didn't ask her to. When he put down the phone he was left wondering if the only thing he had ensured was that Tom never spoke to him ever again.

McQueen had now chalked off two of his personal admin tasks, so now he turned to the final one. His previous message to Olivia hadn't worked. There had been no response at all. Maybe she hadn't even got it or maybe she was not about to reply to a plea for help. He'd tried to play along with her handsome comment as if he was flattered and he'd attempted to appeal to her need to show off, but neither had made her answer. He still wasn't sure if the internet persona of Olivia had been created by a man or a woman, but given Olivia wanted him to believe she was a woman, he had decided to stick with that. It actually didn't matter much.

Whatever the reason for the email silence, he was left feeling frustrated by his own lack of persuasiveness. Tracey also hadn't come back to him yet about all the messages he'd forwarded to her, and he could only think that with Emma's murder still high on the police agenda, she didn't want to have too much to do with him.

As a last-ditch effort, McQueen decided to try to provoke Olivia. He felt like it was all he had left, and if she wasn't going to communicate anyway, he had nothing to lose. In the email subject line, which she would have to see if she received the message, he wrote, "I know who you are." And in the body of the email he typed, "You can't hide any longer." It was a total lie, and not even a clever one, but he hoped it would at least get a reaction of some kind and break the silence.

McQueen was putting on his jacket to head into the office when he got a call from Lia.

'You're off the hook for the Markham murder,' she said by way of introduction.

'That's good to know,' he answered casually, as if it had never been in doubt, although he'd read about enough miscarriages of justice to know you couldn't ever really know how these things were going to pan out. 'Did you turn something up?'

'Better than that,' said Lia, hardly able to contain her joy. 'I'm at the police station right now with Kerry Smith. She came into the office of her own accord this morning, and after a little woman-to-woman chat, she told me what really happened. So then I convinced her that her only option was to come forward with a witness statement. We were right, it was Ross Bailey. Something about a parking dispute that went nuclear.'

'Jeez,' said McQueen. 'A leopard who hadn't changed his spots. A lifetime of brutality clearly not mellowed with age.'

'Kerry's in there now giving her statement to Detective Reed. They are going to put her in a safe house while this is going on. It's going to be a rough ride, but she was at her wit's end.'

They talked a little more about how the case would proceed, and then McQueen said, 'Congratulations by the way, Lia. Your probation is over. You just graduated to full private detective. Your single-handed dedication and focus have broken this case.'

'Oh, I had some luck,' she said, trying to downplay how ecstatic she was feeling.

'No, this one's on you, not Lady Luck.' What he was thinking was that he was the one who had benefitted from luck. He'd advertised for an office administrator and he'd found a talented business partner.

McQueen was just shutting his front door when his phone rang again. He fished his handset out of his pocket thinking it must be Lia again but he was surprised to see it was Tracey.

'You at your office?' she asked, without any preamble.

'Just leaving my flat, actually.' He slammed the door so she'd be able to hear it down the line. He was keen to hear what she thought about the emails he'd forwarded to her, certain that's why she was calling him now, but he also wanted to get back to his office. He wanted to be there when Lia got back from the police station.

'Wait there,' said Tracey. 'I'm coming to get you. I've found Olivia.'

Forty

It was a risky decision that she might regret when her brothers in the police family found out, but McQueen was the one she had chosen to back her up. She looked at him sitting in the passenger seat of the police car and didn't have any doubts it was the right choice. He had no gun and he had no police authority but he was the one Olivia had chosen to talk to, and Tracey was hoping he would provide the key.

On the drive over, she outlined what she had found out about Ian Bridger: the complaint by Harold Kaylor, the suspiciously inherited house, and the name Olivia. But it still wasn't much. Their mission was only to talk to him. They had no evidence to bring him in, and he might not be willing to say a word, but they needed to see him face-to-face.

Tracey had taken one of the marked police vehicles from the pool because she wasn't trying to hide her identity. In fact, she wanted the weight of the law to be visible. She parked outside the address and turned to McQueen. They had been in similar situations before, and McQueen was feeling it as a trigger for his trauma. He breathed deeply.

'You okay?' she asked.

'Never better,' he said through a false smile. 'Let's do this.'

Tracey led the way down the path, through the messy, unkempt garden, and knocked at the door. They both stood and waited. McQueen was looking at the windows to see if there were any signs of life. Tracey knocked again, harder this time, and crouched down to look through the letterbox. She shouted his name and that she was from the police, but there was still no answer.

She stood back from the door, hands on hips.

'Well,' she said. 'If we're right about this guy, we need to get in there.'

McQueen had just started to say that they would have to come back later when Tracey did something McQueen could never have predicted. She lunged forward with all her weight, and in a flat-footed kicking motion, she aimed her boot at the lock area near the handle. The door sprung open and clattered back on its hinges.

McQueen was open-mouthed. 'When did you start breaking the rules, Tracey? I mean, isn't that breaking and entering?'

In the past, Tracey had always been one for playing everything by the book, but it seemed that police life had changed some of her values.

'I thought I heard the cries of someone in distress,' she answered flatly. 'You heard them, didn't you?'

McQueen was uncomfortable about being drawn into criminal behaviour by a police officer and he wasn't entirely sure how he felt about it, but after all the messages from Olivia, he too was eager to see what was in the house.

'Yeah,' he said, making his decision. 'I heard them. We'd better check.'

As they stepped into the hall, Tracey shouted, 'Ian Bridger, are you here? It's the police. We've come to see if you are okay.'

With Tracey leading the way, they walked down the wooden hallway strewn with junk mail that had dropped through the letterbox but had never been picked up. The letters and free newspapers had been trodden down and kicked aside, forming a crazy multicoloured carpet. It flitted across McQueen's mind given the comments about Emma Cullen that Ian had made, there was a slim chance he had a gun, but McQueen pushed that thought to the back of his mind.

On the left of the hall, they found the living room, where a large sofa was the dominant piece of furniture. It was facing the front window and bore the indentation of the last person to sit on it, presumably Bridger, and a dirty plate of what looked like baked beans on the floor in front of it. Against the wall, near to the electricity socket, was a computer printer and an internet router, both plugged into the dull black minitower of a computer with tiny flashing red and green lights. They stood out as modern and incongruous things in a bare room that didn't even have a TV. Tracey checked, but there was nothing in the output tray of the printer.

Still shouting out Ian's name, they both went up the stairs to look in the rooms. There were three bedrooms but only one had been used recently. The double bed was unmade, but there was little else in the room to give any clue about the person who slept there. There were some discarded jogging bottoms on the floor and two identical black hoodies, but there was nothing on the nightstand except a bedside light. In the chest of drawers under the window, they found some neatly folded older woman's clothes that must have belonged to the elderly woman whose room it had once been. They were looking for anything that might have a recent picture of Ian Bridger on it but they didn't find anything, no driver's licence or passport hidden under the clothes.

Judging by the musty smell and the thickness of the dust, the other bedroom doors hadn't been opened in quite a while. In the bathroom, there was one toothbrush, a squeezed tube of toothpaste and an electric razor, no other products. No soap, no creams, no shower gel.

McQueen was feeling more and more uneasy about them being in the house. If Bridger turned up now and proved to be a strange but totally innocent individual, he and Tracey could be in a lot of trouble.

'It's like a house where no one lives,' said Tracey, her voice echoing slightly in the tiled room.

'Looks like the old woman died, he moved in, and apart from the bedroom and his toothbrush, he hasn't touched anything else.'

Back in the hall, they made their way to the kitchen. So far, they hadn't found a single thing that could be said to be suspicious, and McQueen was starting to worry they had broken in for nothing. When they got to the kitchen, everything changed. Looking down the room, McQueen could see the sink piled high with dirty dishes, and in the corner of the room there was a pile of empty baked bean cans.

'Ian's got a somewhat limited diet,' said McQueen, trying to inject some levity.'

Tracey had stopped at the kitchen table. 'Look,' she said, almost in a whisper.

On the table was a laptop, and next to it, printed on cheap A4 paper, was the infamous picture of Emma and McQueen in the restaurant. Emma's face had a large black cross drawn through it, and around McQueen's head was a circle that had been traced so many times it had almost gone through the paper. In the centre of the circle was a clear quartz crystal. One word was written at the top of the page in block capitals: **THREATS**. The black marker pen was lying next to the picture.

'That'll do it,' whispered Tracey, moving into professional mode. 'Circumstantial but compelling.' She opened her coat, and from her inside pocket, she took out some thin rubber gloves which she put on. She also took out some evidence bags. She carefully put the picture into one and put the marker pen and the crystal into another. She went back upstairs and came down with a see-through plastic evidence bag with hair from the shaver.

She held up the bag with the pen in it and said, "Fingerprints," and then the other bag and said, "DNA."

She opened the laptop, and when it burst into life, she

was met by the password screen. She shrugged. There was no point typing in random password guesses. It was one for the IT geeks back at the station. She unplugged the laptop. It was too big to put into one of her bags, so she tucked it under her arm.

'And this is coming with us,' she said. 'I'll get it straight to the lab, and we'll see what they can find on it.'

'He's going to think he's been burgled,' said McQueen with an uneasy smile.

'Good. Maybe it will make him contact the police and we can invite him to come and get his stuff back. Can you carry the computer from the living room?'

McQueen went and disconnected the PC tower from its various wires, leaving them in a tangle on the floor, and then lifted the box out into the hall.

'I think we'd better get out of here,' she said, moving quickly now. 'There's a good chance that he has a gun, and based on that picture, there's also a possibility that you are the next victim.'

As Ian walked towards his house, he could see the police car parked right outside his gate. He carried on walking at the same steady pace, but his hand had closed on the gun in his pocket. He had taken to carrying it with him all the time now. As he approached the garden, he looked quickly down the path. He could see that his front door was wide open but couldn't see the police inside. He didn't look twice. He carried on walking like any other passerby would, past his house and down to the end of the street. He didn't quicken his stride and he didn't look back. The laptop was a big loss, but he would get another once he could get his hands on some cash. He had numerous hidden bank accounts but he needed a computer to access them. He needed some money fast and he knew where to get some.

Ian walked on until he reached a park where he sat down heavily on a bench. It was very clear now what had to happen. He would go to McQueen's office bright and early and wait for him to arrive. Then he would balance the universe and he would start all over again.

He took out his burner phone and wrote a message from his fake pilot Sebastian: *My love, my only love. I am so lost. Things are so bad for me, and I need you so much. I am flying to Manchester tonight. I will be in Leeds by tomorrow. Yes, it's true! I can hardly believe it. You have already been so generous. You have been my saviour. Bring the £5,000, more if you have it, and we can go away and start again together. xxx*

Within minutes, he had the reply: *Yes, yes, yes, Sebastian. I love you so much. Just tell me where.*

He told her he had to get his flight and that he was making some final arrangements and would send her the address in the morning. He didn't like having to meet this woman but he needed the cash, and once he'd killed her and taken the money, there would be no way to trace him and everything would realign.

Forty-one

McQueen hadn't gone back to his office. Tracey had dropped him at his flat before she headed to the police station to log the evidence. She'd said she wanted the various lab reports back as soon as possible so she needed to get the paperwork done and the process moving. McQueen messaged Lia, but she was also still at the station, lending support to Kerry.

Suddenly, alone in his flat, a mixture of emotions surfaced as it all hit home. He had possibly been in the house of the man who had killed Emma, a man who may have killed others like Harry Kaylor. So far, the evidence was circumstantial and sketchy, probably not enough to arrest the man for, but there wasn't much doubt in McQueen's mind. But why had he done it?

McQueen opened his laptop. For the thousandth time, he read through the emails from Olivia, who was now revealed as Ian. This time, he could read them and visualise the very kitchen they had been sent from. There had been no answer to his last email in which he had tried to taunt Ian. He couldn't even tell if Ian had read it.

Perceived threats, was that all this was about? Had Bridger's warped mind seen Emma and her media crusades against criminals as a personal threat? The human fight, flight, freeze, or fawn set of responses to threats had evolved over thousands of years. It could be a very powerful motivator, but had it been twisted out of shape in the brain of Ian Bridger? And where did that leave McQueen?

Ian was out there and he had to be caught and questioned by the police. McQueen wanted to be part of that process. He had a lot of questions himself, but the man might disappear now, never to be seen again. Sometimes serial killers went tens of years between murders and sometimes they were never caught, their crimes becoming mysteries for new generations to theorise over. Jack the Ripper was never uncovered but he was still selling books and inspiring tours more than a hundred years after his last known victim. McQueen didn't want Emma's murder to become nothing more than an unanswered riddle.

He didn't have much leverage, and he didn't know if Ian was able to read his emails now that they had taken his laptop and computer, but he wrote and sent a message anyway: "Come and get me, Ian. I'm waiting."

It was getting late, but McQueen didn't think he was going to get much of a night's sleep again. Exhaustion was starting to overtake him, and with it, his fears were growing. Maggie, the therapist, had given him some simple coping mechanisms to use until he could start their proper trauma sessions, and he tried one of her grounding exercises. He sat comfortably on his sofa and thought back to what Maggie had told him over the phone.

First, he identified his main fear. Surprisingly, it wasn't that Ian would kill him. It was that Ian would escape. He then put the fear on a mental shelf to look at it. He visualised it outside himself, like a specimen, something that wasn't part of him. Then for step two, he made physical contact with his own body. He breathed deeply, noticing the air fill his lungs and the feel of his feet on the floor beneath him. Then he took step three: he opened his eyes, glanced around the room and made himself notice the colour of the walls, the temperature of the air and the sounds in the distance.

He went through the exercise several times until he could feel the fear subsiding. Suddenly, his phone pinged with a message. Without hesitation, he picked it up and saw it was a message from Lia.

Hi, it read. *Quick update. Kerry has given her full witness statement. It took ages, but she's at the safe house now. She's still scared, but I think she's relieved. Bailey has been arrested. He kicked off big time but he's now in custody. I'm going home. I'll see you in the office tomorrow.*

McQueen replied, *Great news. Thanks. See you tomorrow.* He then flopped over onto the sofa to try to sleep.

Forty-two

Bright and early and not feeling too bad after a reasonable six hours of sleep, McQueen drove into the carpark. His was the only car so far, so he knew he'd beaten Lia in this morning. As he parked, he got a text message from Tracey, who also seemed to have pulled an early shift.

We're still working on his computers, the message read, *but the DNA is back. We have a match with DNA found on the scarf that was used to strangle one of our unsolved cases. It's starting to come together. Be careful. He is very dangerous.*

Wow, thought McQueen, *how many more victims?*

The carpark was surrounded by a wall of neatly spaced poplar trees that were part of the landlord's attempt at country landscaping. As McQueen got out of his car, he saw a man emerge from behind one of the trees. McQueen assumed it was one of the reporters who had been staking out the office, but by now Emma's story was growing cold, and they had largely given up on trying to get a statement out of him. McQueen walked to the front door and started to punch in the security code as the man got closer. He had something in his hand, which McQueen guessed was a voice recorder.

McQueen held up his hand. 'Still no comment I'm afraid,' he said to the man, who was now about fifty metres away. As he got the door open but before he could step inside, McQueen looked again and saw that the man had a gun in his hand. They both stopped and stared at each other, and the door's closing mechanism pulled it shut again.

'Ian,' said McQueen. 'Or is it 'Olivia'? We need to talk.' He tried to make it sound friendly and calm, but his scattered mind was racing. His best move would have been to run inside the security door and close it behind him, but now it had relocked, that would mean entering the eight-digit code again with his back to the gun. He didn't think he had the time so he stayed still.

At that moment, Lia's car pulled into the carpark, and Ian swung round to face it. Lia must have seen the man with the gun that he'd been pointing at McQueen and had reacted instinctively. She turned her car towards Ian and drove at him. He fired once, the gun making a shockingly loud bang sound, and Lia's windscreen shattered. She swerved to the right, smashing into the back of McQueen's parked car. From where he was standing, McQueen could see that Lia's airbag had deployed but he couldn't see if she was moving. Ian was still pointing the gun at the car and he started to walk towards it.

McQueen had a decision to make. With Ian distracted, it was possible he might get inside the building, but Ian was getting closer to Lia, and Tom flashed through McQueen's mind. He couldn't let that happen again. A woman who had tried to drive a car at Ian was a threat he might be about to eliminate.

McQueen took the laptop bag from his shoulder and threw it at Ian. The heavy bag hit him on the back, and he turned around to McQueen.

'I thought it was me you wanted?' shouted McQueen. 'Aren't you interested to know how we found you?' McQueen was hoping to start some sort of dialogue, to give himself the chance to talk his way out of it, but Ian wasn't even listening.

McQueen wasn't exactly sure where the bullet had struck him but he felt a sharp stinging pain in his right side, followed by a dull ache. His legs went from under him, and he fell to the gravel. As he did so, he heard another shot and the sound of glass breaking. Had he been hit again? All the fears of his dreams swam before him now. Was this his death? Was he finally sinking below the waves?

He tried to get up, to make it to the door, but he couldn't. He passed out, though he couldn't tell for how long. He lurched back into consciousness as he heard footsteps approaching, crunching across the surface. A hand took him roughly by the collar and pulled him onto his back. He looked up into Lia's face. It struck him that she was lovely, but right now she looked distraught, and a thin trickle of blood had run down from her nose. He tried to tell her that the airbag had given her a nosebleed, but his tongue wouldn't work.

'Are you okay?' she shouted.

He tried to say, 'I'm shot,' but the words remained in his

mouth.

'I've called an ambulance,' she said.

McQueen managed to croak out the question, 'Where?' He still wasn't really grasping what was happening.

'He's gone,' she said. 'I'm not sure what happened. He pointed the gun at you and then he stopped and ran.'

Lia opened McQueen's coat and he saw the grimace on her face.

'We've got to stop the bleeding.' She pressed hard on his chest, sending a burst of pain through his body.

'Where's that ambulance?' she said, her voice on the edge of a sob, before McQueen lost consciousness again.

Forty-three

It had not gone to plan at all. The forces of the universe had turned against him. He had tried to rebalance everything with one sacrificial gesture but he had not enjoyed the good fortune that had blessed him through the years. Ian had waited all night outside McQueen's office, crouched down behind one of the trees, sleeping intermittently in the cold. When McQueen had eventually arrived, Ian should have run up to the car and shot him right there and then. Instead, he'd let McQueen get out and walk to the door. Too far away. He had needed to be closer. And then, unexpectedly, the other car had come in, the one with the woman in it. That wasn't supposed to happen at all. He'd been torn. Was she another sign? Was he being given her to kill as well? The bag that had hit him in the back had awoken him to the danger. She was a distraction. McQueen was the threat.

When he had turned and shot McQueen, Ian had been too distant and he'd pulled at the trigger rather than squeezing it. The gun had dipped in his fist, and the shot missed McQueen's head and hit him in the body. Ian had tried to shoot him again, but the falling McQueen was a moving target, and the bullet completely missed and hit the door, breaking the glass panel. Then the useless gun had jammed. The trigger wouldn't move. It was an old gun, maybe military issue, and Ian had no idea what to do to make it work so he had run. He had never run away before. But this time, he wasn't in control and he had to get away. He had shot McQueen once, and McQueen might be dead, but Ian couldn't be sure the balance had been restored.

Now what he needed was cash. He could soon reconnect to his secret online networks but first he needed to get a new computer and somewhere to stay. He had messaged Cynthia and told her where to meet him. It was good she had wanted to start using the messaging app. That was something the universe had given him. Maybe it was already turning in his favour. He made up a lie about being chased by the gangsters who were after him so he couldn't risk being in the centre of the city or anywhere where there were a lot of people. What he wanted was to get her somewhere he felt comfortable and safe.

In the past, he had spent a lot of time around the old Holbeck Managed Zone. A couple of his early victims had been sex workers; he'd felt threatened by their boldness and the way they approached him as if they knew him. It meant he knew the tight streets and dark alleyways very well. He could get in and away again once he had killed Cynthia. The gun wouldn't fire but it would still be heavy enough to serve as a useful hammer.

Ian approached the corner where he had told Cynthia to

meet him and checked all around for any police. There were some terraced houses nearby, but everyone in this area kept their curtains closed and their doors locked after dark. On the other side of the street, there was a young boy, maybe fifteen or sixteen, who was slouching along in the opposite direction. Ian studied him just in case, but like most people, he didn't notice Ian. Once the kid had gone, the street and corner were empty. Ian needed the money but he wasn't prepared to wait around for too long. He took out his phone to tell her he was only going to wait five minutes, and as he did, it buzzed in his hand with a message from Cynthia. She was on her way and she had the money.

His head was down reading the message and he didn't hear the soft trainers approaching from behind him until it was too late. As he turned to see the young boy, he felt something whack across his neck. He was fumbling for the gun, but it had snagged in the lining of his pocket. He felt the boy's blade stab at his chest and he fell backwards. The kid was fast and agile and kicked Ian as he fell.

Ian tried to work out what was going on. He guessed he was being mugged, but this was especially violent. As Ian was lying on his back, the kid stood over him. In the dim streetlight, Ian could make out a huge machete in his hand.

'That's my grandma you've been scamming, you piece of shit,' he said. 'She showed me your messages. Sebastian? Pilot? Ha! You don't look much like your picture, mate. She was so happy to find someone who loved her.' He held up his own phone. 'But since she told me about the money, it's me you've been talking to.'

'I can give it back,' gurgled Ian through the blood that

287

was filling his throat.

The young man grinned. 'How thick do you think I am?' His grin turned to rage and he hacked again at Ian's neck. The phone clattered from Ian's hand, and the boy picked it up. Ian's other hand was still buried deep in his coat pocket, tightly clenched around the useless gun.

Forty-three

'Here I am again,' said McQueen to the nurse as she counted out some pills into a small plastic cup for him to swallow. He didn't ask what they were; he trusted her pale blue uniform and efficient manner.

'Been with us before, have you?' she asked pleasantly.

McQueen nodded wearily. 'Once or twice.'

'We don't get that many gunshot victims in here,' she said. 'You're a bit of a celebrity on the ward.'

At the mention of his wounds, he touched his bandages and winced. 'I wouldn't recommend it.'

'Listen,' she said, 'the rapper Fifty Cent got shot nine times at close range and went on to make millions of dollars, so I think you'll be fine.'

That's what McQueen liked about most nurses: They didn't let you lapse into self-pity.

When he had woken after the stitching-up operation, a young doctor had come to the ward to tell him how lucky he was. Not lucky to be shot by a killer, he joked, but lucky the bullet hadn't hit anything vital. McQueen would normally have made a pathetic joke about there not being much that was vital under his skin, but he couldn't raise the energy.

He had lost a lot of blood, he was told by the earnest young medic, who had by now put on his serious bedside manner face. Since his previous heart operation, McQueen had been taking the blood thinner warfarin, and that apparently hadn't helped his situation. Lia, however, had done a fantastic job of keeping what little blood he had left in his body from gushing out until the paramedics had arrived to take over. She'd already been in to visit him and told him she would be putting in a claim for her ruined coat. He promised her a whole new wardrobe -- plus a wage rise.

'Now's the time to get me into a negotiation,' he had said happily. 'Drugged up and glad to be alive.' McQueen had noticed that hospital wards had a way of making light conversation awkward so he didn't blame her when after a while Lia said Carl was waiting downstairs for her so she'd better get going.

As she was leaving, Lia said, 'Oh, by the way, someone called Tom Lewis rang. He said he couldn't visit, so you wouldn't be getting any grapes, but he did want to say 'get well soon' and to tell you that he was staying with his parents for a while. He said you'd know what that meant.'

'I do,' said McQueen, with a close approximation of a wide smile. 'Thank you.'

He was drifting in and out of a dreamless sleep, but the general noise and activity of the ward meant it only came in five-minute bursts. The doctor had said his biggest risk now was infection, and that's why they were keeping him pumped up with strong antibiotics. He was scheduled for a visit from the physio the next day but he'd been warned that he wasn't going to be discharged until his blood pressure started behaving. He closed his eyes to think about that, and when he opened them, Detective Tracey Bingham was walking up to his bed.

'Hi,' she said kindly.

'If you've come for my statement,' he said, 'I'm not up to it yet and I'll want my lawyer with me when I give it too.'

Tracey held up her hand. 'All in good time. I've actually come to see how you are.'

'Have you caught him yet, or do I still need protection?'

Tracey looked down at her hands. 'It's not in the news yet, but there's been a development. Unfortunately, I can't tell you what it is.' Tracey had looked around her at the other beds when she'd said that, but none of McQueen's fellow patients looked in any state to make much sense of anything.

'Come on,' said McQueen in a low voice. 'The person who illegally kicks down doors to get evidence is suddenly a stickler for the rules?'

Tracey leaned in closer, just as McQueen had all those months before with Tom.

'If you get a local paper off the trolley, you'll be able to read that there was a fatal stabbing in Holbeck two nights ago. It's a story by your friend Anne Kirkpatrick. It's a senseless knife crime, the scourge of our age, a 'What are the police doing about it?' kind of story. The name of the victim hasn't been released by the police yet, but between you and me, it was Ian Bridger.'

'What? How?'

Tracey shrugged. 'We don't know. Given the area he was found in, it could be a drug deal gone wrong, or perhaps he was looking for sex from the wrong person. We'll make enquiries but we may never know. What we do know is that he still had the gun on him, the same gun that was used to shoot you and the same gun that killed Emma Cullen.'

Maybe it was the softening effects of the drugs, but McQueen's emotions were very raw, and at the mention of Emma's name, he was close to tears. He tried to change the subject.

'Anything from the computers yet?' he asked.

'Nothing on the emails and contacts. It's all encrypted and tangled in an IT knot, but the geeks in IT have managed to extract a spreadsheet. It's written in some kind of personal code that they don't know if they'll be able to crack, but the dates are interesting. A lot of them seem to correspond to unsolved murders. We'll have to see what comes out of that.'

They talked a little while longer until Tracey glanced at her watch and stood up.

'Anyway,' she said, 'the good news is that you had four bad marks against you in Detective Chambers' book and now you've got none. Plus you've got the perfect alibi for the Bridger stabbing because you were right here, so I think you're in the clear.'

McQueen smiled.

'By the way,' she added as a parting gift. 'I like your new assistant. She's sharp.'

'Well, when you turned down my offer to become my partner, I did the only thing I could do: I got someone even better.'

'Can't argue with that,' she said, her rubber-soled shoes squeaking on the polished floor as she turned away.

ACKNOWLEDGEMENTS

I'd like to thank Tricia, Holly, and Alex for their never-ending support. I'd also like to thank novelist, Sophie Morton-Thomas, whose tenacity and encouragement during the long publishing journey was an inspiration.

SRL Publishing don't just publish books, we also do our best in keeping this world sustainable. In the UK alone, over 77 million books are destroyed each year, unsold and unread, due to overproduction and bigger profit margins.

Our business model is inherently sustainable by only printing what we sell. While this means our cost price is much higher, it means we have minimum waste and zero returns. We made a public promise in 2020 to never overprint our books for the sake of profit.

We give back to our planet by calculating the number of trees used for our products so we can then replace them. We also calculate our carbon emissions and support projects which reduce CO_2. These same projects also support the United Nations Sustainable Development Goals.

The way we operate means we knowingly waive our profit margins for the sake of the environment. Every book sold via the SRL website plants at least one tree.

To find out more, please visit
www.srlpublishing.co.uk/responsibility

Milton Keynes UK
Ingram Content Group UK Ltd.
UKHW042220120224
437699UK00001B/8

9 781915 073310